BEWARE

THE

SHEEP

M. LEWIS-LERMAN

OPTA ARDUA

NEW YORK, NEW YORK

Opta Ardua.
New York, New York
ISBN: 978 0 9863 4236 3 FIRST EDITION: March 2015

For Hannah
&
Oliver

BEWARE

THE

SHEEP

1

TRUTHS
&
TRIFLES

MR. MCCLOUD'S PINGS AND THINGS was one of many clever little shops along the old main street. Its door was large and red, its ceiling was arched and high, and its perfume was a neat combination of mothballs and overripe bananas. It was a narrow, dust-filled shop, crowded with the largest wheels and the smallest cranks, extravagant masks and strange, warping mirrors, all teetering precariously from the misaligned shelves, dangling from the ceiling, and looming out from the darkest of corners.

Though in utter disarray, the small shop had an order to it, that much was clear, and Livi Dixon gasped as her friend Benny reached out carelessly for a peculiar metal object sitting on one of the highest shelves.

"Would you be careful with that?" she hissed through the dusty, dim light.

"But just look at it, will you?" He slapped the metal box into Livi's palm. Its texture was smooth and its metallic color seemed to change at every angle. It felt unusually heavy as Livi turned it in her hand, watching the cogs underneath move together.

"What do you think it is?"

"Oh, it is a complicated contraption -- many wheels and whistles," a detached voice muttered from behind a stack of old magazines. "Pick it up, give it a whirl. I expect you'll like it very much.

"Mr. McCloud? Mr. McCloud, is that you?"

"Just turn the handle," the voice insisted. "No, nope, not that one -- *yes*, there you have it." The handle was painted red and it was tiny enough for Livi to grip successfully between her thumb and forefinger. As she turned the handle, a quiet melody began to play from within.

Just then, a little old man with wispy white hair extending past his ears popped up from behind a long mahogany desk. "Just lovely, isn't it now?"

"Mr. McCloud! Do you remember me? I'm Benjamin Shaw. We met once, when you came through Primareaux to do some trading."

"It's called a music box, isn't it lovely?" the man asked again, smiling brightly. He reached toward Livi and collected the box from her hands, enveloping it within his own. "It plays something different for every person who turns the knob."

Mr. McCloud cranked the little red handle eagerly, clutching the box up to his ear as it began to play. "Intuitive, you see, *intuitive*. It's one of a kind," he cooed happily over the music that was playing -- an entirely different melody from the one that had played for Livi, just moments ago.

The cogs slowed and the song came to a stop. "I traded an old Trilinian gypsy the finest silver tea kettle this world has ever seen, and I'll tell you it was well worth it, *well* worth it. And it can be yours -- for the right price." He grinned mischievously at the two young friends. "What's your best offer? It's one of a kind, handcrafted -- a masterpiece, really."

"We're not here to buy anything, Mr. McCloud. We've only come to talk to you. Don't you remember me? We met just last month."

As Benny tried to stir the shopkeeper's memory, Livi moved across the narrow store, to something silver that caught her eye: coiled up at the end of a long chain, was a shining silver medallion. It was round and practically weightless, fit neatly in the palm of her small hand, and had a curious insignia cast on the front. The hinge on one side said it was meant to be opened, and Livi was glad to oblige.

She turned the silver toggle and the locket sprung open. Out popped a clock.

"A beauty isn't it?" said Mr. McCloud eagerly. "That's real silver."

Livi smiled politely and closed the locket, returning the toggle to its original station. He grunted unhappily at another missed sale and then returned his attention to Benny, who had been reduced to begging:

"Please, you *must* talk to us -- not for me, but for my sister. She's in real trouble, she's sick-"

"Does this look like an apothecary to you, boy?"

"But we're not here for medicine, sir," said Livi. "Just information -- about Mathilda Battlebee."

"What do you want with Mathilda? She's not been in Eaux for over a decade."

"I wish that was true, but she's back. Been back for almost two weeks."

"That's impossible."

"I've seen her myself," said Benny. "She's been nursing my sister."

Mr. McCloud's eyes shifted up and down. "Go home, Mr. Shaw. You have no business here."

"But please, we need your help. We wouldn't ask if it weren't absolutely imperative."

"And what's Mathilda got to do with you anyhow, boy?"

"Not with me -- with my sister, Violet. She's very sick, you see, and we're afraid that-"

"Mrs. Battlebee's a witch and everyone know it," Livi blurted out, casting an impatient stare Benny's way.

"Hah! Mathilda Battlebee is no witch."

It was not a secret that Livi held more than a little contempt for the small woman who was nursing her best friend, and she was dumbstruck at Mr. McCloud's vehement denial of the facts. "But sir, everyone knows-"

"*You* -- you're the Dixon girl. You've got a lot of nerve coming here, asking questions when your family has about as bad of a reputation as the Battlebees."

"Sir, you have no right-" began Benny, impassioned, but Livi silenced him with a stern glance.

"My family's got nothing to do with this."

"Is that so, missy? Well, I think I'll disagree."

"Please, Mr. McCloud," Benny cut in, "we've got to know the truth about her, my whole family depends on it."

Mr. McCloud narrowed his eyes. "And what makes you think that I have the answer?"

Benny swallowed nervously. "Everyone this side of the Blue Mountains knows that Mathilda Battlebee was from Trifle. They say she passed through here before she disappeared. Just tell us what you know and we'll stop bothering you. We've got money."

Mr. McCloud's eyes lit up at the sight of the coins that Benny withdrew from his pocket. He reached greedily forward, but Benny batted his hands away.

"I have ten pieces here. Tell us what we need to know and then they're all yours."

"*Ten*? Are you mad?"

"It's all I have."

"You're holding out on me, boy. Give me twenty and I'll throw in that pretty silver charm little missy here had her eyes on."

Benny looked nervous; he was not used to bartering. He reached into his pocket to retrieve the coins.

"Wait," Livi cried, pulling his hand back. "Don't give him the money until he's told us everything."

Mr. McCloud scowled. "Listen here, Miss *Dixon*, I'm a business man, first and foremost. I'll tell you what you want to know, but not before I have that stack of coins you carry."

Benny thought for a moment, and then he said, "You get half now. You'll have the rest later -- *after* you've answered all our questions."

Mr. McCloud seemed annoyed but he did not protest. He took ten gold coins from Benny and slipped them into his pocket. "Your sister, you say she's sick? What are her symptoms?"

"Pain, the worst I've ever seen -- than *anyone's* ever seen. Lately she's been blacking out from it, but no one can find a cause. And the more Mrs. Battlebee tries to help, the worse Violet gets."

"And so you think Mathilda's to blame? Hmm, yes, a logical conclusion, I suppose, with Mathilda's reputation. But quite wrong. You know, she always came to me with the most interesting of objects -- from places far from here, that's for certain. I was sad to see her go, sad indeed. Now, I cannot say where she went, for despite what you have heard, Mathilda did not return to Trifle that day. *Ah, ah, ah* -- calm yourself boy, you'll get your money's worth yet," Mr. McCloud added, responding to Benny's indignant expression.

"We've all heard the same stories: Mathilda Battlebee set a whole village aflame the day she ran, though no one could tell you where that village was. Mathilda was a spy, passing code on to the dark witches in the Midlands, though besides her strange disappearance on the day of her execution, no one ever saw Mathilda Battlebee so much as stick her big toe out of line."

"Well, she obviously did something. She was sentenced to die, after-all."

"Mathilda was a good woman, a strong woman. But she got involved in some trouble that was over even *her* head, I dare admit.

She knew things she shouldn't have, about some very powerful people, and *that's* why she was sentenced to death. Alas, the only crime of which she was truly guilty, was being a coward. Ah, but then, who am I to judge?" Mr. McCloud added after a brief pause. "After all, what other option did she have?"

"She could have faced her death with honor," Livi argued.

"Like your parents faced their deaths? That was not honor, little girl; that was idiocy."

Livi's face grew hot and her eyes burned, but she clamped her mouth shut, afraid that if she spoke she would lose her temper and then the whole trip would be for nothing.

Mr. McCloud drew a heavy breath and shifted his stare from Livi to Benny. "In any case, Mathilda's not the cause of your sister's ailments, of that I can assure you."

"How do you know?"

The old man scowled. "Isn't it *you* who came to *me*, boy? Yes that's what I thought. So listen here, and don't you go interrupting: Mathilda's many things, but you know what she is the most? She's a protector. She protects weak things like you from all the rotten beasts out there. I trust Mathilda Battlebee, and you should too. She's had a hard run of things -- harder than most everyone else I know -- but it's not been her fault. And she might prove quite useful, you just never know."

Benny shifted slightly, looking especially alert. Then he poured the rest of the coins into the old man's waiting hands.

"Hold on there a minute. Aren't you forgetting something?" Mr. McCloud tossed the silver necklace to Livi, completing their bargain. "Take it; it's known to bring luck."

• • •

Despite taking a shortcut through the Garga Forest, the trip from the tiny village of Trifle, back home, to Primareaux, took all afternoon. The Garga trees were known for their enormous size, as well as for their bright amber bark and sweet sap, tappable only in the dead of winter. They were the rarest and most robust trees in all of Eaux, and though Livi normally found them beautiful, today as she waded through piles of fallen autumn leaves that were as large as her whole torso, Livi only saw the Garga Forest as a nuisance.

Where the forest ended, the harsh, barren landscape of Quarries Way began, winding unceremoniously through the flattened yellow farmland that made up Outer Primareaux. Quarries Way was the longest and most tedious leg of their journey, but at the end of the road, Livi and Benny were rewarded with the paved roads and the sparkling fountains of Central Primareaux, arriving home just as the stars were creeping into the navy sky.

They lived in the Old Town, on a winding, cobbled street that had no name. Everything here was misaligned cobblestone and ancient brick paths, narrow streets and twisting alleyways. The roads weren't ten steps wide, the roofs were laid in old terra cotta, and you couldn't tell where one man's house ended and where his neighbor's began.

The Shaw home was the third faded brick house in a crooked row of faded brick houses. As they rounded the corner they saw Mrs. Shaw standing on the front stoop with her hands on her hips. "Skipping school! Disobeying my direct orders! *Lying.*"

"How'd you-"

"Never you mind how I knew, Benjamin Powell Shaw. You went behind my back talking to Peatree McCloud after I specifically told you not to!" She paused suddenly and pulled them both into her plump arms.

"Running all the way to Trifle by yourselves -- I don't know what you were thinking. Do you have any idea how worried I was?"

Releasing them, she smacked Benny hard on the back of his head. "*Peatree McCloud*, Benjamin. Of *all* people. Oh, you're just lucky your father isn't home."

"But we didn't tell him anything, Mother, honest. We didn't even mention the trip."

"And anyway," said Livi, "aren't you curious about what we found out?"

"I am *not*. Mathilda is my friend and the past is the past."

"But Mr. McCloud said-"

"It is none of my business what Peatree McCloud is gossiping about this week, Benjamin -- and it's none of yours either. And as for *you*, Olivia," Mrs. Shaw fixed her glare at Livi, "I expected *more* from you -- some common sense, perhaps? If only your parents could see you now. They left you with me for safekeeping, and here you are gallivanting around with no regard for anybody else!"

Livi felt the familiar prickle of guilt surface in her chest. "But Jane, Mr. McCloud didn't tell us anything bad."

"Olivia, I thought I made myself very clear: I have no use for that man's slimy second rate information. I've known Peatree for years and he'd sell out his own grandmother for the right price. The fact that *he* of all people knows that Mathilda's back in town -- it makes me sick, just sick."

"He won't say anything, Mother -- and even if he does, who cares? We'll be gone soon and then it won't matter."

Mrs. Shaw looked puzzled. "So now you're all set to go, are you? After just a few words with Peatree McCloud? And you, Livi? I suppose you're done fighting me as well?"

Livi hung her head. "We were only trying to do the right thing."

"The right thing would have been to trust me ... Oh, but what's done is done -- no use crying about it now. Off to yours rooms, the both of you; I don't want to see your faces until supper."

The Shaw house, like all the other houses in Primareaux's Old Town, was much taller than it was wide, and was made up of four small, square floors, piled on top of each other like building blocks. Livi's room was in the attic. Though Mrs. Shaw tried very hard to make it nice for Livi when she moved in nearly a decade ago, it remained windowless and dusty and swelteringly hot no matter what the season. It was for these reasons that Livi decided not to go up to her room just yet, instead sneaking out the back door, to Mrs. Shaw's garden.

The back garden was fertile, but poorly tended, and weeds bloomed alongside the flowers in great, greedy bushels. It wasn't a very large space, or even a particularly beautiful one, but the little square of green was Livi's favorite place in all of Primareaux and she looked forward to the many blooming dandelions as much as the well-groomed roses that sprung up in arbitrary patches throughout the garden.

The sun had gone down, but the early autumn air was still warm. A rickety wooden bench sat neatly between a dogwood tree and a bush of lively indigo colored berries, which as Mrs. Shaw frequently warned, were as noxious as they were blue. Livi was surprised to see Violet sitting on the bench, bundled under a heavy winter quilt, despite the fine evening.

"What are you doing out of bed?" Livi asked.

"I needed fresh air; the whole house positively reeks."

Violet wasn't wrong. For many weeks now, the Shaw home had smelled like boiled skunk cabbage.

Livi suspected that it had something to do with the strange infusions Mrs. Battlebee was always coming up with, but she didn't dare acknowledge this truth to Violet, who was always looking for an excuse not to take her medicine. Instead, she simply shrugged and told Violet again that she shouldn't be out of bed.

"Well, that's easy for you to say, isn't it? You're not the one cooped up all the time."

"You look better today." It wasn't a perfect truth, for Violet still seemed very weak, and her cheeks were gaunt and drained of color, but she was awake and aware, and these days that was the most anybody could hope for. "How are you feeling?"

"I feel good. I took a little walk around the garden. Mother helped, of course."

"She knows you're out here?"

Violet hesitated. "No, not exactly anymore. Ned helped me back outside when she went to fix dinner."

"Well, she's in a terrible mood; you'd better sneak back in before she realizes."

Violet rolled her eyes, apparently unconcerned. "So did you do it? Did you talk to him?"

"Why do you think she's in such an awful mood?" Benny's voice echoed off the garden walls. He clomped through the flowerbed and sat down cross-legged in the grass in front of the bench. "Mom saw you sneak out here, Livi -- sent me to hurl you back inside. And you shouldn't be out here either, little sister."

Livi laughed. Benny took his role as eldest sibling very seriously -- too seriously, in her opinion, since he was only a few minutes older than his sister, Violet, and he bickered like a child with his younger brother, Nedrick.

"It's almost dinnertime anyway, so just come in, okay?"

"In a minute. Livi was just telling me what happened at Mr. McCloud's."

"Right, well he seemed very sure Mrs. Battlebee's not the problem. And he seemed to know what he was talking about, too."

"So I guess we're really going then?"

Livi shrugged. "I bet it'll be okay, Violet. The Midlands can't be all that bad, now can it? And besides, it's not forever."

"But what if something happens while we're out there? It'll be all my fault."

"You're being ridiculous, Violet. No one thinks this is your fault, and even if-" Benny stopped short as his sister's face contorted in pain. "*Violet?* Violet, are you okay?"

She answered in a scream so piercing, so full of agony, that it did not seem human. Her whole body shook; she collapsed to the garden floor and then went still.

2

TERROR IN THE FIRST COURT

THE MORNING SUN FELT UNSEASONABLY WARM as Livi wove
quickly through the narrow residential streets on her way to
school. She was up half the night with Violet, nursing her
fever, and trying to make her comfortable until the attack
passed, and now Livi could barely keep her eyes open as she
crossed beneath the ancient stone wall that divided the city.

Here the old movie houses and green copper fountains
of the Old Town were traded for the shining office buildings
and tall towers that decorated the New Town. The roads
turned from cobblestone to bright, slick marble, the streets
widened, and the buildings grew thick. Central Station was
the largest and most impressive building in the New Town,
and Livi cut through it nearly every morning. Usually she
shot straight through the throngs of commuters, unbothered
by the bustle, but today Livi stopped in the middle of the
main terminal and found her way to the ticket box.

The ticket she purchased was for a train to Brighton, a little beach town a hundred miles east of Primareaux. The train departed right after school, at four sharp, and with her ticket in hand, she crossed the terminal and was back on her way to school.

At the very the edge of the New Town, right before the road turned to dust, there were the schoolhouses. The street was swarming with children and a few yards ahead, Nedrick Shaw's laughter echoed through the crowd.

"Ned, hey, Ned!"

Through the indistinct mob of schoolchildren, Nedrick turned and waved. "Well hiya, Livi." Nedrick was pale and lightly freckled with the same wide brown eyes and sandy hair as his brother, Benny. He was taller than every other boy in his class (and the next three classes above him) but scrawnier, too, which made for the most gangly, uncoordinated boy in nearly all of Primareaux.

"Where were you this morning, Ned? Did you skip breakfast?"

"Woke up early to meet some of the boys in the park. We were going to play a round of stickball before the bell but then we stopped at the pond to catch some frogs -- I caught a huge green warty one -- and then Billy Keen threw up and then it was just too late to play."

"Benny went too, I guess?"

"Naw, I haven't seen him this morning. Anyway, I have to go, the bell's about to-" Nedrick stopped short as the school bells began to chime. "Gotta go, see ya!"

Livi waved goodbye and ran toward the schoolyard, where three white-brick buildings stood side-by-side. She rushed by Primareaux Preschool, where half a dozen chubby-faced toddlers played in the yard, and passed Primareaux Primary, where Nedrick had just sprinted. Then, she pushed through the large double doors of Primareaux Secondary School, and into her classroom, where the professor had already begun calling roll.

"Late again, Miss Dixon," said Professor Stodge, crossly.

"Sorry," she mumbled as she slipped into the seat next

to Benny. "Benny, where were you this morning? I needed to talk you."

"Sorry -- I had a thing," Benny said, barely glancing up from his notebook. "Why, what's up?" Benny was handsome, with a serious face, hard cheekbones, and a nose just a bit large and slightly crooked. His good looks and nice personality would have made him very popular, had not been for his close association with Livi, who too often found herself on the outside looking in.

Livi waited for their teacher to pass before talking again. "I'm going to visit my Uncle Dean."

"*What?*" Benny whispered loudly enough to elicit a glare from Professor Stodge, who had just finished calling roll. "When?"

"I want to say goodbye to him before we leave."

"We're going to come back."

"I know, but just in case. Anyway, you'll come, won't you?"

"When? Today?"

"Right after school. I already bought the tickets."

"I can't today, and you can't either," he whispered sharply. "Dad's telling Ned everything tonight at dinner. We all have to be there."

"*Tonight?* But -- oh, we should have told Nedrick the plan *weeks* ago. Now we're out of time and-"

"Miss Dixon, Mr. Shaw -- another word from either one of you and I'll send you both to the Headmistress's office."

"Sorry professor," the pair recited. Normally such a threat would have silenced Livi for the duration of class, but today was different: it was the last day of school before she left Primareaux behind, maybe forever, and these threats no longer mattered.

Benny must have felt the same because the moment Professor Stodge turned away, he spoke again: "Have you *met* Nedrick, Livi? That boy can't keep a secret for anything, and you know it."

"You've never given him a chance, that's the problem."

Benny rolled his eyes. "Well, you can stop worrying, we're telling him tonight. Don't be late, all right? Dad's going to explain everything right after dinner."

Livi slouched sullenly into the hard wooden chair. She didn't care what Benny said -- she was going to see her uncle tonight, even if she had to do it alone. By now class had commenced and Livi was vaguely aware of Professor Stodge as he recited the names of the last century's Third Crowns, and their subsequent years of reign.

"And a bonus question," Stodge was saying enthusiastically, "who can tell me the name of the Third Crown at the beginning of the Second Continental War?"

It was a trick question. Professor Stodge loved his trick questions, but halfway through the trimester, the class nearly always saw them coming. In this case, the right answer (which a pupil in the front row promptly gave) was that there was no Third Crown (or First, or Second, for that matter) during the Second Continental War. There was one King then, and his name was Marcous Astor.

The Great Triangulation, as it was called, was what permanently divided the Eauxian crown into three parts, and it happened half a millennium ago, the year King Astor took the throne. After almost a century at war, Astor approached his reign with fresh eyes, and a vision of peace. King Astor found resolution with their warring neighbor, Trilinia, just weeks into his reign. Then, to ensure such blood-loss never again befell his country, Astor split his crown in three -- split his *power* in three -- thus allowing for fair and balanced rule throughout the kingdom.

To this very day, Eauxian law still demanded that there be three crowns in Eaux at all times -- three separate leaders, three separate monarchies -- each with their own set of rights and duties.

Livi let her mind wander as Professor Stodge wrote a list of the Third Crown's duties on the blackboard. Before she knew it, the bell for lunch was ringing.

The end of the day arrived not too long after that, and Livi soon found herself back in Primareux Station's large, dome-like main terminal.

The train to Brighton was bright red and had steam flowing from its engine. Livi could feel her stomach flutter as she stepped on board. She had ridden in trains many times before, but never such a far distance, and never alone. But this was important: she was going to see her Uncle Dean.

Dean Dixon was an old and lonely man. He never married and had no children of his own, and though Livi barely knew him, they were each other's only family, and she thought he deserved a proper goodbye.

She was thinking about Dean, and how old and frail he must be by now (it had been ten years since she'd seen him last), when she overheard a piece of the conversation being had by two school-aged girls in the seats directly in front of her.

Livi had not meant to eavesdrop, but now that she was, she seemed unable to stop. The girls were talking about a recent trip they took to Eterneaux, the nation's capital city. One of the girls had family there -- a brother, it seemed -- and so she'd gone on a visit just last week.

"And you wouldn't believe it!" the girl was saying. "Everything's exactly as bad as they say on the radio. Bradley," the girl's brother, Livi presumed, "has a friend whose cousin knew a man whose neighbor just up and disappeared one day! Can you believe it?" She asked excitedly.

"Oh I don't know," said the second girl skeptically, "he probably just went on a vacation or something. Or maybe he moved."

The first girl let out a frustrated huff. "He did not *move*, Sally. He was taken, I just know it!"

"But who would take him?"

"The same people who took all the others, of course. A dozen people have been reported missing in the past few weeks, and that's just from Eterneaux!"

To Livi's great disappointment, the girls got off at the next stop, and so she did not get to hear who they theorized was doing the kidnapping. Livi had read stories in the newspaper about the strange disappearances but like most people, she didn't really believe them. And besides, they were happening so far away from here, it didn't seem to matter much.

The sun had already set by the time Livi arrived in Brighton, and any vague hope of getting home in time for supper was shattered. There was no moon tonight, and barely any stars, and she walked the half-mile to Dean's cottage in near-perfect darkness. She had not told him she was coming and now, as she stood in front of his little stone house, she regretted the surprise.

Before Livi could lift her hand to knock, the door swung open and a small, shrunken-in man was standing in front of her. Nearly bald, with patches of grey on either side of his head, Dean Dixon grinned broadly at his visitor.

"Well, I'll be -- is that little Livi Dixon? Come in, come in." Dean ushered her in to his small kitchen where a tea kettle was whistling.

He removed the tea from the stove and then placed his hands firmly on Livi's shoulders. "Just look at you! You know who you look like, don't you? Your mother -- you look just like your mother." He hobbled across the small room and took down a photo of Livi's parents off a nearby shelf. "Oh, yes indeed, you're Anne's mirror image. And wait just a second, stand just like that -- yup there's a bit of your dad in there too, up in the shoulders. Not too much, and thank the sweet stars for that -- my brother wasn't much of a looker. Oh but Anne, oh now *she* was a beauty. Too good for old Peter, if ya ask me. Turn around for me, won't you? Turn around."

Livi blushed a deep crimson as she spun once in a circle for her uncle. His words were kind, but they were not true. Livi's nose was too pointy, and her hips were too square, and Livi's dark, unruly hair looked nothing like her mother's shining sable locks.

"I'm sorry to just show up like this, Uncle Dean," she mumbled once he had finished examining her and they were both sitting across from each other at the small square kitchen table. "It's just, I wanted to see you and I didn't have your telephone number and then I found your address in the filing drawer in the kitchen and so-"

"No explanation needed my dear, none at all. In fact, I'm very pleased to see you. I've been meaning to visit, but I've got the gout, you see, and it's damn painful. I'm trying to remember now, when's the last time I saw you? Three years ago? Four?"

"It was ten years ago, Uncle Dean."

"*Ten?* No, no, that can't be right. That would make you -- why in Astor's name, could you really be sixteen?"

"I turned sixteen last month."

"Well, that's a shame, a shame indeed -- not you, of course, oh you're just lovely. But it's a shame all that time's passed. I meant to come see you after what happened. I even talked to Jane Shaw about you coming here to live. But in the end -- well, it worked out in the end, now didn't it? It is a shame, though, a sure shame. And now with you leaving -- well I've been meaning to visit, like I said, but it's a might hard to travel in my state, at my age."

"You know we're leaving, then?"

"Jane's been kind enough to keep me informed. Now there's a fine woman! Better to you than I've ever been. Now that's not to say blood doesn't matter, of course, for it most certainly does. But then, what could I have ever offered a little girl? I'm an old man. I'm *tired*. You were better off, better off, that's for certain."

He seemed to be talking more to himself than to Livi, and she sat politely, hands crossed in her lap, as he argued with himself. "So tell me child, when are you leaving?"

"In two days."

"Two days? But that's Eaurival."

Livi shrugged her shoulders. She didn't like the idea of missing Eaurival either, but it was their best option. "It makes the most sense. And Violet can't wait much longer."

"Poor creature. When she first got sick I called up and shared my sympathies; I even offered to take you off their hands. But may the Good King bless 'em, that family wouldn't hear of it. Those are fine people you've fallen in with, Livi. You're very lucky."

Livi's mouth tightened. "Yes, well, I should get going. I'd only come to tell you I was leaving, but I see now that's not necessary."

"I've upset you! Forgive me, I'm an old man, I don't what I'm saying. Now you listen, it's true the Shaws are a fine family, but you are even finer. You're a pretty thing like your mother, and of a strong mind like your father. Jane Shaw is as lucky to have you as you are to have her."

"You're being kind."

"I'm being honest. Now tell me, dear, who is it you're meeting out in the Midlands? I trust they're expecting you?"

"Yes, they're expecting us. They're some friends of Violet's nurse. She thinks they'll know what's wrong; she says that if anybody can help Violet, it's them."

"They're doctors, then?"

"Yes, well sort of. I don't know all the details exactly, but Jane really believes it's going to work ... and so do I," she added hastily.

"Humph, well you'll be careful out in the Midlands, won't you? Some of those natives can be mighty peculiar. You had better watch out."

"Have you ever been to the Midlands?"

Dean screwed up his face. "*Me*? No, no, certainly not. But you hear stories. They're not quite civilized out there -- a good group of folks, I expect, but not civilized, from what I gather. They don't have the sort of technology we do, you see. Not that technology makes a man civilized, of course. But it helps, I do think it helps." Again Dean Dixon argued with himself; again Livi listened politely to the debate. "And in any case," he concluded, "I think it's the right decision; you'll be safer in the Midlands, I expect."

"Why do you say that?"

"Oh, it's nothing -- just more rumors, really -- about Crown Horridor. Same old gossip that's been going around for ages. Still, you just never know, especially nowadays ... difficult times we're in ... complicated and such, with May-back..." Dean's voice trailed off, and he looked exhausted. "You'll have to forgive me, I'm not used to company; let me pour you some tea."

• • •

Livi caught the last train back to Primareaux, arriving home at nearly midnight. The lights were off all over the house and she planned to run straight to her bedroom and deal with Jane Shaw's inevitable wrath in the morning. But the moment she walked in the front door, the quiet voice of Mr. Shaw called out to her from his workshop.

George Shaw was a tall and lanky man with hair a few shades darker than his children. He worked as an engineer specializing in air-transport design, which meant he divided his time between his office in the New Town, the landing docks where he tested out his latest prototype, and here, in his home workshop -- a small, and poorly lit room right behind the kitchen.

Mr. Shaw was bent over his worktable, sorting through a pile of cogs and wires, when Livi entered. He pushed his glasses up on the bridge of his too-large nose and cleared his throat.

"I'm very glad to see you, Livi; I was worried there for a minute."

"I'm sorry about missing dinner and everything, but-"

"But you wanted to see your uncle, I understand. Still, you should have let us know."

"Benny *told* you?"

"Oh he lied up and down for you, don't you worry. Dean gave us a call a few hours ago -- said you had just left and not to worry; he said to expect you home late. He's a good man, for thinking of us."

"Well, I'm sorry he made you worry."

"Livi Dixon you know perfectly well that it was not your uncle who made us worry."

"Can I just go to bed?"

"You missed quite the event this afternoon," Mr. Shaw said, ignoring her plea.

"Ned took it badly, then?"

"Just the contrary. It turns out he's known about our little trip for weeks. Apparently he'd overheard some things and put it all together. Funny boy, my son is. And sensible, really sensible. He told us he'd been waiting until Mother and I brought it up to say anything -- said he knew we'd talk to him when we were ready."

This news came as no surprise to Livi, who often thought that, because Nedrick was the youngest in the family, he was never given the proper respect.

She feigned surprise. "Well, I'm happy it all worked out."

"It seemed to, didn't it? You know, Benjamin and I went down to the docks this morning; we had a nice little stroll."

"Is that where he was? He wouldn't tell me."

Mr. Shaw grinned. "Seems he's a good secret-keeper all around. We were going over some plans. And I have news I think will please you: we're not going to leave until the afternoon, just before the parade."

Livi's face lit up. In some ways missing Eaurival was the hardest part of leaving. "So we'll have the morning, then?"

"You can go to the festival, if that's what you're asking. But you must be at the docks by twelve o'clock, understand?"

Livi nodded. She glanced down at Mr. Shaw's desk, to where a bundle of newspapers lay. The Shaw household subscribed to three newspapers: *The Daily Quotidian*, *Eterneaux Times*, and *The Stretch*, an offbeat local paper that Livi read strictly for entertainment purposes, as its pages rarely held any real news at all. Tonight, however, all three papers were dedicated to the fire at the royal compound in Mayback County.

Livi's eyes scrolled the headlines, each more dire than the last:

18 DEAD IN MAYBACK TRAGEDY; FIRST MINISTER AMONG SLAIN

TERROR IN FIRST COURT: CROWN SAINTRIGHT PICKS UP PIECES

IN WAKE OF MAYBACK, SOME SUSPECT
FOUL-PLAY

"Come now, Livi, don't read those things before bed -- you'll have bad dreams." Mr. Shaw's gentle voice snapped Livi out of the fiery daze. Grateful to see he was done lecturing her, Livi slipped out of his workshop and up to her attic bedroom without another word.

• • •

Livi didn't sleep at all that night. The words of her uncle, and of Mr. Shaw, and the newspapers' inky-black headlines bumped around loudly in her head, making her pillow feel leaden and her bones restless.
Finally, she snuck quietly from her bed, stepping carefully down the old, creaking staircase. She would make a cup of tea or sit in the garden or take a walk -- anything to stop her mind from spinning.
But when she arrived in the kitchen, all thoughts of tea or gardens or midnight strolls disappeared; there, amid the shadows, Mathilda Battlebee stood quietly, wielding a large, silver knife.

3

EAURIVAL

MATHILDA BATTLEBEE stood at the kitchen counter, carving through a large red apple. She was a short, narrow-faced woman with graying hair and black, unreadable eyes. And though Livi knew with certainty that Mrs. Battlebee was the same age, exactly, as Jane Shaw, Mathilda looked much older, and *much* wearier.

Livi had never been alone with Mathilda before. She could still turn around, still get back up the stairs before Mrs. Battlebee saw her, but something -- Fear? Curiosity? -- held her legs in place. For several long moments, Mathilda didn't seem to notice Livi at all, but suddenly her head flickered up and she met Livi squarely in the eye. "I see you over there, wondering about me." She motioned for Livi to come over, and Livi felt her eyes grow wide, but Mathilda only smiled. "I was like you once. Always curious."

"And now?"

"Oh, now I'm too old to be curious."

"Well, I'm sorry for intruding. I'll leave you alone-"

"Your mother was curious, too, you know."

Livi frowned. Her mother's history with Mathilda Battlebee was yet another blemish on her family's already spoiled reputation, and it was a piece of the past that Livi worked hard to forget. "You know, everyone thinks you're a witch," she blurted out in an angry attempt to change the subject.

"And what do you think?"

"I think it too, of course."

Mrs. Battlebee laughed heartily. "And here I thought you had some common sense. Well, aren't I a fool?" She reached out her palm and offered Livi a slice of apple. "Did Peatree tell you I was a witch?"

"You know about that?"

"It seems I do."

Livi frowned. "No, but he said you were a coward."

"Did he now? Well, perhaps I was a coward."

"But not anymore?"

"No, not anymore," said Mathilda.

"Is that why you're helping us -- to make up for before?"

"That's part of it."

"What's the other part? You don't owe us anything."

"Well, you're wrong on that count. I owe a great deal to a great many, this family included."

"What do you mean?"

"Oh, the details aren't important. But I have my reasons for wanting to help."

It was true, the details weren't important, not anymore. In two days' time, Livi would have a new set of problems, and Eaux would just be a memory. She sighed deeply, all thoughts now turned to the Midlands. "These people we're going to -- your friends in the Midlands -- you know them well?"

"I would not send you to them if I had any doubts."

"*Send* us?"

"Oh, I won't be going with you, dear. Of course, I wish I was. I miss the Petrichor terribly these days. It's been my home ever since I left Eaux. It's a real sanctuary for people like me -- for those who don't quite belong."

Mathilda promised that the Petrichor would hold a cure for Violet, but that did little to soothe Livi's anxiety, who knew almost nothing about the place, except that it was hidden deep in the Midlands.

"If you like it there so much why don't you come with us?" Livi asked.

"Well, things are a bit hairy at the moment, and I go where I'm needed. For now, that means heading up to the boarder."

"What's up at the boarder?"

Mrs. Battlebee reached into her dress pocket, retrieved a folded sheet of paper, and handed it to Livi. "There's some conflict brewing between a few of the local tribes. It's my job to try to settle things."

Livi examined the thin slip. Where did Mathilda get it, she wondered, and from whom? The notice gave little information, but sent Mathilda to a territory just a few miles north of the Noauxware River. The river was the borderline between Eaux and the Midlands. It was a narrow strip of land but one notorious (on *both* sides of the boarder) for its frequent and violent disputes.

Mathilda glanced at the clock that hung over the kitchen stove. "I'm leaving in the morning -- in just a few hours, in fact."

Livi frowned. She did not like Mathilda, and she most certainly didn't trust her, but she liked the idea of going to the Midlands without her even less.

"You're not afraid, are you?" Mathilda said, reading Livi's worried brow.

"Of *course* I'm afraid. Anybody would be afraid. There are monster in the Midlands. And witches, and thieves."

"Witches maybe," she agreed, "but there are no more thieves out there than there are right here in Primareaux. And the only monsters I've met look the same as you and me -- although they're usually dressed better," she added with a wink.

"So none of it's true?"

"Oh, I'm not saying that. The Midlands are like any-where else: they're exactly as dangerous as you make them. If you go looking for monsters, you'll find them, and that's a promise."

. . .

In a flurry of good smells and familiar sounds, Eaurival, Eaux's most revered national holiday, arrived both too soon and not fast enough. The sun had barely risen and the morning air was cool, but the cobbled streets of the Old Town were already mobbed with people dressed head-to-toe in the traditional pure white costumes of Eaurival.

Jugglers and acrobats, stilt-walkers and clowns, packed the narrow streets, all dressed in airy white linens, translucent satins, and the finest of creamy white silks. The Eauxian flag was flying high and traditional music poured into the streets. Flanked by Benny and Nedrick, Livi made her way through the crowds, to Primareaux Square, which was full to the brim with festival booths and street performers.

The brothers were dressed identically, in matching white sweaters, and Livi wore a dress made of cotton and lace, with straps so thin that they nearly disappeared against her pale skin. A trail of crystals curled beneath her wide blue eyes and her usually wild, untamed hair was pulled back into a long, dark braid.

"Can we get gingered pears?" asked Nedrick excitedly, running over to the pear stand. "Oh, and how about a sweet tea?" he asked, already bolting across the square, slowed down only by his sweater's stiff embroidery. With teas in one hand and pears in the other, the trio wandered through the busy square. They stopped to watch some drummers play and danced with a troop of belly dancers, wiggling their hips to the beat.

They shopped for souvenirs in the festival bazaar and they ate until their stomachs hurt, sampling every local food they could get their hands on. They only had the morning, after all, and no excess was too great.

All of Livi's friends from school were there, all of her neighbors and her professors. What would they think when she disappeared? Would they think of her at all? Her eyes drifted from the familiar faces of her school friends, to the walls of the courtyard, where projection machines were in constant rotation, flashing the royal portraits of the Three Crowns of Eaux onto the city walls.

She watched as the face of First Crown, Mavis Saintright, flashed across the gray stone wall. A tiara perched delicately at the front of her tight copper bun and her eyes were steely and unflinching, projected three stories high onto Primareaux Square. Though new to the throne, Crown Saintright had already garnered an impressive reputation, as her looks were as lethal as her words, and her confidence was unsettling.

With a *click*, the projection machines rotated and Crown Saintright's portrait faded to black. Half a second later, the image of Crown Hubert Horridor, Second Crown of Eaux (and the oldest by nearly fifty years) flashed across the square. Th Horridors ruled with arrogance and birthright, and Crown Hubert Horridor was no exception. He knew his legacy and he made certain that all of Eaux knew it too.

Livi watched as the near silent *click* of the projection machines erased Crown Horridor from the walls of Primareaux Square. As he faded to black, the image of a child flashed across the square. Raven-haired and bright eyed, Livi recognized the girl as Crown Petterina Whispen, the Third Crown of Eaux.

Though the Whispens as whole were an old and well respected Crownship, Petterina's legacy was obscured by tragedy.

An orphan by the age of eight, Petterina was the youngest crown to ever actively reign. Now Crown Whispen was twenty, though she had not been seen in public in nine long years.

It's not that she vanished completely: she was alive and well, at least according to the Third Court. But she never showed her face. Some speculated that Crown Whispen couldn't handle the pressure of the Crownship, and so she retreated to the shadows of her palace. Some thought she was so distraught from the loss of her parents that she went mad. Others, like Livi, thought that she was simply shy, and preferred to make decisions out of the public eye.

Whatever the true reason for her absence, it had become customary at public events for Crown Whispen's representative, Mary Lucidon, to take her place. And, *click*, the image of Representative Lucidon, a plain-faced woman with streaks of silver in her otherwise dull brown hair, danced across the walls of the square.

Mary Lucidon was a point of pride for the small east-coast city of Primareaux. She was a local girl, who thanks to good old fashioned hard work, rose to the very top of an otherwise nepotistic and often unscrupulous government. Livi's own mother was schoolmates with Representative Lucidon, and so was Benny and Violet's; Mrs. Shaw frequently spoke of the times she and Anne Dixon and Mary Lucidon had together as children.

Eaurival was in full swing now, and Primareaux Square was only the beginning. Benny and Nedrick had gone to the prize tent to play some games, and so Livi wandered alone through the crowded kiosk-lined streets. Everywhere, people were dancing and singing, playing music and clapping their hands. The festival wound all through the Old Town, up to and concluding in Primareaux Castle, where a costume contest would be held in the courtyard at sunset.

The castle courtyard was a wide, open space, with light bouncing off every corner. The white stone pillars extended two stories high, supporting the balcony that peered into the lush green center. Every bend, every arch, and every pillar, was built with a twin, both below and across, mirroring the original at all angles. The courtyard was slightly longer than it was wide, and had ivy growing up its walls and into its corners, making it a beautiful escape from the rest of the world.

The courtyard was already flooded with people and lined with vendors by the time Livi arrived. She pushed through the crowds and made her way up the narrow, winding staircase, to the balcony, where she could get a better view of the spectacle below.

Livi loved Eaurival. She loved her city and her country, and she didn't want to say goodbye. She had not allowed herself to grieve, always pushing forward, ignoring the ache of impending loss, but now watching her city below -- so alive, so steeped in culture and celebration -- she suddenly wanted to cry. The ceiling above was like spiders' webs, casting long, strange shadows around the balcony level. But below, it was bright. Faces painted in white, bodies draped in white, reflecting the sunlight -- pristine against the gray stone castle.

Livi meandered back toward the spiral staircase, preparing to rejoin the celebration, but then a disturbance in the castle gallery drew her back up.

The gallery was a drab sort of place, its walls lined with fruit bowls and sunsets and portraits of dead people in large, funny hats. It was unusual to hear any noise at all coming from its walls. Today, however, the gallery was overcrowded and sweltering and buzzing with excitement.

Livi entered reluctantly, slipping into the room and finding as space by the door. Someone was addressing the crowd, but she couldn't see who it was. She pushed a bit further into the mob-scene, catching a glimpse of the agitator between gaps in the crowd.

"We demand answers!" a large, angry-eyed man was shouting, gesturing fervently at a portrait of Crown Horridor.

The Horridors had always been a controversial crownship, and Livi was not surprised that Hubert Horridor was the target of this burgeoning riot. Throughout the ages, the First and Third royal families had changed with relative frequency, but the Second Crown was different: the Horridor family held the Second Crownship since the Triangulation's inception, five hundred years ago.

Livi guessed that the Horridor family's longevity was a big part of why there were always rumors circulating about them. The rumors were generally crude, always outlandish, and rarely held any truth at all. Livi knew that, of course, but they were still interesting to hear.

"We demand the truth!" An eruption of applause followed.

The truth about what? Livi thought to herself. What awful rumor had they heard, which she had not?

"Murderer!" someone shouted from the crowd. "Tyrant!" Then *splat*, a tomato was hurled from the mob, exploding against Horridor's oily canvas cheek.

The energy around her felt frenetic, almost addictive in speed and ferocity. Livi felt herself pushed left, then right, moving in swarm-like synchronicity with the angry crowd. Something sharper than melancholy rose up in her now: A feverish heat crept into her body, flushing her cheeks and turning her hands into fists. She was angry, feeling what the crowd felt, moving as they moved. More people were yelling now, and more things were being thrown and smashed.

Members of the Guard arrived, their royal purple uniforms standing in stark contrast to the glowing white civilians. The Guard blew their whistles, calling for order, but it wasn't doing any good: Hands tore through century-old canvas; marble busts smashed to the floor.

If Livi stayed any longer the riot would swallow her whole. She ran.

She sprinted out of the gallery and down to the courtyard, through the maze of people, who were heartily unaware of the chaos erupting just one floor up. She left the castle and ran toward the square, her eyes peeled for Benny and Nedrick. She'd overstayed her welcome; now her city was pushing her out.

Benny and Nedrick were not in the prize tent. It was almost noon, they had to get going. She was starting to panic when someone shouted her name:

"Livi, come on, hurry!" Nedrick's head popped out of the mob of people.

"Ned! Where's Benny?"

Nedrick shook his head and yanked her by the arm, urging her to follow. "Just come on, come quick."

He led her down a narrow arcade that sat right off Primareaux Square. A wide circle had formed in the middle of the alley. People were yelling and calling out names and Livi pushed her way to the front of the crowd just in time to watch Benny get punched squarely in the jaw.

The person punching Benny was their classmate, Gregory Wilcox -- a triple-chinned boy, at least twice the size of Benny in both height and girth.

"Take it back," Benny demanded as blood streamed from his lip.

Gregory laughed. "Or what? Or you'll *bleed* all over my nice white sweater?"

"*Take it back!*" Benny shouted again, lunging toward the overgrown boy.

Gregory stopped him with one punch to the gut, knocking Benny flat on his back. "I'm only saying what everyone's thinking. Your sister's getting what she deserves. What your whole family deserves. I mean what do you expect, surrounding yourself with traitor trash like Livi *Dixon* and that crazy old witch, Mathilda Battlebee. We all know she's back. We all know what your family's up to." Gregory looked down at Benny, strewn pathetically in the middle of the alley. "Now stay out of my way, Shaw. I mean it this time."

Gregory had made his point; he clomped away and the crowd of onlookers disbanded, leaving Livi, Benny, and Nedrick alone in the near-deserted alleyway.

"Benny!" Livi cried, kneeling beside him. His left eye was swollen shut and his lip was split in two. "Benny, are you okay?"

"I'm fine," he grumbled. "Oh, I mean it, Livi, I'm fine. Just quit looking at me like that."

"You don't *look* fine," said Nedrick, wrinkling his nose.

"Aw shut up, Ned -- just for once in your life, I'm begging you."

"Let's get you out of here, all right? Come on, Ned, help me get him up."

4

FLY
AWAY

IT WAS TWELVE-PAST-TWELVE by the time Livi and Nedrick
got Benny, limping and bleeding, past the gatehouse and
onto the docks. In front of them a clean line of arks, some
new, some ancient, hovered in the distance. Livi hadn't
been on the landing docks since their renovation a few years
back, and the once rickety wooden planks had been replaced
with smooth metal platforms, extending for what seemed
like miles, beneath unnatural florescent spotlights.

In the past, the docked arks had reminded Livi of birds
in their nests, but now the enormous flying machines more
closely resembled tombs in a cemetery: neat and square, and
somehow foreign. They made their way to the number
twenty-two lot, where a shining silver ship glowed bright
under the midday sun.

The ark was modern, long and narrow, with a lean,
curving body, cast of steel and impenetrable glass. The
door sealed tightly behind them as they stepped on board.
Everything here was shiny and new, every surface reflective
and sanitized. The cabin was dim, lit only by a strange
golden glow, which emanated off the slick, curving walls.
Windows lined the way, but through them, Livi could see

only black.

Her eyes adjusted slowly to her new surroundings. It was a modest space -- large enough to accommodate Livi and the five Shaws, but not many more.

There were rows of pod-like reclining chairs and a small, square kitchen in the far right corner. Then, neatly hidden away in the far left corner of the cabin, Jane Shaw was perched at the side of an already reclined seat.

Livi crouched beside Mrs. Shaw, glancing down at Violet. "How is she?"

"Oh Livi, there you are," Mrs. Shaw exclaimed, jumping up from her kneeled position. "We were beginning to worry. George -- they're here, George."

Mr. Shaw came clomping out from small door on the far wall of the cabin. "I said *twelve*. It's going to be hell getting out of here now. You know, it wasn't kind worrying your mother like that, either." Without waiting for apology or explanation, Mr. Shaw disappeared behind the door again, leaving Livi, Benny, and Nedrick face-to-face with a scowling Mrs. Shaw.

"We're sorry, Mother, but it wasn't our fault," Nedrick said.

"It's true," said Livi. "There was this crazy riot at the castle and then Benny got into a-" Livi stopped short as Benny nudged her hard in the side. "Anyway, we're really sorry, Jane."

"What do you mean there was a riot?" Mrs. Shaw asked, ignoring the rest.

"In the gallery on the second floor," Livi explained. "People were throwing things and shouting. I think it had to do with Crown Horridor."

"Sounds like we're getting out just in time," said Mrs. Shaw nervously, resting her hand on Violet's forehead.

"So how is she?" Benny asked.

Mrs. Shaw frowned. "The past few hours haven't been kind to her. Her fever's grown worse; she's not been lucid."

Livi crouched down again and took Violet's hand in her own. Her palm was sweaty and her wrist was limp.

"Come on, now, Vi. Hang on, just a little longer."

Nedrick touched his hand to Violet's cheek. "What's lucid mean, Mother?"

"Not well, dear. Your sister's simply not well." Mrs. Shaw gasped suddenly as her eyes surveyed her eldest son. "What happened, Benjamin?"

"It's nothing."

"He got in a fight."

"*Nedrick*," Benny hissed.

"A fight? Benjamin, just what were you thinking?"

"I -- well, it wasn't a fight, I mean, not really."

Nedrick laughed. "Yeah, only because you didn't get in a single punch. Gregory knocked the daylights outta you."

"That's quite enough Nedrick," snapped Mrs. Shaw. "And Benjamin, none of my children will be getting in fist fights, not as long as I'm alive and breathing, is that clear?"

"But-"

"Have I made myself clear?"

"Yes, Mother."

"Fine. Now, I'm just glad you're in one piece. Come now, all three of you, let's leave Violet be. We'll be taking off any second, so you had better find a seat."

Livi took a seat by the window, resting her head against the cool, paneled glass. She felt the engine start, and then a deep vibration. Benny slumped into the chair next to her, and Nedrick plopped down by the window across the way.

"Will you lie down and give yourself a chance to heal properly?" Mrs. Shaw ordered Benny from her place at Violet's side.

"But I'm fine, Mother, honestly. I mean, I'm a bit sore, maybe, but I've always been a quick healer. Tell her, Livi, wasn't I worse before?"

Livi glared at Benny, but looked him over and nodded. "Well, he *was* worse a little while ago."

"Aw, yeah, way worse," agreed Nedrick enthusiastically. "He was all bloody -- couldn't even walk right."

"Would you shut up?"

"*What*? I'm only trying to help."

"Hush, now, the both of you. You're going to disturb your sister."

"Sorry Mother," Benny and Nedrick said together.

"Anyway, can I go check on how Dad's doing in the cockpit?" Nedrick asked. "I'm going to be his first mate."

"No need," Mr. Shaw said, appearing suddenly behind them. "I am happy to report that we have made a safe and successful liftoff."

"I missed it!" cried Nedrick, pressing his face against the window. Sure enough, they were no longer stationed at the dock. Instead, they were up in the air, flying high among the clouds. "But I could have helped, Dad! You should have let me help."

"I'm sorry, but we had to move quickly. Now, the good news is that we are on due course, on direct route for the Midlands." Mr. Shaw's mouth broadened, his thin lips spreading into a wide smile. Benny stood up and clapped him hard on the back, grinning proudly at his father.

Mr. Shaw had worked as an engineer for the last two decades. He took his arks from pure concept, all the way to manufacturing and distribution. He was an expert in so many ways. But whether he had any practical knowledge on how to captain one of his very own flying ships, was up for debate, until today.

"With some luck, we will arrive safely in the Midlands early tomorrow morning. Any questions? Good. Well, I suggest you all get as much rest as possible in these coming hours, for tomorrow will be a very long day."

Livi watched through her window as they sailed through the clouds, the world below flying by in miniatures. Cities and tiny villages, farms and mountains -- from here they were all just playthings: toys designed for a small child. They were certainly not real places, real cities, real *homes* to which she once belonged.

The ark was quiet now, and the lights had dimmed all around her. The hours ticked by, the sky turned from blue to black, and the excitement of the day faded into a foggy memory.

5

THE
PETRICHOR

LIVI WOKE TO SUNSHINE ON HER FACE. Still in the ark but no longer amid the clouds, she was alone in the thick of a meadow, with only Benny by her side. Her body felt stiff as she shifted her weight off his shoulder; it was a small movement but he reacted to it instantly: "You're up? Livi, are you up?"

"Huh? Yeah, I'm awake. What time is it? Where is everyone?"

"We tried to wake you when we arrived but you wouldn't budge. Finally Dad just said to let you sleep. That was hours ago, though; I'm not sure what time it is now."

"You stayed with me this whole time?"

Benny's cheeks flushed pink. "Well, it was either me or Nedrick, and did you really want to wake up to his ugly face?"

Livi grinned. "Well, thanks."

"Doesn't matter. We didn't miss anything important, I don't think." Benny yawned widely and rubbed his eyes, wincing a little when he touched the black and blue area where Gregory had punched him. "Well, anyway, if you're ready I can show you the way to the Petrichor."

The Petrichor. Livi had heard it mentioned countless times over the last several weeks. It was Mathilda's home. It was where Violet would get better.

It was in the Midlands. But that was all she knew about the place they'd left everything for. And what about the Midlands? She had been hearing stories about the Midlands for as long as she could remember, but now that she was here, she realized she had no idea what to expect.

So far, however, the Midlands did not seem very different from the farmland in Outer Primareaux. The meadow in which they landed was full of a bristly and slightly sticky sort of plant that grew higher than Livi was tall. Fortunately, a trail had already been stamped out, leading them into the nearby forest. *This place isn't so strange*, she reassured herself as they walked. *Where are all the monsters? Where are the savages?*

Livi had just finished convincing herself of how perfectly ordinary the Midlands were, when they arrived at the forest. In most ways the Garga forest felt familiar to Livi: The trees were endless and massive and thick. They appeared healthy from root to tip, their rich amber bark, growing coarse around their trunks, and their four-pointed leaves extending from their heavy branches in bright, lively bushels. In *most* ways the trees were exactly as they should have been for autumn, growing thick and dense and full.

In fact, there was only one thing that set this forest apart from the countless other Garga trees that Livi had seen in her lifetime, but it was something *so* unique, *so* different, that it changed everything: Every tree in this forest was slumped over, as if one day they each grew tired of standing tall and so they simply fell right where they were, never to rise again.

Many trees were piled on top of each other and some were lying all alone. Some trees were drooping and others were arching and still others were more flat to the ground. None were uprooted, though; instead they were collapsed over themselves, still extended, still fully attached and growing from the deep, dark forest soil.

"What is this place?" Livi wondered out loud, her jaw nearly on the ground.

"Why, it's home, of course," answered an unattached voice coming from somewhere nearby. A second later a funny little man plowed through the brush. "Welcome to the Befallen Forest! You must be Livi -- I've heard all about you. And may I say, my dear sleeping girl, you are even more ravishing than they warned. But -- *oh my*," the strange man gasped, his gaze suddenly transfixed on Livi's neck, "what a splendid necklace. Where ever did you get it?"

Livi reached to her chest and felt for Mr. McCloud's silver locket. "It was a gift."

"A *gift*? How very nice, indeed. Ah, and you must be Benjamin. Your brother described you a bit differently -- something about a wart under your chin and a peg-leg -- hm, well, it's no bother."

"You know Nedrick?" said Benny.

"I'm sorry, sir, but who *are* you?" asked Livi.

"No need for apologies. Nor need for sirs. Wallace is my name," he proclaimed in a song-like manner, raising his chin slightly as if to let Livi examine him properly. "I've had the marvelous pleasure of showing your family around this morning, and Nedrick is a fine young man. A delight, in fact."

Wallace was a somewhat shabby looking man, but there was something distinctly charming about him. His eyes were green, and they looked very wise. His hair was black and it was sitting in a thick, disheveled mop on the top of his head. He was wearing many layers, and Livi thought that he must have been hot, as it was a warm day, even in the shade of the forest.

"Well, you won't just stand there. Or will you? The rest of your party is just this way."

Even on their sides, the Garga were many times the height of any man, and the trio was well hidden as they trekked further into the forest. Wallace led the way, easily dodging bushels of leaves and leaping gracefully over roots, apparently oblivious that Livi and Benny were behin-

-d him, struggling to keep up.

Finally, they arrived at a pile of six or seven slumped over Garga trees, all crisscrossed on top of each other, creating an enormous weaving, knotting formation in the middle of the forest. Wallace walked up to the knot of trees and placed his hand flat against the amber bark. At his touch, a panel pushed back, creating a doorway leading into the trees. "This way, right through here."

The moment Wallace closed the door behind them, Livi understood why he was wearing so many layers, for it was at least twenty degrees cooler inside the tree-trunk, and barely any sunlight snuck through. "Welcome to the Petrichor! To Tymken more precisely. To Olinda's Passway, *most* precisely. Do come along -- or don't. Whatever *does* suit you."

Under the dim lantern light, the red wooden tunnel twisted and turned in countless directions, but Wallace was a confident guide and never seemed to take a wrong step. "Bewildering at first, this is certain. But you'll learn your way eventually, it only takes some practice and some proper motivation."

Wallace pointed this way as that as they walked, passing countless doors and passages and stairwells, and offering explanations for each: "the old dormitories are down that way; this here is storage; go three doors to the right for the clock room; three doors to the left for the conservatory; down that hall's the cellar; down that one's the arboretum."

"There's an *arboretum* inside of a *tree?*" Benny said looking around wildly for confirmation that this was indeed a bizarre and impossible claim.

But Wallace only chuckled. "A bit of a paradox isn't it? You'll get used to it."

The planked wooden tunnel finally deposited them into a large, light-filled room. The room -- though also carved directly from the wood of the Garga -- was nothing like the tunnel, which was dimly lit and narrow.

It had a high beamed ceiling and rows of peculiar shaded windows, where most of the tree was etched away, letting light seep in. The windows went all the way around the large, domed room, ducking in between the vaults and casting strange, beautiful shadows all around.

A mural ran along the concaving inner wall, portraying a bright and exotic landscape: there were waterfalls as green as grass and flowers as large as mountains, and strange animals with three heads and five eyes.

"The picture? That's not a real place?" Livi asked, remembering again the stories she'd heard of the beasts and monsters that lived in the Midlands.

"To the artist I suspect it's very real," said Wallace casually. Then, tapping a finger to his temple: "Imagination, dear Sleeping Girl -- it can take you so much farther than reality. *If* you let it.

"This is Olinda's Circle," the peculiar little man continued. "It's used for meetings and gatherings -- things of that like. Today it's rather quiet, I see. Except for Penelope, of course."

Sitting on a small stool set up on the periphery of the otherwise empty room was a barefooted woman in a floor-length amber colored dress. Her back was to them, and her long ponytail (which was an unusual ashen color) dusted the floor. She sat very still, and she was looking through some sort of scope. As long as Livi watched her, the woman's eyes never moved from the scope, which -- after some observation -- Livi figured out, was just a long pipe that led from her eye all the way up the wall, past the shaded windows. From there, it connected with a number of other pipes, running in various directions, some wider, and others very thin.

"Ah, the pipe-station," said Wallace, answering Livi's unasked question. "It *is* intriguing, isn't it?"

"What's it for?"

Wallace walked over to the woman on the stool and patted her on the shoulder. "Penelope here is on patrol. From just this pipe, she can monitor nearly all of Tymken, and the forest to the West."

Penelope smiled, but she did not remove her eye from the pipe.

"Pull down the auditory pipe, won't you, Penelope?"

The young woman leaned slightly off her stool and reached out toward the wall, tapping and prodding slightly, until one of the pipes released from the wall. Then she pulled the second pipe to her ear so she now had one pipe stationed at her eye and a second at her ear.

"This pipe sends messages to the other stations," Penelope explained. "Of course, it only works inside the Petrichor. But if you need to send a message somewhere else, just let anyone on patrol know and we'll get it to where it needs to go."

Livi's eyes widened. She had so many questions; she didn't know where to start. "Wallace, how do the trees stay growing -- all bent over and carved out like they are?"

"A gypsy curse. We have good relations with the gypsy families now, you see, but it hasn't always been that way. Let's continue, shall we?"

Livi and Benny followed dutifully through a complicated series of tunnels and hallways and rooms and doors. As they walked, Wallace filled their heads with endless facts and figures about the Petrichor. He told them the proper names of all seven of the trees that the Petrichor was made up of -- from Tymken to Esker -- and the differences between them. He explained that the people who lived here were called Petchlings, and that law here was kept by the Elders.

Finally, he told them the story about when the Elders first came to the Midlands ("From Eaux, just like you!") during the First Continental War: "In the early days the Petrichor was tiny -- minute -- *nothing* even.

But since that first winter (people died left and right that first winter) we've tripled, quadrupled, and multiplied from there. We're a bit of a hodgepodge, that I'll admit. A handful of gypsies live among us, and several aged witches, too. And of course, there are those like you -- travelers from Eaux, and places far beyond, who have found their way to us. Its a charming way of life, you'll see. There are things to learn at every turn, and someone to talk with at all hours of the day."

After a lengthy trek down a number of grainy amber

corridors, they reached a place called the Atrium. Livi could tell right away that the Atrium was a central location. It was loud and busy, and its organized chaos reminded her quite a bit of the main terminal back in Primareaux Central Station.

In the very center of the enormous, cylindrical room, there was a seemingly endless spiraled staircase, swirling up, connecting with dozens and dozens of floors. In every direction, at every height, the Atrium was swarming with people and Livi watched with intrigue as the countless unfamiliar faces moved swiftly around the building. Most of the people Livi saw were dressed in shades of red and amber and nearly all of them -- old and young alike -- had the same strange ashen hair that the girl, Penelope, had.

"The Atrium is the very heart of the Petrichor," Wallace explained. "It is where all seven trees intersect, allowing for the most liberal amount of space. The dining hall, the kitchen, the infirmary -- why many and most practicalities -- can be accessed from this one single staircase. I've got to be off now -- business elsewhere, you see -- but you're dormitories are on the eighteenth floor, down the third hallway, to the right."

"Is that where Violet is?" asked Benny.

Wallace shook his head. "You'll find Violet in the infirmary -- seventh floor, across the foyer, and to the left."

As they began rounding the stairs, Livi noticed that the banister was carved with an elaborate design, which seemed to be telling some sort of history. But the symbols and figures were all foreign, so the story was impossible to read. When they reached the seventh floor, they were dispensed into large, ring-like foyer, with a wide-open center. Livi inched up to the guardrail and peaked over. From here, the people below looked like ants, busy and bustling, and entirely indistinct.

Then she looked up. Even as high as Livi was now, she was no closer to seeing the top of the tremendous staircase. *I must look like an ant to someone just a few floors up.* The thought was strangely comforting.

As Wallace had promised, the infirmary was just

across the foyer, and to the left. Nedrick was sitting alone in the waiting room when Livi and Benny arrived. "Mother and Dad are in with the doctor," he said, sounding unusually dejected.

"And Violet?"

"She's in *there*." Nedrick pointed an unmarked door that Livi thought must be the sickroom. "We're still not allowed in."

"What do you mean not *allowed*?"

"They took Violet in right when we arrived. That was hours ago, and they haven't let us see her since. Mother was about ready to murder the nurse who kept stopping her. Finally, just a few minutes ago, a lady came in to talk to them, but she made me wait out here."

All the excitement and anticipation Livi felt moments ago drained from her as she and Benny took the two remaining seats against the wall of the small, rectangular waiting room. They sat there for nearly three-quarters of an hour until finally, at ten-to-noon, the door to the waiting room swung open and a small, stout woman beckoned them to follow.

The woman introduced herself as Wren and explained that she was the doctor here, though she did not look like any doctor Livi had ever seen. She was round and somewhat dowdy, with wild ashen hair falling well past her shoulders. And instead of a proper medic's uniform, Wren wore an apron-like dress and an amber shawl over her shoulders.

Wren led Livi, Benny, and Nedrick into a room down the hall, in which Mr. and Mrs. Shaw were already waiting. This room was even smaller than the last, and it felt terribly congested, with elbows poking out in every direction, as the four Shaws, plus Livi, crammed themselves into the ever-tightening space.

"Now, as I've explained to your parents," Wren began, turning to face everyone, "Violet is suffering from a severe case of Empath's Fever. It's an extremely rare affliction, but one that can be treated. How much do you all know about Empaths?"

Livi had never even heard the word before. Fortunately Wren seemed to be expecting confusion, falling into a rehearsed speech about the properties of an Empath. According to Wren, Empathy was a rare and wonderful trait. Empaths could heal the injured, nurse the ill, and cure the incurable. But for those like Violet, who had been left without any guidance or training, the pain could be unendurable, leading to fever, hallucination, and even death.

"I've given Violet a sedative to help with the pain; she's asleep, and for the time being, stable."

"What's going to happen to her? You can help her right?"

Wren smiled tightly. "The usual treatment for Empath's Fever is a heavy dosing of mooncalf's milk, but in very progressed cases, like Violet's, the root of the Emickus plant is necessary to make a full recovery. And I'm sorry to say, Emickus is nearly extinct."

There were only two places in the world where Emickus still grew. The first was in the Western Wince, a vile and dangerous part of the Midlands. And the second was in Eaux's capital city, Eterneaux, in the private greenhouse of the First Crown.

"But just because Emickus is out of the question," continued Wren, "does not mean there is no hope. I suggest that we proceed with the usual treatment; at the very least, it will slow down the progression of the fever."

"Well, that's a start," said Mrs. Shaw. "You can give her the milk today?"

"Generally, powdered milk is used, but what I suggest is that we use fresher, more potent supplies; it will take an extra day or two to procure, but it could make all the difference. There is a nearby Oracian village, Tiethe, that can supply us with the fresh milk. With this treatment, Violet could have several months left -- maybe even years; she could still live a happy and productive life."

Months? Livi thought. *We came all this way for just a few extra months?* "And what if we got the Emickus?" she asked out loud. "Then how long would Violet have?"

Wren frowned. "The Emickus would cure her, dear.

But as I explained, it's impossible to get."

· · ·

The next few hours passed in a daze. They visited briefly with Violet (who, as Wren had assured them, was fast asleep); they were shown to their dormitories; they were fed, and given new, warmer clothes.

After the tour, the group dismantled and Livi was left alone in her dormitory. There was so much here that she did not understand. The words *Empath* and *Mooncalf* and *Death* danced in her head as she tried to make sense of it all. After coming so far, and giving up so much, was it really possible that Violet would still die? The thought was inconceivable.

6

ZIGZAGS
& MOONCALVES

"WELL, THAT'S NOT HOW I LEARNED IT," Livi said frowning
at the red and black checked playing board. It was after
supper and she and Benny were lying on their stomachs on
the floor of her room playing a game of Simple Pins.

"Then ya learned it wrong. That's the Guardian. It
can only move left and right. If you wanna move forward
you've got to use a Crown Pin."

Livi was about to argue that the Guardian could move
forward when it was threatened by the Court, but then
Nedrick burst into the room. "There you are! Do wanna see
something neat? It's the Elders -- they're all out. Come on
-- come look."

Livi and Benny followed Nedrick as he ran down the
hallway and then bolted down the eighteen flights of stairs
to the main level of the Atrium. There, a troop of twelve
men in brilliant emerald robes were mingling with other
Petchlings, answering questions and asking some of their
own.

"That one there's Emble," said Nedrick, pointing to a
friendly looking man with a long face and a hooked nose.
"And that one's Quizzle." He pointed to a round, gentle-

faced man. "That's Turvy, and there's Rolf."

Each of the men had ash-colored hair and light eyes and skin the color of soft, sweet olives.

They wore bright green robes, and around each of their necks, strings of salmon-colored beads hung congenially.

"You talked to them?" asked Livi, impressed.

"Well, not exactly," Nedrick admitted, "but I've been watching them for a while and they seem pretty all right. They're nice, I mean; they're like us: they're sort of normal."

Livi watched the interactions more closely now, and Nedrick seemed correct. The Elders were leaders but not feared, salient but not separate. The one Nedrick pointed out as Quizzle was kneeling down, laughing with a little boy and his mother. The one named Emble was being bombarded with questions by three grouchy looking women, one of whom was angrily wielding a bucket of green slime. Some Petchlings were stopping to talk with the Elders; others were continuing on with their evening. Socializing with the Elders appeared an unexceptional event, an observation that Livi found reassuring.

"Well, should we talk to them?" said Nedrick.

"What, you mean just walk right up to them? *Right now*?" asked Benny skeptically.

"Sure, why not?"

"I bet they'd be nice," Livi said.

"You guys are crazy. I think I'll stay here, thanks."

"Aw, come on, Benny, come with us," Livi said, tugging gently on his arm.

Benny turned beet red. "Fine, let's just get this over with."

Nedrick, looking unabashed, waltzed right up Elder Emble (who by now had resolved his dispute with the three angry women and ended up with green goop on his shirtfront) and tapped him on the shoulder. "Hiya!"

"Why hello!" said Elder Emble, smiling brightly and wiping a bit of the slimy substance off his cheek. "And who are you?"

"I'm Nedrick."

"Nedrick, what a peculiar name!" Emble said, shaking Ned's hand heartily. "I do like odd things! We'll get along well, I expect. And who are you?" he asked, looking at Livi.

"I'm Livi. And that's Benny."

"Livi and Benny and Nedrick. A fine group, indeed. You will excuse my appearance, won't you? I had a slight disagreement with the ladies, you see. As it happens, no one told them the pipes in the wash rooms on the third level would be congealing overnight -- weather related -- totally normal for this time of year. Unfortunately, the memo got lost and they -- well, they had a bit of an *experience* while running their showers this morning. These things happen, you know. No ones fault, really. And utterly reversible!"

Livi stifled a giggle. The image of those three grouchy women showering in slime was enough to satiate her hungry imagination for the rest of her life.

Emble introduced a few other Elders who were standing nearby and exchanged the usual pleasantries one exchanged with house guests: *Are you finding everything all right? -- How have your travels been? -- If there's anything you need, please do ask.* And Livi and Benny and Nedrick offered polite and conservative answers: *Just fine, thank you -- A bit tiring, but we're happy to have made it -- We will, and thank you.*

In this backwards place, with these backwards people, it felt strange to be acting so normal, so reserved. Here in the Petrichor, however, strange seemed to be normal ... *so normal would feel strange, now wouldn't it?* Livi smiled as she worked this out in her head.

Her brain was on overload, introduced to new, fascinating things practically every minute. Tonight it was Elder Emble, and his gang of gentle leaders. Tomorrow she could only imagine what it would be.

• • •

The next morning Emble joined them at the breakfast

table, and so did Violet's doctor, Wren. Conversation remained polite, but superficial, straight through morning tea, but by the time the dishes had been cleared, all talk had turned Violet and things were getting tense:

"A trip to the Oracian village of Tiethe has been arranged for first thing tomorrow," Wren explained, "at which time, we will collect the mooncalf's milk. All we require now, is a party for the journey. Wallace -- I believe you met him yesterday -- will be leading the effort, but we ask for two more." An uncomfortable silence filled the room as Wren's eyes darted expectantly from Livi, to Benny, to Nedrick.

Livi could barely contain her excitement. She had learned all about the Orac people back in Primareaux. They were one of several native tribes that used to inhabit the continent, but now they lived exclusively in the Midlands. Her professors had always described them as animalistic and primitive. *But since when have my professors ever been right about anything?* She thought wryly. The idea of seeing an Oracian village for herself was too exciting a prospect to imagine.

But when Mrs. Shaw finally caught on to what Wren was asking, she let out a gasp of horror. "Absolutely not. None of *my* children will be traipsing out into the wilderness, not in this lifetime."

"We are a community of *doers*, Mrs. Shaw," Wren said sharply. "There is no laziness permitted here, and no fear-mongering either. At least two more are required to make the journey to Tiethe, and they *shall* be from your group. You may choose for yourself, if you like, but do so quickly."

"And I can assure you, Madam, that whomever you select will be watched over most astutely," added Emble graciously. "Wallace will be a wonderful guide. He gets along marvelously with Chief Pax; he really seems to understand the Oracian culture. Wren, perhaps you would like to go down Tymken and locate Wallace? I expect he'll have an opinion in all this."

"Tymken? So early?"

"He's helping Missander with pigments down in the Yownth Tunnel. I expect he'll be delighted to be relieved -- he does hate that stench!" Emble looked at his wrist as if to check an invisible wrist watch. "Oh my, it seems I'm late as usual. Wren, let's scurry on now. Much to do, busy, busy!"

• • •

It was mid-afternoon by the time Wren arrived back with Wallace. The dining hall was deserted now, except for the table where Livi and the others sat waiting. Wallace and Wren took seats near the front of the long, square table, smiling pleasantly as they settled in.

"The little cannon kinglet tells me an adventure's to be had," Wallace sang, his eyes wandering wildly around the room until focusing decidedly Livi. "Well, do follow -- or don't -- as I am your guide, and there's a journey to be had, you see. A mooooooncalf to be milked!"

Wren rolled her eyes. "Ignore him, won't you? He's just pleased to be free from pigmentation duty for the day."

"Never any fun, the little bird is," chortled Wallace, who looked even shabbier than he had yesterday, and now carried with him an awful, almost otherworldly, stench. "Yes, it's true I'm glad to breathe clean air again, but do I really need an excuse to be agreeable?"

"Pigmentation duty?" Nedrick said, wrinkling up his nose. "Is that what stinks?"

"My, my, even the boy recognizes foolishness when he smells it! Yes, good sir, the stench you so wisely detect is from the pigments."

"What are pigments? What are they used for?"

Wallace inhaled deeply. "Ah the aroma of fresh curiosity. It veils even the foulest of odors. Pigmentation, dear boy, is a wretched, useless process, but it tugs at the heartstrings of the fool in us all: the man who desires tradition over progress, sameness over singularity."

Wren let out an exasperated huff. "Nedrick, not only do we live within the Garga trees, but we live off them, as well. We use their leaves in our salads and their sap in our puddings, we use their roots in our medicine and, in the case of pigmentation, we crush up their bark to dye our clothing. It is arduous work, but necessary in our way of life."

"*Alas*, she lies," Emble wailed dramatically. "Nothing is necessary about the pigments. No, my boy, the process continues for tradition and tradition alone, which would be just fine if the dyes didn't smell as rotten as the worst witch in the Western Wince."

Wren pursed her lips. "Now then, everything is prepared for tomorrow morning. We've sent word to the village and they should be expecting us. Mrs. Shaw, have you decided-"

"Yes, yes, let's get to business, shall we?" Wallace cut in. "Hm, let's see here, as a first-rate guide, I must have enthusiastic, if not intrepid, followers. The Sleeping Girl will come with me. The Curious Boy, as well, if he likes?"

"Yes!" exclaimed Nedrick, jumping up from his seat.

"Absolutely not," said Mrs. Shaw yanking a very eager Nedrick out of Wallace's reach. "Nedrick's just a child. And *Olivia* -- well, I'm not risking another daughter -- I'm just not."

Although Livi was moved, (as she always was, whenever Mrs. Shaw referred to her as a daughter) she was also profoundly annoyed (as she always was by Mrs. Shaw's coddling), and today she had no patience for it. "I can do it, Jane. I *want* to. Besides, what other choice do we have? Somebody's got to go."

"Well, not any of *my* children. I'm sorry but I forbid it-"

"Livi's right, Jane, and so is Wren," said Mr. Shaw suddenly, silencing his wife.

"We're here now, and we'll earn our keep."

"Then you and I will go. I'm not sending the children-"

"You need to stay here and look after Violet, and as for me -- well, I wouldn't make it a mile with my old knees. Livi and Benny will go. They are growing up, they can do this." Mr. Shaw rarely had an opinion that wasn't directly in line with his wife's, but when he did, not even Mrs. Shaw dared argue with him.

"Now listen very carefully," Mr. Shaw went on, "you two are going to look after each-other. You'll listen to Wallace, and you won't leave his side, not even for a moment. Is that understood?"

"Yes!" the pair exclaimed in unison.

"But what about me Dad?" whined Nedrick. "How come *they* get to go?"

Mr. Shaw smiled at his youngest son. "They are older, Nedrick. You'll get your day."

• • •

"Adventures abound, wonders ahead, look straight and stay steady, keep your mind ready," Wallace sang gleefully as they marched through the Befallen Forest. With Wallace in the lead, then Livi, and then finally Benny rounding out the back, the trio trekked west, toward Orac Territory.

Livi was in such a good mood today that not even Violet's worsening state could damper her spirits. *Maybe the mooncalf's milk will be enough*, she thought hopefully to herself. *Maybe we'll be headed home soon.* She felt content as she followed Wallace's trail, and happy knowing that Benny was right behind her.

Despite Wallace's promise of adventure, there was nothing much remarkable about their hike into the village, other than the excessively complicated route that he chose through the trees:

Instead of taking the straightest path through the Garga, Wallace led them in winding loops and zigzags, figure-eights and ins and outs, climbing high in the branches, and crawling flat on their stomachs through the brush. He never consulted a map or glanced at compass; he never even paused to consider the way.

It was the middle of the afternoon when they emerged from the Befallen Forest, arriving at the beginning of a dusty dirt road. Wallace pointed to some indistinct markings in the dirt. "Hm, yes. This here is Orac-built. You see this treading in the dirt? It's not far now, I'll tell you that much. Come now, my friends, no adventure's too great for our valiant hearts."

Weary now, the trio moved slowly along the dirt road. Livi's feet were dragging and her back was aching; she was not used to such long journeys, and her whole body felt the strain. Still, she kept on for what seemed like hours, until they finally reached a small cluster of thatched roofs sitting at the bottom of a steep, grassy hill. The dirt path they had been following widened, and straight ahead of them there was a small market where a handful of villagers gathered.

Wallace spread his arms out. "Welcome to Tiethe! It's a small village, as you can plainly see, especially compared to some of the cities the Oracians built farther north, but it has its uses. And the people here are good to us."

Tiethe was not extraordinary. It had no downward growing trees or men in green cloaks. There were fewer than twelve little cottages in the whole village, built of mud and straw and clay, and even the market was small, neat, and perfectly ordinary. But in a strange way, Tiethe was like no place else Livi had ever been. She couldn't say exactly what it was, but it was as if the air was different here, or the people, or the land. The village was quiet, and out of the dozen or more villagers that passed by them, only a few seemed to notice her at all.

Wallace nodded to a local woman he seemed to recognize. "Umbra, you glorious creature. I was just coming to see you."

Umbra was tall and her presence was commanding. Her cheekbones were high, her nose was wide, and she had wrinkles creeping out from the corners of her eyes, that gave away her age. "It's been a long time, friend."

Wallace took Umbra's large hand in his. "*Too* long, too *tragically* long. How are you?"

"Busy. The crops came late this year; we only finished harvesting last month."

"And your father?"

"Father is well. He'll be happy to learn of your visit."

"Umbra is Chief Pax's eldest daughter," Wallace explained to Livi and Benny. "She'll be Chief herself one day. Umbra, this strapping young lad is Benny, and his lady is called Olivia."

"Livi," Livi corrected him sharply. "And I'm not his lady."

"I am happy to meet you both. And on behalf of Chief Pax, I welcome you to Tiethe."

"And what a fine welcome, indeed," Wallace said, "but I'm afraid this is not a social call."

"You're here about the fleet," Umbra interrupted.

"You received my letter, then."

She shook her head. "You're predictable, that's all."

Wallace grinned, and for a moment Livi glimpsed how handsome the tired, shabby man must once have been. "We're in need of some fresh milk. Not a lot -- a liter, at the most. Will he see me?"

Umbra crossed her long, slender arms. "A number of our youth is joining the Guard tonight and the chief will not delay the celebration for you. You may stay the night, of course, and tomorrow, once the feast is through, I'm sure Father will help you."

"Has a year passed already?"

"We're inducting them early, and I expect your people will want to do the same. The Shepherd's numbers are rising, Wallace. Without a proper Guard-"

"You know I have no control over such matters."

"Still, it must be dealt with."

"Now is not the time." Wallace glanced meaningfully at Benny and Livi, who had been listening to the exchange with rabid curiosity.

"Come then, I'll show you to your lodging."

They crossed the small village in a few wide steps and stopped in front of a small cottage. "I'll leave you now. But Wallace, find me later; we have a lot to discuss."

"It'll be too cramped for all three of us," said Wallace once Umbra had left them. "But when the weather is fair like this, I prefer to sleep under the stars anyhow. You two get settled; I've got some things to take care of across the village."

Livi wanted to stop Wallace from leaving. She wanted to demand an explanation for the things she'd overheard, but something told her that this was not the time, and when she glanced over at Benny, it seemed that he felt it too.

The room was cool and dark. A redbrick fireplace took up nearly the whole length of the farthest wall, and across from the door sat a large, low bed. Finally, in the far corner, there was a plain wooden chair with an unlit candelabra balancing on its seat.

Livi dug around in her rucksack, pulling out a book of matches, and Benny crouched in front of the fireplace. Several minutes later, once the fire was raging and the candles were lit, the two friends sat down next to each other on the hard straw mattress.

"Your face -- you're all healed," she said, brushing her fingers lightly against his cheekbone. Only this morning the area had been purple and puffy.

"Yeah, I guess so." He pulled up his shirt and examined his once-bruised torso. "That's funny -- I mean, I've always been a quick healer, but it's not even been three days. Maybe it's the Midlands. The air out here does seem fresher, maybe it's that."

"Or maybe it's Violet," said Livi, ignoring the way that Benny winced at the sound of his dying sister's name. "Wren did say that Violet had the power to heal people."

"Do you think?"

"You are twins. That's got to mean something."

Benny shrugged vaguely.

"Hey, I've been thinking," she began again, carefully. "Remember what Wren said about that other medicine?"

"The Emickus stuff?"

"Yes, exactly. I was thinking that if -- well, you know, if the mooncalf's milk doesn't work out, then we should go and track down the Emickus ourselves. Wren said it would *cure* her, Ben."

"Yeah, and Wren also said it was a suicide mission."

"But the risk's worth it, isn't it?"

Benny hesitated. "You're serious?"

"Of course I'm serious. Violet's like a sister to me. I can't let her-"

"She won't. She's going to be fine. This mooncalf milk is gonna fix her right up and then we're going get back to Primareaux where we belong and that'll be that."

Benny was deadly stubborn when he wanted to be, and Livi didn't see a point in arguing. She hoped that he was right, of course, but if he wasn't -- if the mooncalf's milk *wasn't* enough -- then she promised herself she'd be prepared.

7

UNTHINKING

IT WAS A PECULIAR HOUR: the day was over, but except for a few early stars, night hadn't yet fallen. The feast would begin soon and they still had lots to prepare. When Wallace returned to the guest cottage he was accompanied by a large Oracian man named Petu. Petu helped Benny and Wallace get ready for the feast in the guest cottage, and Livi was sent across the village, to Umbra's home.

Umbra and her sisters drew a warm bath and scrubbed Livi clean. They braided feathers into her hair and dressed her in a fine turquoise skirt and a matching beaded blouse that revealed most of her mid-drift. It was an outfit that Mrs. Shaw would undoubtedly find indecent, but Livi thought it was wonderful.

By the time she stepped out of the Umbra's cottage, the party was in full swing. An enormous bonfire raged in the center of town, and the smell of roasting boar filled the air. Drummers drummed and songstresses belted out proud tribal anthems; men and women danced together, their bare feet apparently unbothered by the hard, rocky ground; little girls held hands, twirling in circles under the wide, navy sky, and little boys ran wild through the village.

Livi spotted Benny squatting on one of the many colorful blankets spread out around the fire. Like her, Benny donned traditional Oracian clothing, and his bare chest was covered in rich red and turquoise paint.

The feast tonight was in honor the boys and girls in the village who were being inducted into something called the Midlands Guard. Tonight, children as young as Nedrick would become men, as they accepted the great honor of serving Tiethe, and the lands beyond. Speeches would be made and traditions would unfold, and by the end of night, every eligible boy and girl in the village would be inducted into the Guard.

Livi watched with reverence as the first inductee (a little girl with rosy cheeks and two long sable braids) began the walk down the fire-laden aisle, to stand in front of Chief Pax. But she was just halfway down the aisle when the ceremony was brought to a sudden and untimely end: a screech -- sharper and more potent than a lamb at slaughter -- filled the air, and sent the village into mayhem.

Men and women were running in every direction, shielding their children or shoving them into nearby houses. Torches were lit and bows were drawn. Some of the younger boys wielded slingshots and rocks, and some of the older men shouted for order. The music was replaced with wails of terror and the bonfire (which only moments ago, felt warm and safe and welcoming) became a deadly welt in the earth.

The Guard formed chains of protection around the circumference of the village, but Livi could not tell what they were protecting the village *from*. She was frozen and confused and had no idea where she belonged. Thankfully, someone was there to take charge:

"Get back!" Wallace screamed, running toward Livi and Benny. "Get down, now, hurry."

"What is it?" Benny cried. "What's going on?"

"Come -- this way!" He pulled them into the nearest cottage and pushed them to ground. "Stay down, and stay quiet. I'll be back as soon as I can." Wallace disappeared before they could protest, and the pair was left alone on the floor of the dark cottage.

But the chaos melted away as quickly as it had risen. Through a crack in the door, Livi watched as the tumult ceased; the yelling had been replaced with eery silence, and the mob of villagers had broken up completely. Most people had fled indoors, and those who remained were hidden and silent. There was no sign of intrusion, no sound that shouldn't be. But the horrible fear remained. The uncertainty was overpowering, and though Livi had no idea what she was afraid of, she was gripped -- nearly paralyzed -- by the unknown.

Wallace came back several long minutes later. "The Guard is holding control, but barely. We're going to have to move."

"I'm not going anywhere until you tell us what's out there," Livi demanded.

Wallace pointed beyond the warriors, whose colorful war paint Livi could just make out, and directed her to look into the now pitch-back forest. "Look there, through the shadows."

She leaned over Wallace to get a better look through the ajar door. "Where? There's nothing."

"Look *properly*. Look properly and perhaps you may even see."

From the cottage, she had a clear view all the way out to the edge of the village. Except for the warriors, who had stationed themselves around the periphery, not a soul remained in sight. Then, just beyond the line of soldiers, something moved that shouldn't have: an indistinct mass of shadows, moving in perfect synchronicity, shifted left, inching closer. Not quite anything, as hard as she tried, Livi couldn't find a word for what they were, or where they might belong.

She pointed at the collection of dark little creatures. "There, is that what you mean?"

"*Yes, yes*. Now don't draw attention to us. They might be as dense as night-rats, but they'll know us if they see us."

Benny snickered. "What happened to our *valiant* hearts?"

"The Unthinkers will take our hearts, and our minds too. *Stay down.*" As he spoke, something happened at the front line: first one warrior, then two, then four, and soon half the Guard broke formation and began a slow stride toward the strange clump of shadows. "It's too late, the Guard has fallen. We must go. Now, *now* -- we must go!"

This time no protests were uttered, no questions called. Livi and Benny followed obediently behind Wallace as he sprinted out of hiding and joined the mob of desperate, terrified Oracians already crowding the narrow dirt roads, running toward safety.

But the creatures moved swiftly. In a blink, hundreds -- maybe thousands -- of Unthinkers swarmed the village. A dozen or more burley Oracian soldiers walked among them now, bleary-eyed and slack-jawed and dazed. The creatures themselves had no identifiable form -- no mouths or hooves, no eyes or snouts -- which made them even more terrifying to Livi, who glanced back fearfully as she ran.

And then something very strange happened: Livi stopped running. And so did Benny. And Wallace. All around, wild expressions of fear were replaced with quiet, glazed over eyes. An uncomfortable calm had sedated the whole village, making legs heavy and minds tired.

Next to her Benny held the same vacant, almost peaceful expression as all the others. *Something terrible is happening*, she thought tiredly.

Fear grabbed her, cutting through the false calm, the vague peace, the impossible exhaustion. But it lasted only seconds. Then she was in a daze again, falling backward into a warm, empty contentment.

But fear clawed its way up again, and this time it went nowhere. She was alert and terrified; there was a shooting pain and a second later, her mind -- her whole *soul* -- pulled out from her body.
A rush of wind blew her up and up, higher and faster, past the small group of clay houses, and into the starry night sky.

8

LUMAE

LIVI COULDN'T FEEL HER BODY. She couldn't move her fingers or wiggle her toes. She had no ground to walk on and no legs to carry her, and when she tried to look down at herself, she saw only a blast of impossibly bright light. Livi was someplace else, someplace outside of herself, and the view from here was extraordinary.

Dying isn't so hard, she thought vaguely as she floated amid the hazy purple clouds. *It didn't hurt at all, and besides, things are so pretty up here.* But her peace was interrupted when somewhere down below voices spoke her name:

"Livi, no!" Benny sobbed. *"No, no, no,* not you. Please, not you."

"What's happened?" called another voice.

"What's going on?" called a third. "What's the meaning of this?"

"It's Livi, she's-"

"She's a Luma!" proclaimed Wallace. "How spectacular. How wonderfully, marvelously good! Why, she's saved us all."

Shouts of unbridled joy mottled the air, and Livi struggled to hold on to the familiar voices of Benny and

Wallace, listening blindly as they discussed her fate:

"Lumae are so very rare that no one goes looking for signs anymore," Wallace explained to Benny.

"Livi might have lived out all her years without knowing what she was. Luckily for her -- luckily for us all -- it seems that she was scared straight out of her body."

Wallace explained about the Lumae, their history, and as he put it, their gift of metamorphosis: While Livi's body remained earth-bound, her soul had condensed itself outside of her body. All the important bits -- all the things that made her *her*, had flown away. Of course, she would not be stuck in two parts forever; she only needed to learn how to put herself back together again.

So I'm not dead? Livi thought quizzically. *But then, what-?* Livi knew no suitable way to finish that thought, for if she wasn't dead then something very peculiar was happening. Fear swelled within her yet again.

"So where is she?" Benny asked anxiously. "I don't understand. Where has she gone to?"

"Now, son, the danger has passed, so *should* the dramatics. She is probably frightened -- hiding somewhere -- in the clouds or under the sea. Stop pouting boy, she'll find us soon enough."

But Livi was not so certain. She stared hopelessly into the great darkness and tried to focus on the direction the voices were coming from. How could she find them when she could not see them? And how could she go to them when she could not move?

The longer she stared into the dark night clouds, the more things came into focus. Everything was different in her new form. Sounds and tastes and feelings and smells -- they all came from someplace outside of her body -- someplace guttural. Everything felt more potent and more precise, especially her new sense of sight.

In this form, she could see farther and stronger. She could look past things that were in her way. If Livi focused, she could see through the dense night's sky and into the village of Tiethe, where the night's festivities had been abandoned.

Most people had retreated indoors and those that remained were huddled in groups of two and three, talking quietly about what had happened.

She found them -- Benny and Wallace -- leaning up against the side of a cottage. And there was a third among them: it was her, *Livi*! Well, it was her body at least, resting on Benny's wadded up sweater. A deep longing rose within her, and half a second later she was moving down and down and down, and back to earth.

What drove her, she did not know, but as fast as lightening, she was hovering above the pair of men. Wallace and Benny stared wide-eyed at the strange form before them: a creature carved from light, like a star that somehow came alive and floated down to earth.

"Glorious, *simply* glorious."

"Livi, is that you?"

"I -- I ... well, yes. I *think* I'm me." She stumbled over her words as her voice rippled through the air like music, only vaguely resembling her harsh human tone.

"What happened? Where'd you go?"

"I don't know. I was trapped among those shadow animals, just like the rest of you, and then the next thing I knew, I was being pulled up into the air. I thought I had died."

"Not dead, my Sleeping Girl. Not dead, not close."

"Wallace, what's happened to me? What -- what's a *Luma*?"

"You've been eavesdropping, I see."

Wallace explained again all he knew about the Lumae, their mysterious origins, and how very rare they were: "Lumae are human, plain and simple. They need air to breathe and food on their plates. They need friendship and love and they come from mothers and fathers, just the same as all the rest of us. But they -- *you* -- are a bit more than all that. You are not limited by the physical. You are not stuck in a pitiful, half-able human body until the day you die."

"But how do I fix it?"

"*Fix* it? Are you mad? There's nothing to *fix*, child. You are perfect -- *better*, even. You are a Luma. You can fly, you can float, change shape, melt and mold. What you are -- what you can do-"

"But my *body*. I'm split in two!" And indeed, Livi *was* split in two: her body lay limp on the ground while the rest of her hovered brilliantly above her friends.

"Only temporarily, dear," Wallace reassured her. "You can put yourself back together anytime you wish, it will only take some practice."

Well, I'm ready right now, she thought stubbornly. With a sudden and magnificent thrust, Livi propelled herself toward her vacant body, only to bounce right off of it and back up into the clouds.

"What *was* that?" cried Benny. "What just happened?"

"She can't break the barrier between her soul and her body. She doesn't know how."

"But she's done it before."

"Not consciously. Don't worry, Benjamin, she'll learn. It will only take time."

"How *much* time?" said Livi in a huff, flying back into their eyesight.

"Ah, a very good question, very good indeed. But it's a question that you, and you alone, will have to answer."

• • •

Ever since Livi floated back into the village, a crowd had been growing around her. Now practically ever person in Tiethe was there -- every eye drawn to the strange light-form above them, every face eagerly awaiting Livi's next attempt to put herself back together. Livi had no interest in indulging the nosy villagers, however, and so she abandoned her quest to rejoin her body and went on talking to Wallace as if nobody was watching: "Wallace, what was it that attacked us back before I changed?"

"That dear, was a herd of Unthinkers -- a very large, very powerful herd. Unthinkers are the darkest and most terrible creatures in all the Midlands. They are not human but they were once, long ago for most of them. And they do not kill, like most monsters; they trap. Unthinkers will trap you, hold you, and turn you without any effort at all. One walk among a herd and you will lose yourself forever."

A murmur of agreement floated through the crowd, but Livi didn't understand. "What do you mean, *lose* yourself?"

Wallace shuddered, as if he was remembering something painful. "First you will move like the rest, then you will look like the rest, then finally, you will unthink like the rest. Once that happens your only business will be stealing others' souls -- making new Unthinkers, just like you. I was close to joining them tonight, my dear, closer than I ever thought I'd be. I owe you a great deal. We all do."

"You owe *me*?"

"Oh yes, my Sleeping Girl. The Unthinkers would have taken us all if it weren't for you. I'd say you gave them quite a startle."

"Startled? By *me*?"

"I wish you'd seen it, Livi," Benny exclaimed. Until then, Livi had been so entranced by Wallace's story, and so preoccupied with her attempt to ignore the large group of strangers crowding her, that she had nearly forgotten Benny was there. She smiled inwardly at the sight of him, calmed slightly by his presence. "The second you burst out of your body, they all scattered, scared as ever, as if *they* were the ones running for their lives. It was amazing. I just wish you could've seen it."

Scared of me? Running from me? she thought, bewildered. Then, aloud: "I don't get it. I just don't get what they were afraid of."

"I'll admit, my insight into the *how* and the *why* is somewhat limited, (you're the first Luma I've ever had the pleasure to meet, you see) but the concept is simple enough: the moment you transitioned into your Luma-form, the Unthinkers scattered; they ran for their lives. You've saved us, Olivia, and from a hand far worse than death."

"It's true," said Umbra, emerging abruptly from the crowd of onlookers. "If it weren't for you, our whole village might be at the mercy of the Shepherd right now."

The Shepherd. It was a name Livi had heard only once before: just a few hours ago when Umbra first came to greet them. "Who's the Shepherd? You've mentioned him before, who his he?"

Suddenly the whole crowd was speaking at once. No one knew where exactly the Shepherd came from, but no one could remember a time before him. And no one seemed able to agree who the creature really was: "The Shepherd's an animal" -- "He is a vicious, heartless man" -- "The Shepherd is evil" -- "He does not feel at all" -- "He knows no better" -- "He knows everything!"

But one voice rose above the rest: "The Shepherd's got the wit of a man and the claws of a lion," said Wallace. "He pulls the strings and controls the curtain. The Shepherd is master of those Unthinkers. Those, and all the others."

The Unthinkers were the Shepherd's great weapon, and their numbers were growing every day. The Midlands Guard was put in place to fight off the Shepherd's growing herd, but lately they were failing.

"Livi, you will join the Guard, won't you?" said Umbra. "You -- your gift -- could change everything."

Join the Guard? That was not the plan, not all. How could Umbra ask that of her? And now of all times -- when she was split in half. Right now she did not care about the tribe, or the Midlands, or even the kind people at the Petrichor. She was afraid and confused and utterly exhausted. All she wanted was for things to go back to nor--mal. And although Livi said none of this, her silence spoke for her.

"Forgive me; now is not the time for such talk. But please know, we are so grateful for what you've done. If there's anything we can do-"

"You can take us to the mooncalves."

"Of course. The moment you are ready I'll take you there myself."

• • •

Over the next several hours Livi tried all sorts of tactics to rejoin her body: she hovered above and tried to push herself back in; she slunk lower and lower, only to pass right through her body all together; finally she resorted back to pushing as hard as she could, certain that the next time would heed different results than the last.

"This isn't working," Benny said, sighing loudly. It was the dead of night and the village was quiet. By now even Wallace had retired, leaving Livi and Benny alone in the center of the deserted village market.

"You're clearly doing something wrong, Livi, so just stop. Take a break."

"Well, I've got to try something--or do you *want* me to be stuck like this forever?"

"You never have been very patient, have you? Here, I have an idea: no more charging and banging and trying to force yourself back into your body. Just relax. When the time is right it'll happen on its own."

"That's not an idea; that's giving up."

"Come on now, just try it."

Livi was exhausted now and she had little patience for Benny's gentle ways. But she was also bruised and weakened, and too tired to argue.

"So what do ya think Ned'll say once he finds out about you?" Benny asked once Livi had begun to relax.

To that question, Livi had to laugh, which, in her new voice, sounded more like she was trying to sing. "He'll probably faint or something -- or try to run away."

"Can't *I* be a Luma?" Benny continued in a mocking, high pitched whine. "Nothing exciting ever happens to *me*."

Here, laughing with Benny, everything seemed easy and familiar. He didn't seem to mind talking to a light in the sky, and she no longer felt embarrassed to be one. They talked about everything, the words *Shepherd* and *Unthinker* and *Luma* and *Guard* moving back and forth between them so frequently that they stopped feeling foreign.

Then, when everything felt safe and calm and quiet, she began to melt. She didn't notice at first. But then, the angle of Benny's face began to change: she was no longer hovering high above him. Instead, she was lower and wider and her voice was liquid smooth. "Something's happened isn't it? Am I?-"

"Don't think about it, Livi. It's happening all on its own."

"Well, what does it look like?"

Benny watched as she went lower and lower, molding around her lifeless body. Soon every inch of her body was coated in white light. "It's beautiful."

With those words, and a sudden twist of pain, Livi was whole again.

• • •

An hour later, Livi was on her way to the pasture to find the mooncalves. It was still night, but she could feel dawn coming; if they were going to catch the mooncalves, they would have to hurry. Wallace walked next to Umbra, Benny next to Livi, and leading the pack was Chief Pax himself. Squat, with a bulbous center, the chief had long silver hair, ruddy skin, and kind, sparkling eyes. Though he hadn't said a single word since their initial meeting, Livi liked the chief, and felt comfortable as she followed him down the dirt road.

The trail was lined with rows of tall, skinny trees with flaking, white bark and paper thin leaves. They walked until the road ended and the trees thinned, arriving in a wide open pasture. The moon was already beginning to fade, and there were no mooncalves in sight. The chief took a few steps forward and pulled out of his satchel a pointed, iridescent horn.

"Very rare," muttered Wallace. "Carved out of moonstone."

Chief Pax put the horn to his lips and blew three times.

Several tense seconds passed. Finally, a warm wind blew through the pasture and the sky filled with light.

First, there was only one -- a newborn, trotting elegantly across the dark night's sky, descending into the soft green pasture. Its smooth hide shone prismatically and its new legs wobbled nervously on the earthy ground. Another and another landed, trotting into Livi's world from somewhere else.

Soon the pasture was full of them, their enormous golden eyes shining brightly in the dark night. Some, like the first, were just babies; the smallest of the bunch barely came up to her waist. But most were grown, and stood large and hearty. Their snouts were square and blush, their ears, offset from their heads, were pearly white, and their eyes were as mysterious as the very surface of the moon, from which they haled.

"They're beautiful," Benny whispered.

"Beautiful, but dim," said Wallace. "Their souls are shaped differently. No need for a mind like ours where they come from."

"You underestimate them," spoke the chief. "One man's dunce is another's teacher. Befriend a mooncalf and you will never be short a sage."

Chief Pax moved approached the fleet cautiously, his head bowed, his hands together.

Not the largest or the proudest, the calf who came forward showed no clear indicator of being leader, except perhaps hidden well behind her eyes. She bowed her head slightly, and Chief Pax did the same.

"There is a sick child, sick with the Fever," the chief explained, speaking directly to the animal. "We need your milk to heal her."

At the Chief's command, Umbra knelt beside the mooncalf and took out a tin canister from her satchel. She whispered something and then pressed her hand to the calf's belly. Then she began to milk.

9

HOPE

THE INFIRMARY WAS QUIET today. It had been five days since they arrived back with the mooncalf's milk, and Violet's health was steadily improving. This morning, Livi sat at her bedside, listening patiently as Violet chirped away, just like the old days:

"And once I'm feeling completely better, Wren's going to teach me how to harness my energy, whatever *that* means. Isn't it wonderful?"

"Is Wren an Empath too?"

"I don't think so, but she knows all about us. Oh, she's just *amazing*, Livi. I've never met anybody even half as brave as Wren. She knows all sorts of things and has been practically *every*where. And you've *got* to ask her about the time she travelled to Northern Trilinia to treat an ailing Curmudgeon, whatever *that* is."

Livi was working hard to focus on Violet's rapid speech, but her mind kept wandering. Her eyes darted aimlessly across the sickroom, past the line of empty white cots, and then back to Violet, who looked annoyed.

"Are you even listening?" Violet said. "Wren says I could be fully on my feet by the spring! Isn't that wonderful?"

"It's not that simple," interjected Wren, who had just walked in. "You mustn't push yourself too hard; we still don't know how you're going to handle things in the long term."

"But I don't *feel* sick."

"Then the medicine is doing its job. But there is simply no telling what's to come."

"Oh, let's not think about that now. Come sit next me and tell Livi about that time you rescued the fallen Small."

• • •

By the end of the second week, Violet's fever had broken entirely, and her pain was practically nonexistent. Wren still preached caution, but even she grew optimistic as the days went on and Violet kept growing stronger.

As they became more secure in her recovery, Livi and the others began to embrace their roles as Petchlings, involving themselves in the regular chores and duties that kept the Petrichor afloat. Mr. Shaw utilized his skills as an engineer, working as a communications officer at a pipe-station down on the leaf-end of Esker; Mrs. Shaw helped in the nursery on the second floor of the Atrium, tending to the babies and toddlers who weren't yet ready to begin their schooling. Nedrick, as the only member of the family who was still of school-age here, spent his days with the other children on the ground floor of the Atrium, where classes commenced; and Benny spent his time in the outfields on the south-side of the Petrichor, learning about farming.

Livi spent some days in the fields with Benny, and some days shadowing a woman named Mrs. Mewlik as she patrolled the grounds. Of course, Wallace managed to cross paths with her nearly every day, and he never failed to pester her about joining Midlands Guard:

"But we need all our young people," he argued. "Has what happened in Tiethe already left your mind? Benny's willing -- eager, even -- to join up, and I expect I can count on Nedrick soon enough."

"They don't know what they're agreeing to, Wallace. And besides we'll only be here for a few more weeks. The moment Violet's strong enough, we'll be going home."

"But a few weeks could make all the difference."

"It's not happening, I'm sorry."

It wasn't exactly the Midlands Guard to which Livi was so sharply apposed; more-so, it was why the Guard wanted her: the only reason they were so eager for her to join them was because she had some freakish thing inside her that could drive off the Unthinkers, and she just wanted to forget all that.

Livi had hoped that when Mrs. Shaw heard what happened in the Oracian village, she would forbid Livi from ever transitioning into her Luma-form again; she had even counted on that as her excuse. But strangely, Mrs. Shaw was not the least bit surprised when she found out:

"Oh, is that what it's called? Livi, your mother was like that too, only we never knew what to call it. I think it's a wonderful thing. I hope you'll nurture it."

Livi found no solace in the discovery that her mother had been a Luma. In fact, she was less eager than ever to address her newly discovered talent. Wallace, however, was thrilled by Mrs. Shaw's reaction, and he went out of his way to make that known. It was the first time Wallace and Mrs. Shaw had found themselves on the same side of an argument, and the pair was excruciating.

Trying to explain things to Wallace or Mrs. Shaw separately was enough of a challenge; going up against them both at the same time was nearly impossible, and so for the next week and a half, Livi spent nearly all her time trying to avoid Wallace and Jane Shaw. She threw herself into her chores, explored the nooks and crannies and secret back alleyways of the Petrichor, and snuck to the infirmary as often as she could to check in on Violet.

Even the chores she detested were better than sitting idly by and waiting for Wallace or Mrs. Shaw (or *worse* -- both of them!) to sneak up and pester her, and with that in mind, Livi woke up briskly on Wednesday morning, skipped breakfast, and moved hurriedly through the crowd-

ed Atrium and down the chilly sloped path, to the
Yownth Tunnel.

The Yownth Tunnel was home to the most arduous
and archaic chore in all the Petrichor: Pigmentation Duty.
There were many elements to the process of pigmentation,
but the worst by far, was the quern-stone. Taking the rough
outer layer of Garga bark, crushing it down, and then
squeezing out the acrid amber dye was a three person job,
and it took hours. Today was Livi's first time working the
quern-stone and she had no idea with whom she would be
partnered, but as long as it wasn't Wallace or Mrs. Shaw,
she didn't care.

The Yownth Tunnel was much as she expected it to
be: dark and chilly and rather uninviting. It was a somewhat
narrow space, which felt especially cramped because it was
crowded with grumpy looking Petchlings rolling barrels and
loading hand trucks and stirring pots of a foul smelling liquid which Livi assumed to be the Garga dye. And so she
was very pleased when she saw the sunny, smiling face of
Elder Emble marching toward her.

Only, Livi had to do a double-take, because at the exact moment that Emble popped up in front of her, a second
man, dressed identically to Emble from head-to-toe, with an
identical mop of messy ashen hair, and the same large,
slightly hooked nose in the middle of the same long face,
also arrived. Except across this man's distinctly Emble-like
face was the most unpleasant scowl Livi had ever seen.

Emble slapped Livi heartily on the back, jolting her
out of her surprised daze. "Livi, dear girl, so pleased you've
made it. You know my brother -- or perhaps you don't.
This is Imble. Don't be alarmed, he's a disagreeable fool at
first, but once you get to him he's nearly tolerable!" Emble's laughter echoed through the tunnel.

Imble pouted and stuck out his hand begrudgingly,
which Livi took with distinct discomfort. "Humph. She
appears perfectly unexceptional to me."

"*Pardon?*" said Livi.

"I *said* you appear unexceptional."

"You're being rude Imble," Emble interjected before

the exchange could escalate. "Forgive him, please, my dear. All my foolish brother means is that we've been hearing so very much about your marvelous encounter with the Un-thinkers and we've been on pins and needles waiting to see it for ourselves. You will show us, won't you? You will change into your Luma?"

"Is that what this is about?" Livi snapped. "I was wondering, you know ... I was wondering what two *Elders* were doing on pigmentation duty. You're just trying to cor-ner me. Oh I'm going to *kill* Wallace."

"Wallace? You think Wallace set this up?" said Em-ble, looking confused. "Oh no, Livi, I'm sure you're mis-taken. Even we Elders must suffer pigmentation duty once a month. Being paired with you was merely a fortuitous coincidence."

Livi felt blood rush to her cheeks. "I see."

"Hah!" Imble scoffed. "You think I'd spend a whole day stuck down here just to get a chance to talk to you? *Hah!*"

"Let's just get to work, okay?" All around them eve-ryone was already hard at work. Livi walked hurriedly over to the only unmanned station left in the tunnel and rested her hand inexpertly on the long wooden handle that jutted out from the side of the ancient looking contraption.

The quern-stone was large (nearly three feet in diame-ter), and as its name suggested, was made almost entirely of stone. Over the next hour, Emble patiently explained to Livi how the quern-stone worked, reviewing its various components, from the two wheel-like pieces of stone that sat one on top of the other, to the wooden crank that jutted off the side of the top wheel, to the hole in the center, where the bark was poured in. All the while Imble moaned and groaned and paced irritably back and forth, whining about wasting time, and getting in the way of the many other Petchlings working nearby.

By quarter-after-ten in the morning Livi had ground up her first batch of bark and was getting ready to make it into dye. An hour after that, she was plugging her nose as the first drizzling of dye dripped into the empty barrel that

Emble had put in place at the spout carved into the stone wheel. By half-past-one they'd filled three barrels, and it was time for lunch.

Sandwiches were sent down from the kitchen, and the trio retreated to a small apple orchard near the outfields on the south-side of the Petrichor, finding a comfortable spot in the sun to eat. But before Livi's eyes had time to adjust to the midday sun, Imble had disappeared back inside, complaining that his sandwich smelled rancid, and leaving Livi alone with the more agreeable brother.

The pair made smalltalk for a while, and Emble complimented Livi on her hard work in the tunnel. But Livi had never been very good at smalltalk, especially when she had more interesting things on her mind.

"Emble, may I ask you something?"

"Certainly."

"I've noticed that most of you here have grayish, sort of ash colored hair. Even the children. Why is that?"

"Hm, yes. That would seem odd to you, wouldn't it? Let's see, how shall I explain it? Well, you live here in the Petrichor long enough -- taking shelter within it, seeking nourishment from it -- and the Petrichor starts to bargain a bit with you, to ask for something in return."

"You talk about the Petrichor like it's alive."

"Well, of course it's alive! Stand up my dear, follow me."

Livi followed Emble as he hobbled across the orchard, back to the Petrichor. He pressed his hand against a low point on the outer wall and Livi did the same. "Feel that, my girl? Do you feel it?" Beneath the warm, rough amber bark was a gentle, steady pulsing, much like a heartbeat.

"What is that?"

"It's just what you think, Olivia -- it's the Petrichor's heart. It's been beating long before any us, and it'll keep on going after we're gone."

The pair retreated back into the sunny spot in orchard.

"So the Petrichor takes your coloring?"

"She's doesn't take it. We give to her as a sort of tribute. Those of us with pale eyes and ashen hair have pledged ourselves to her service, to her protection. It is our way of honoring her, and of giving a little bit back of what she's given to us."

"It is our bondage, our branding," said Elder Imble grumpily, reemerging from the Petrichor and sitting down next to his brother.

"It's our *choice*," Emble snapped in retort. "And one I'm proud to make. No one is obligated to serve the Petrichor, but we live longer than anyone in Eaux or Trilinia or anywhere else in the Midlands, even. We are safe within these walls, we have been blessed with so much. So the Petrichor asks something from us in return? It's a small sacrifice, I think."

Livi nodded somewhat absently. "It sounds like a fair trade."

"Oh, but *fair* is a funny thing, isn't it?" said Imble sourly. Though physically identical, there were such irreconcilable differences in the brothers' dispositions that it was easy to forget Imble and Emble were related at all. "Anything worth doing is likely not to work itself out quite *fairly*, now is it? Life and death? Love? Hatred? Injustice? Have we each shared in such experiences *fairly*? I should say not!

"So you see an unfair life is as fair as any other, and in this way they are not opposing words at all, but sad and disappointing synonyms." He ended lightly, almost carelessly in tone, and then smiled at his somewhat convoluted proclamation, apparently pleased with himself.

Emble, looking unamused, glared sharply at his brother. "Fair or foul, or then perhaps both, why trouble the girl, brother? For today life is glorious."

And life was glorious for many days to follow. Livi worked hard all day, and watched happily as Violet continued to get stronger. And in her free time, she explored the Petrichor. She wandered delightedly through its secrets halls and trap doors, its vast libraries and winding corridors. There were books in languages she'd never heard of and maps of places she'd never been; there were trees growing within trees; rows of stores with interesting confections;

candlemakers and glassblowers and potters. And Livi loved it all.

Then one evening, right as she was really beginning to feel comfortable, the peace was shattered: halfway through supper, Wren stormed into the dining room and charged at full-speed toward the Elders' table. Strangely Quizzle seemed to have been anticipating Wren's interruption, and he got up immediately to let her whisper in his ear. A moment later, the entire table stood up to leave.

A sick feeling formed in the pit of Livi's stomach as she watched as the twelve men in green file out of the crowded dining hall. Something was wrong, she could feel it.

That night, well, after midnight, Violet's fever spiked, and her pain came back raging; her screams shredded the air, ringing up and down the Atrium, and waking Livi from an uneasy slumber.

Though the sound was vague and diluted by the time it reached the dormitories, Livi recognized Violet's scream immediately, for it was the sound of true agony. After such a great (though brief) period of convalescence, Violet's new wave of misery was too much for Livi to bear. As she approached the seventh floor infirmary, she heard Violet's cries more clearly -- her curses and her prayers for death -- and for the first time, Livi wished them to come true.

Livi was the last of the group to find her way to the dull gray waiting-room. Mr. Shaw looked red-faced and stoic as usual, but poor Mrs. Shaw looked sick to her stomach, and Nedrick was practically wild with grief. Worst of all was Benny, who sat in the corner looking shrunken and vacant and nearly dead himself.

"She's dying, Livi, she's dying," Nedrick wailed, jumping from his seat and throwing himself into her arms, but Livi pushed him away.

"Stop crying. I said *stop it.*"

"But-"

"Don't you think everyone's got enough to deal with without you wailing about like a newborn baby? It's going to be fine; I'm going to take care of everything, so just shut up already. Now where's Wren?"

"She's dealing with something else, apparently," Mr. Shaw said. "Something more important than a dying girl."

"A nurse has been helping," explained Mrs. Shaw, "but she can't seem to calm Violet down, not the way Wren can."

For once Livi was thankful that she wasn't allowed in Violet's room during treatment. No matter what the young nurse did, Violet would not be soothed. Her cries carried on through sedatives and pain killers and it wasn't until Wren showed up at dawn that the cries finally ceased. Within the hour, Violet was fast asleep.

• • •

"I was afraid this would happen," said Wren the next evening as she sat with Livi in the eleventh floor library. "A battle was fought last night, just a little way's south of here. Half a dozen of our people were lost, and even more from the other side. Poor Violet's taken all that pain on herself ... we're lucky the trauma didn't do even more damage."

"*Lucky?*"

"She's alive isn't she? She's even leveled out a bit since last night."

"Is the battle why you called all the Elders out of dinner yesterday?"

Wren nodded. "There was a small skirmish between some local tribes -- well, we had expected it to be small ... it's become quite the mess -- a real war."

"What's that got to do with the Petrichor? We're not at war, are we?"

"No, we're not at war. But we have an alliance with the Oracs so we sent in a few of our people to aid them, and to try to keep the peace. It certainly seems we've failed on that count, now doesn't it?"

"Who were the Oracs fighting?"

"The Soophecs -- *again*."

"I've never heard of them."

"Well, it's not likely you would have. Unless of course you've been strolling around the Western Wince recently," she added with a wink.

According to Wren the Soophecs were a vicious, clandestine people. They were born on the West Coast, right off the Wince but they'd been expanding eastward for some time now. The Oracs were trying to stop them, but so far they'd had little success. "The Soophecs are brutal fighters, brilliant strategists. The Oracians are strong, but they're no match for the Soophec army. Mathilda's team has been helping enormously, but this can't go on forever."

"You don't mean Mathilda Battlebee?"

"That's the one. If it weren't for her, the Soophecs would have pushed east a long time ago. How do you know her?"

"She used to live near me in Primareaux. She was the one who sent us here."

"Well, you'll be reunited soon enough. Mathilda's on her way back here as we speak. And you know, she's always been a talented nurse, maybe she can-"

"Mrs. Battlebee can't do anything. She's already tried to help Violet, and she didn't get anywhere."

Wren sighed loudly. "Well, like I said, she's stable for now, and of course, we'll get her some more milk and keep her sedated as much of the time as possible; assuming no more battles are raged close by she'll likely be okay for another few months. But in the long stretch, I'm afraid it's not looking good."

"What about the Emickus. The Emickus would help, wouldn't it?"

"I've already told you, that is not an option."

"But if it were-"

"*It isn't.* Now why don't you make yourself useful and run down to the infirmary to relieve Jane."

10

HARD BARGAINS

WHEN LIVI FIRST OFFERED her services to Midlands Guard in exchange for help getting the Violet the medicine she needed, Wallace looked at his precious Sleeping Girl as if she had lost her mind. It took a long evening of hard negotiation for him to even consider the idea, but once he did, the rest of the plan fell smoothly into place.

They decided that out of the two places that Emickus still grew (in Eterneaux, inside the First Palace, and in the Midlands, on the Western Wince), getting into the First Palace would prove a slightly less dangerous journey. Wallace agreed to act as her guide, but to have any hope of success, they would need the support of the Petrichor and the Elders. The Elders could provide things like maps and weapons and links to safe houses along the way. They could grant the use of an ark and even provide a small team to help them.

Wallace promised to present their plan to the Elders as soon as the sun rose, and Livi left their meeting feeling almost gleeful. Morning was still a few hours off, but she was too excited to wait until then to share her plans. She ran straight to Benny's dormitory to wake him, but to her surprise Benny was already up, reading a book at his desk.

"Break into the First Palace!" he bellowed once Livi had shared her plans with him. "That's the craziest thing I've ever heard. And especially now -- with people disappearing in Etnereaux left and right -- you can't seriously be considering it?"

"It was my idea, of course I'm considering it."

"Well, you're not going."

"I thought you'd be happy; this is the only real chance Violet's got."

Benny scoffed. "*Happy*? You thought I'd be happy about you running out like a fool, trying to play the hero? There's a reason no one's tried this before -- it's just too dangerous. We'll have to find another way."

"There is no other way, Benny; I'm Violet's only chance."

"But she's already so much better from last night. She might not even need the Emickus."

"I know you don't believe that."

"Well, fine, then I'm going with you," Benny concluded after a second's hesitation.

"Oh no you're not. You'll stay here and take care of Violet, and you're going to join the Guard too, just like you planned."

"Am I?"

"You are. Because it's the right thing -- and I've never seen you do anything but that."

"And what will Mother say? She barely let us go to Tiethe, for Astor's sake! Do you really think-"

"She'd do anything to save Violet."

"She wouldn't risk you."

"Of course she would."

"That's not true."

"Of *course* it is. And besides, it's not up to her. I'm sorry, Benny, but I'm going."

• • •

As certain as she had acted while talking to Benny, deep down Livi was not sure what Mrs. Shaw would think about her plan, and after she and Benny parted, she decided to find out.

"Good morning," Livi said quietly, surprising Mrs. Shaw, who was slouched in a chair next to Violet's bed.

"What are you doing up so early, dear?" Jane asked, a thin, nervous vale of sweat covering her pale forehead. "It's not even dawn -- you should be in bed."

"I couldn't sleep. How is she?"

"Her fever's gone down a bit more, but she's still not making any sense. Wren says the hallucinations are a good thing, though -- they mean she's still with us. Oh, Livi, stop looking at me like that."

"Like what?"

"Like my daughter's dying. There's been a setback, that's all. But Wren says that as long as there's not another incident, Violet will be just fine. Come now, let's go back upstairs; I don't want to wake her."

Livi followed Jane out of the sick room, but with every step she took, she lost some nerve; she had to tell Jane about her plan right now, or she never would. She stopped abruptly halfway up the staircase, making Mrs. Shaw stop too. "I've got to talk to you," Livi blurted out. "I've decided to join the Guard, like you wanted."

Mrs. Shaw pursed her lips. "So it's true, then? You're going to Eterneaux?"

"How do you know about that already?"

"I'm a mother; I know everything." Then, answering Livi's quizzical stare: "Wallace came and found me after you two talked. He thought I'd try to put a stop to it."

"But you're not going to?"

"No, dear, I'm not. Don't misunderstand -- I'm not happy about it, and I'll be worried sick while you're gone, but you're not like the rest of us, Livi. You're very brave; you've always been very brave."

"Well why can't Benny see that? He was so awful about it, Jane. He's scared for me, I guess, but I've tried to explain that Wallace wouldn't agree unless he really thought I could do it. He just doesn't understand."

"You know, Benny only resists it so much because he

loves you."

"And I love him, but if things were reversed I wouldn't ever be so stubborn."

"No, dear, I mean he *loves* you. That's why he's so afraid; that's why he doesn't want you to go."

"*Benny?* Oh, you don't know what you're talking about."

Mrs. Shaw laughed. "My son loves you, Livi; he has for ages."

Livi didn't know what to say. If Mrs. Shaw was right, then everything would be different. Benny was her best friend in the world; she grew up with him, she loved him like a brother. But she never even considered him in a romantic sort of way, and she never would.

• • •

Over the next several days, Benny's anxiety and worry grew into bitterness and rage. Livi could not understand why he was taking it so badly, and she didn't care -- or at least she tried very hard to convince herself she didn't care. After all, she had too much to concern herself with, without worrying about what Benny thought of her.

It had been five days since Wallace presented Livi's plan to the Elders, and they were only now getting ready to discuss it. But they would agree to it, Livi *knew* they would agree; there was no other option.

She had already told Mr. and Mrs. Shaw about her plan: she had already promised them she would cure their daughter; she had ruined things with Benny, and she'd made Nedrick cry too many times to count. And poor Violet! Her condition had leveled out for now, but who knew when she would start to get worse again? Livi had to do something soon, or else it would be too late.

There were a few areas of the Petrichor that were off limits, the most curious of which being the top floor of the Atrium, which was off limits to everybody except the Elders. Wallace said it was where they went to meet about important or controversial issues. This morning the Elders were gathering there to discuss Livi's proposal, and she intended on being present.

Since Benny was still too angry to help her, Livi enlisted Nedrick to act as accomplice -- a duty that he accepted enthusiastically.

It was still early morning, and most of the Petrichor was still fast asleep, when the pair tiptoed up the great staircase in the center of the Atrium. A teenager, skinny and disorganized, with a great mop of ashen hair coming down to his chin, stood on patrol in front of the final flight of stairs that led to the Elders' private quarters. Livi and Nedrick ducked around the corner, out of view from the young officer.

"See I knew it -- I *knew* they'd leave it unguarded at night."

Nedrick made a face. "But it's *not* unguarded. *Or* night."

"Well, it's close enough. Anyway, you cause a distraction and I'll slip past when he's not looking."

"Are you sure this is a good idea? What if there's no place to hide once you get up there? Then what do you do?"

"Then I'll come back down. Don't worry, Ned, it'll be fine, I promise." Livi rustled Nedrick's hair, and then, without any warning, she shoved him out of hiding and into the patrolman's line of vision.

"Good -- good morning," Nedrick stuttered. "Whatcha up to?"

The bleary-eyed officer blinked several times before responding. "A bit early, isn't it? What brings ya up this way?"

"Oh, just exploring ... taking a little stroll," Ned improvised, shifting his body right, hoping the officer's eyes would follow. "Been here all night?"

"'Fraid so. It's a formality, really -- no one ever comes up this way. Quite boring, you know? I keep hoping to get moved to a more exciting location -- maybe a pipe station or patrolling the forest."

"Oh yeah? Any uhh ... any pipe station in particular?"

As Nedrick was regaled with stories about the most

exciting stations in the Petrichor, Livi tiptoed around the patrolman and up the stairs. She was nearly out of sight when the stair beneath her foot let out a loud *creak*. Nedrick cleared his throat trying to the cover up the noise, but it was too late: the patrolman was already turning around.

Livi froze, terrified.

"Hey you -- you there! No one's allowed up that way."

"Oh -- oh, well the Elders invited me. Quizzle himself, in fact. He wants me to, um..."

"No way -- *no* you've gotta come down from there right now. The Elders don't allow anyone up there."

"Maybe not any of *us*," said Nedrick seriously, "but do you know who she is? She's a *Luma*. She's probably up there on private business -- business she can't share with the likes of us. Isn't that right?"

"It is. I'm sorry, but my business is my own -- mine and the Elders, of course. You can come on up with me and ask them, if you must. They won't *like* it, but if you really don't trust me..."

The officer hesitated. As he stared up at Livi, looking wide eyed and uncertain, she could see just how young he really was: thirteen, maybe fourteen, at the most. It felt wrong to deceive him but she saw no alternative.

"I guess just go ahead," the boy said finally.

Livi nodded a thank you to the guard and sent an appreciative grin to Nedrick, before slipping quickly up the final few stairs, and stepping onto the Elders' Floor.

The top level of the Atrium was similar to all the rest, except it felt somewhat grander, with higher ceilings and more brightly polished floors. There were many, many doors, and countless corridors, and as Livi wandered, she began to worry that she wouldn't be able to find the room where the Elders would be holding their meeting.

Fortunately, she didn't have to worry about that for very long: halfway down the first, long corridor, she heard Emble's familiar voice bellowing out from behind a pair of large yellow double-doors. She leaned her ear up against the doors and listened. To her surprise, it seemed the meeting was already in full swing:

"Wallace is no fool," Emble was saying. "If he thinks she can do it, then it's something to consider. And if she does make it -- well, it certainly wouldn't hurt to have the seeds of the Emickus growing in our garden."

"But it's not safe in Eterneaux, especially now," snapped a hard, unpleasant voice that Livi didn't recognize. "The Crowns can't be trusted; she'll die before she ever gets back."

"Maybe. But if we don't help her, she'll go by herself, and then she'll have no chance at all."

"But asking us to spare our resources so that she may *die* undertaking the impossible -- it's an audacious request."

"I for one *like* some audacity in the morning," countered a voice that sounded like Elder Quizzle. A flutter of laughter swept through the room. "She's acted rashly, surely, but she's a young girl, what are we to expect? And aren't we forgetting -- Livi can help us in return. We've all heard what happened in Tiethe."

"We've heard the tale, certainly, but where's the proof?"

"Wallace saw the whole thing."

"Hah! I for one am not willing to endanger a single citizen on the word of a glorified vagabond," argued Imble, his words landing perniciously on Livi's ever impatient ear.

"Wallace is a respected member of our community -- a pillar, some might say," said Emble.

"Wallace is a liar and a rogue," Imble countered. "And even if he *is* telling the truth -- if the girl really *is* a Luma-"

"I *am* a Luma!" Livi shouted, unable to contain herself a moment longer. She flung the door open and stomped unabashedly into the large, bare room.

"Well, gentlemen, it appears we have an intruder," Quizzle said, maintaining a perfect calm. "Olivia, dear girl, what are you doing here?"

Twelve sets of eyes bore into her. She had no plan, no reasonable excuse for spying on the Elders. Her only hope was the mercy of the men whose trust she just invaded. "I *am* a Luma. And I *can* help you. But the more time you waste, the worse everything-"

"Sit, please," interrupted Quizzle, standing up from his chair and motioning for her to take it. Livi's breathing slowed down enough for her to look around at the large, rectangular room: it was plainly decorated and had no furniture, except for twelve enormous armchairs that were set up in a circle, and in each sat an ashen-haired, green-robed stranger.

Quizzle's chair felt hard and unnatural under Livi's backside. Like the staircase in the Atrium, the chair was carved with an intricate design, telling a story that Livi could not read. She traced the characters that were carved into the armrest with her forefinger. The wood was clearly worn down, but the story -- every character, even each of their tiny, carefully carved out faces -- was still perfectly preserved, somehow unmarred by years of wear.

"You like our chairs," said Quizzle.

"They look like the staircase."

"Both were gifts from the gypsy family who lent us this land. The carvings tell our shared history." The rabid bickering from a few moments ago had ceased now, and the Elders were quiet, watching Quizzle eagerly as he spoke: "I understand why you are angry, Olivia. You are like Toremme."

"Toremme?"

Quizzle pointed to Livi's left hand. "Underneath." Carved into Livi's left armrest was a picture of a boy standing in between many angry men.

"Long ago, when we first settled in the Midlands, the natives of this land nearly ran us out: the witches covens cursed us; the native tribes banished us; the gypsy caravans hunted us. We would never have survived the first winter, had it not been for Toremme.

"Toremme was a gentle young gypsy who befriended the Elders. He brought us food and helped us build shelter, and he was even younger than you are now when he stood between the Elders and his gypsy family, and demanded peace."

"What happened to him?" Livi asked.

"Peace came, but not before war; Toremme died, and so did many others. You are like Toremme, Olivia: you fight blindly for what you believe. But not everyone is as brave as you; some of us rely on reason to guide us, not instinct."

Livi suddenly felt hot. The Elders thought she was being reckless, just like Benny did. Why couldn't any of them see that this was the only option?

"I *am* a Luma," she repeated fiercely, "whether you believe it or not, I am. You want to stop the Unthinkers so badly? Well, this is your chance. I've scared them away before and I can do it again."

"You've given us a lot to consider, Olivia, truly. But we cannot be hasty."

"You don't know better," Livi said, through gritted teeth and narrowed eyes. "You're not wiser than me, or stronger, and you've admitted yourself that you're not as brave. If you won't help me, I'll find another way; I'll do it by myself, and then there's not a chance I'll join your Guard, not even if King Astor himself asked me to."

A disgruntled murmur went around the room. "It's time you left us, Livi; you'll have your answer by sundown."

• • •

The rest of the day crept by. Wallace didn't seem the least bit surprised when Livi filled him on the details of the morning, and all he did was laugh when she told him what Imble had said about him.

"Well, you can't be mad at a dog for barking," he said simply. "Cheer up, my Sleeping Girl. You did well for yourself. Now we just have to wait and see."

They finally called her back after supper. This time, they gathered in one of the library rooms on the ground floor, far away from the off-limits area she had snuck into earlier that day. The library was long and narrow and dimly lit, filled with bookshelves and desks and important-looking leather-bound volumes.

There was lot of frowning and nodding when she entered, but no one spoke. Finally, Quizzle rose from his seat and began: "Well, we'll have to send word to Tess and Hickory. They are the only people who are qualified to make this journey."

"You mean you're going to help me?" Livi exclaimed.

Quizzle nodded. "But we'll have to wait until spring; the voyage will be arduous enough in the fairest of weather -- let's not add unnecessary hardships."

"But Violet can't wait that long."

"Violet will survive the winter, and then some."

"But-"

"Let's be very clear, Livi, if you do this, you do it on *our* terms. It will take at least one month to get things in order, and then there's your training."

"Training? I don't need any training."

"People *collect* creatures like you, Olivia. If you wish to stay free, you'll need to know how to defend yourself."

"But-"

"You're not going anywhere until you're properly trained -- is that clear?"

"Yes," she answered quickly.

"Good. We'll use the winter to prepare you, and during that time you'll stand with the Guard every night, no exceptions, understood?" Livi nodded. Quizzle extended his hand, which she shook gratefully. "Very good. Then it appears we have a bargain."

11

THE KITCHEN WITCH
FROM THE
WESTERN WINCE

"*NO, NO, NO*. You haven't been practicing have you?" Imble scolded as Livi's arrow missed yet another target. "Shoot straight, Olivia -- *straight*."

"Brother, yelling will only make her nervous. Livi dear, perhaps a different angle? Come this way -- yes, that's right."

For several days now, Livi had spent every morning with the twins out in the Western Clearing -- a great, green lawn that the Elders had outfitted with everything Livi might need for training. There were walls to scramble up and hoops to jump through, meditation mats, and a boxing ring. But most importantly of all, was the area in the far end of the clearing that was set up for Lumae training.

This morning, they were in the archery range: a long stretch of field set up with various targets at different distances.

Livi drew another arrow from her quiver, set it neatly

in her bow, and pulled back the string, just as Imble and Emble had taught her. But instead of flying elegantly across the field -- as the brothers' arrows always did -- Livi's fingers lost the string and it snapped back before she was ready, sending the arrow flying jaggedly toward a nearby tree.

"Could take an eye out shootin' like that," a husky, unfamiliar voice said from behind them.

"Tess!" Emble exclaimed, dropping his bow to the ground and darting toward the two approaching strangers. "Hickory!" One blonde and burly, one dark and small, Hickory and Tess stood side by side as Imble and Emble looked them over adoringly.

"What a fine sight you are, but you were not supposed to arrive until next week."

"Got word about Livi here, so we caught a ride back on Mathilda's Ark -- figured ya could use some help with her training."

"Mathilda Battlebee?" Livi asked. "She's here?"

"Oh yeah, she mentioned she knew you. I'm Hickory, by the way. Glad to meet ya, Livi." Tall and muscular, with pale blue eyes, sun-kissed hair, and just about the fairest skin Livi had ever seen, Hickory was unmistakably Trilinian. Livi blushed as she shook his enormous, calloused hand.

"It's about time you all met!" Emble exclaimed. "Livi, Hickory and Tessajune have agreed to accompany you into Eterneaux come springtime."

"Assuming she *makes* it to the spring," grumbled Imble. "Pitiful excuse for a warrior."

"I'm sure that's not the truth," said Hickory, looking Livi over enthusiastically. "I think it's just great what you're doing to help your friend -- really brave. You know, I've never met a Luma before; can't wait to see what you can do."

"Hah," Imble said, snorting. "The girl can barely shoot an arrow."

Emble glowered at his always-sour twin brother. "You two had a safe journey, I presume? No trouble on the trails?"

"A brief run-in with an unfriendly band of hunters about 100 miles due south of here, but not much trouble, really. Too bad about Mathilda's team though -- real shame. Ya know, they lost the Redcliff brothers in the latest quarrel?"

"An' over just five miles a land -- an' scrappy land at that," Tess added disapprovingly. Then, as if just noticing Livi's presence, she stuck her hand out in greeting. "So you're Livi, eh? How d'ya do?"

Swarthy and wild-eyed, with dark, matted hair, Tess was no doubt a gypsy. And as scrawny as she was short, she was as unlikely a companion for the broad shouldered, fair-haired Trilinian boy standing next to her as there ever could be.

But when Imble and Emble left the trio on the training field that afternoon, Livi quickly learned that Tess and Hickory were a far better match than they first appeared. In fact, they complimented each other perfectly:

Livi had never met anybody like them before. The pair looked barely eighteen, yet they could throw and catch and run and punch; they could shoot arrows and climb walls; they weren't just brave, they were fearless. Livi tried her best to imitate their confidence, to prove that to them that she was worth the effort, but the closest she had ever come to handling a spear or a crossbow was in primary school when she and Benny and Violet carved toy swords from firewood, and her inexperience could not be concealed.

But unlike Livi, Tess and Hickory seemed to be good at everything. By the middle of the afternoon, after watching Livi fail at archery and the obstacle course, they arrived at spear-throwing.

With one great thrust, Hickory sent a spear gliding across the field and into the dummy's chest. "Throwing's easy; the hard part's finding the point of balance." Hickory demonstrated with a second spear, balancing it on his pointer finger, moving it left and right, until the spear stopped inclining one direction or another, and stayed perfectly balanced on his finger. "See that, Livi -- that's your point of balance. Grip it right there and then just chuck it."

Livi watched in awe as the second spear flew easily across the grass, landing millimeters from the last.

"Try it," Tess urged, throwing a spear pointed-end first to Livi, who jumped back to avoid being punctured. "Well c'mon, don't just stand there like a dyin' dung beetle. Pick it up, let's get goin'."

But the grace with which Hickory balanced his spear did not translate to Livi, and after many failed attempts, it seemed that she was as ill-suited for spear throwing as she was for all the rest.

Next Tess showed Livi how to throw knives. With a lift of her elbow and an expert flick of her wrist, Tess hurled knife after knife into the large block of wood set up across the field, eventually splitting the wood in two and sending splinters flying. Livi thought it looked simple enough, but when she went to stab the wood, she could not penetrate its hard surface.

Hickory patted Livi encouragingly on the shoulder. "Don't worry, in a few days it'll be as natural as walking." But after one too many fumbled attempts, even Hickory began to get discouraged, and so they broke from target practice and cartwheeled into the padded arena set up for hand-to-hand combat.

Though Hickory was more than twice Tess's size, Tess moved with a swiftness and ease that her paramour could not match. His punch was strong and his blocks were impossible to break, but Tess had the precision and grace of a mountain lion, and Hickory was her prey.

Hickory was the first to land a punch, socking Tess eagerly in the ribs. She recoiled momentarily, but charged back with power and perseverance, landing punch after punch, kick after kick, until Hickory was limp on the mat.

"Size doesn't matter," Hickory said as he scraped himself off the mat. "And strength isn't so important either. What matters is that you get inside your opponent's head. Tessi here knows what I'll do before even I've figured it out. That's how she beats me."

"And I'm fast. Faster than a big hunk a meat like him'll ever be."

"Okay, your turn now. Who do you wanna take on first?"

• • •

They arrived late for supper that night. Emelda, the elderly witch who ran the kitchen, was waiting with a miserable scowl on her pea green face when Livi, Tess, and Hickory went up to receive their plates.

"I worked *all* day on this fine supper," Emelda wailed. "For you children. Ah, but I can't stay angry, now can I? Not with those bright faces looking back at me. Come, I want to hear all about your travels -- and Tessajune, you look so thin. Have you been eating?"

Emelda was perfectly unique, even as witches go. She had been living among the Elders for more than a century, and in many ways, she was as trusted a source of information as Quizzle himself. She was from a coven in the Western Wince and made the journey east when her sisters destroyed an unfamiliar gypsy caravan that was simply passing through: "Too black, too black for me. That very night I got right up and left. Oh, and how I cried. My sister, Mafalda, tried to get me to stay. Said it was an accident, she said. But that's Mafalda -- always making excuses for the others. I have nineteen sisters in all, but Mafalda's special. A good heart, a good heart, she has."

The dining hall was nearly empty, and the few that remained were gathered at a long narrow table near the back. Included among them was Benny, Violet, and Mathilda Battlebee, who smiled toothily as Livi approached.

Livi was surprised at how pleased she was to see Mrs. Battlebee. So much had changed since their last meeting in Mrs. Shaw's kitchen, and Livi felt like she was finally beginning to understand the anomalous woman.

"What are you doing out of bed, Violet?" Livi asked as she sat down.

"Aren't you happy to see me? Wren said it's good for

me to get out of the infirmary once and a while -- when I'm feeling up to it, I mean."

Livi forced herself to smile. It was true was Violet had been feeling better the past few days, but the hope and relief that everyone felt during Violet's first period of convalescence did not come back with her pink cheeks. This time, everyone knew it was temporary, and they all expected a turn for the worse.

"Where have *you* been anyway?" Benny snapped, glaring at Livi.

"It's our fault," said Hickory, before she could snap back. "We kept her in the training fields too long -- not much time to prepare, you know ... guess we got carried away. I'm Hickory -- I probably should've said that to start -- and this here is Tess."

"They're the ones coming to Eterneaux with me."

Violet's face lit up. "Oh, I'm so pleased we're getting to meet. I've heard absolutely everything about you both, and I think you're just marvelous. And Tessajune, I think you're an absolute *inspiration,* really, I do. You'll sit next to me, won't you?"

Tess looked disconcertedly around the room. "That's her?" she whispered to Hickory, though her voice was loud enough for Livi to hear three seats down. "She doesn't *look* sick."

"And what do they say about looks again? Well, go on, she's waiting; sit down."

It took a hard nudge in the ribs from Hickory, but Tess finally plopped herself down next to Violet, who grinned eagerly at her new dinner companion. Meanwhile, Hickory took the seat beside Benny, who rolled his eyes and then developed an intense interest in the remaining bits of food on his mostly empty plate.

"Livi, I'm so pleased to see you," said Mrs. Battlebee, once the crew had all found seats. "I hear you've made quite the impression. You know, your mother was a-"

"Yes, Jane's told me."

"Well, I think she would be very proud to hear-"

"Mrs. Battlebee, you were down at the Eauxian board-

er, weren't you?" Livi interrupted, eager to change the subject. "Is it true a war's starting?"

"*Starting*? Goodness no. The Soophecs and the Oracs
have been waging these little turf wars with each other for
decades, though I must admit things have be heating up lately ... The Soophecs seem all riled up about something.
Still, I do believe things will calm down soon enough."

"You really think that, Mathilda?" asked Hickory.
"Tessi and me have been down south for a good year now,
and everyone we've met along the boarder says things are
just firing up."

"That's right," Tess agreed. "Not that I care much
either way."

"You don't care if the Soophecs reach us?" asked Violet. "But everyone says they're awful."

"They've a'ready reached *us*, now haven't they?"

"*We've* gone to *them*, Tess," said Hickory. "I expect
things will be very different if they make it all the way up
here."

"Time will tell, won't it?" said Mrs. Battlebee shortly.

"Livi I was just telling Mrs. Battlebee about your trip
to Eterneaux," said Violet. "She thinks it's wonderful, don't
you, Mrs. Battlebee?"

"I think it's very noble ... although, I must ask, have
you really considered all you're taking on?"

"Of course she hasn't," Benny muttered, a deep scowl
mangling his kind face.

"Ah, but if anyone can succeed, it's the Sleeping
Girl!" Livi had not noticed Wallace enter, but she was happy to have his support.

Mathilda nodded as he took a seat next to her, a cloud
of dust rising off his shabby corduroy pants. "Wallace, it's
nice to see time hasn't changed you."

"I'm sorry to hear about the Redcliffs, Mathilda. I
know you were close."

"Yes, well the causalities have felt particularly tragic
as of late -- and far spread, too. I'm sure you heard about
Peatree McCloud?"

"What happened to Mr. McCloud?" Benny asked.

Mrs. Battlebee grimaced. "Peatree was found dead this morning. His shop was torn up badly."

"And you think it was the Soophecs?"

"Well, no one knows for sure, after all Peatree McCloud had more enemies than friends. But with the battles for territory going on just fifty miles north of him, and with so much looting in the area -- well, you just add two and two. Oh, but I do hope Peatree didn't suffer much. He was a kind old fellow deep down, though he'd never let anybody know it."

"You knew him well, did you?" asked Wallace.

"Oh yes, I grew up right down the street from him. Livi, Benny, you never told Wallace about your trip to see him?"

"I guess we didn't," Livi said, fiddling with the shiny silver locket that hung around her neck. The necklace had become a sort of good luck charm since that day, just as Mr. McCloud had predicted.

"I can't believe you still have that old thing," Benny said, glaring. "It's a piece of junk; it doesn't even tell the time."

"Ah, so that's the story of the necklace," said Wallace pleasantly. "I'd always wondered where you'd stumbled upon. I should have guessed it was Mr. McCloud's doing."

"You knew him, too?" asked Violet.

"Briefly," he said, fidgeting. "Alas, he's on to better things."

Dinner wrapped up quickly after that. Livi was too tired to even see straight, but she still had a long night ahead of her, patrolling the grounds with the Midlands Guard.

The Guard wasn't half as tedious as she had initially imagined, especially now that Hickory and Tess were there to keep her company. Livi had expected the land to be flooded with Unthinkers, the way the Elders had explained things, but so far she had yet to encounter anything more dangerous than a burrow of night rats.

• • •

The night started out starry, a near full moon. But the deeper they delved into the forest, the darker the sky became. They talked about nonsensical things -- arguing details in favorite stories and playing games to pass the time -- none of the three paying attention to the wilderness growing around them.

Then a wind rushed in suddenly from behind, knocking the lantern from Livi's hands and sending it crashing to the ground. As the light went out, the three friends noticed how very alone the were. They were deep in the woods now, and the forest was silent. There were no stars, no moon; the blackness was complete.

"Tess -- Hickory? Are you there?"

"We're here Livi," said Hickory. "Hold on just a minute, and I'll relight the lantern."

"Don't ya worry now, Liv. This sorta thing happens," said Tess, and she sounded like she meant it.

Then something dropped from a tree nearby. And then something else. All around them, like apples in an orchard, things were falling to the ground. Through rustling leaves, Livi could hear the crunching of footsteps. It was too dark to see, but she could feel two *no* three *no* four new bodies in the forest. A cackling cut the air.

"What's going on?" Livi cried. "I can't *see* anything. What's happening?"

"Stay calm," Tess ordered.

Livi drew her knife and clutched in inexpertly to her chest.

"Get the girl," a cold, high-pitched voice ordered. Somewhere nearby Tess yelped.

"Not that one you idiot! The tall one -- yes, there."

Something struck Livi promptly over the head and sent her flying to the ground.

She slashed and jabbed and thrashed the air with her knife, fighting back onto her feet, still blinded by the perfect darkness, disoriented by the hit, and so desperately afraid. She felt her knife meet a body, felt it graze skin -- rough, scaly, inhuman skin. What beast stood before her?

"What's wrong with you?" the high-pitched voice

screeched. "Get the girl!"

Livi closed her eyes and listened: Grunting and groaning and thrashing and moaning. Tess was fighting too now, and Hickory. She had to keep going, no matter how pathetic her attempts were. When her mystery attacker charged again, she was ready, knife in hand. He clawed and she jabbed and he wailed and she cried.

She was growing tired, almost too tired to continue, when finally, suddenly, the leader gave orders to retreat.

12

TRIANGLES

"IT COULD HAVE BEEN ONE OF A HUNDRED different species," said Wallace a little while later back at the Petrichor. "Can you remember anything a bit more specific?"

"Not really," said Livi, fighting a yawn. "Just that they were small."

"And brutal," Hickory added. "Incredible fighters."

"The guy I was fightin' had a knife," said Tess. "An' boy he knew how ta use it."

It had been in almost three in the morning when Livi, Tess, and Hickory returned. Wallace made them get checked in the infirmary before he'd listen to what happened. Now it was quarter to five, and everyone was falling asleep in their chairs.

"Somebody was giving the orders, Wallace. It was the Shepherd, wasn't it? He heard what I could do -- how I scared away all of his Unthinkers -- and he came for me, didn't he?"

"Oh no, I serious doubt it. The Shepherd wouldn't come up here, not personally at least."

"Why not?" asked Hickory, who had helped Livi devise this explanation on the walk back from the woods.

Wallace thought for a moment. "The Shepherd is too grisly in heart for such sunny circumstance. Something so dark prefers to stay down below, to makes its lair where the sun doesn't rise."

"Like underground?"

"Or in-between. In any case, what's more likely is that it was somebody working for Shepherd. Still, I can't say why the creature would be after you -- it's impossible the Shepherd would know what you are. *Impossible.*"

"It's the only explanation," said Tess.

"Not the only the one," said Wallace vaguely.

Tess glowered at the small man. "What's that s'posed to mean? Wallace, you know somethin', don' ya? Yep, I know that look an' it's sayin' you know somethin' more than you're lettin' on."

Wallace smiled slightly, but it wasn't his usual jovial grin. "Tess, my Gypsy Princess, I haven't the faintest idea what you are talking about. Ah, but let me reassure you," he continued before she could argue her point any further, "I've never kept a secret without having very good reason." Wallace, remaining tightlipped, smiled mildly at Tess as she contorted her face into the most disagreeable of scowls. "Up to bed now, my weary adventurers. There is nothing more we can do tonight."

· · ·

Livi's head had barely hit her pillow when her alarm sounded the next morning, calling her out of bed. She ignored the first bell, and the second, only rising when the third alarm sounded shrilly in her ear.

She woke aching, tense and tired. The bump on her head from where her attacker had hit her swelled overnight, and the cuts on her arms and legs stung beneath their soft cotton bandages. She wished for a day in bed, but she knew from experience that her injuries weren't bad enough to warrant it, and so her feet dragged and her eyes drooped as she struggled to get ready for the day.

She was very late for breakfast, and on a normal day would have found herself to be the sole occupant left in the dining hall. Rather unusually, however, Mrs. Shaw, Mrs. Battlebee, and Violet were still sitting around the breakfast table, with full bellies and empty plates, chatting and laugh--ing as if they didn't all have places to be.

But the giggles turned to gasps of horror as Livi approached. "It looks worse than it is," she said quickly, sitting down with a full bowl of porridge.

"Oh dear!" Mrs. Shaw cried, jumping up from her seat and rushing to Livi's side. "Oh in Astor's name! What in the world happened to you?"

"It's nothing, just a few scratches. Really, Jane, I'm fine -- just tired."

"Well, what happened?" asked Mrs. Battlebee eyeing Livi worriedly.

"Something attacked us last night -- don't know what. It's nothing though ... looks a lot worse than it is."

"It's not *nothing*," said Violet, looking suddenly very serious. "They hit you -- they hit you hard. Oh, I had the worst headache last night. I *knew* something was wrong. I should have done something, I should have *said* something. I should have tried to help you."

"Headache, Violet?" said Mrs. Shaw, shifting her concern from Livi to Violet. "Why didn't you tell me? Are you okay? Do you need to lie down?"

"I'm fine mother *now*, Mother. I feel fine. It's Livi. They hit you on the head didn't they?"

"They did, but I'm okay, really I am. I've been to the infirmary and I'm perfectly fine -- no concussion, barely even a bump." From the looks around the table this seemed to satisfy everyone enough to end the interrogation.

"And what about you, Violet?" Livi asked, looking over her rosy-cheeked friend. "How are you feeling?" Violet's health had been going up-and-down so much lately that Livi had been finding hard to keep track. For days at a time Violet would be cheerful and talkative, coming to meals and going on walks and acting just like her old self. Then, out of no where, she'd be on the brink of death again. Wren did her best to manage the pain but the only thing that could help Violet in the long term was still the Emickus plant. "Are you really okay to be out of bed this much?"

Violet shrugged. "After breakfast I'm due back in the infirmary."

"Well, it's half-past-nine, you know? We're all going to be late."

"Oh, Livi relax," said Violet. "You really do worry too much."

Livi frowned. She thought she worried just enough.

"You're just like your mother in that way," Jane said wistfully. "She always was the sensible one."

"She kept us in line, that's for sure," Mathilda agreed. "Jane, do you remember the time you and Mary and I tried to get Anne to come cliff diving out on Lover's Peak?"

Jane burst out laughing. "She nearly turned purple lecturing us! She swore she'd run straight to our mothers if we tried."

Livi made a face. "That doesn't sound at all like me."

"Yes, well you're a good bit more adventurous than your mother was, no one could argue with that," said Mrs. Shaw fondly, "but you've got the same heart."

My heart is my own, Livi thought irritably. These days it seemed the comparisons to her mother were endless, and they often left Livi with a sort of dreary, sinking feeling. Livi barely remembered her mother; she died so long ago. Who cared if she bore Anne Dixon's smile, or shared her fondness for elderflower tea, or that Livi could also shape-shift into a weightless blob of white light? Livi found none of these anecdotes soothing, and she often wished she could retreat back to the time before they left Primareaux, when her parents were almost never mentioned.

Livi remembered from spending time with the pair back in Primareaux that once Jane and Mathilda began reminiscing about the old days it was impossible to make them stop, and she sat grumpily, eating her porridge as fast as she could, as the two old friends told an eager-eared Vio-

-let about the day they met Mary Lucidon.

"Your mothers and I all lived on the same street nearly our whole lives," said Mathilda to Violet and Livi. "We were inseparable before we were crawling."

"But Mary lived on the other side of town," Jane cut in, "so we didn't meet her until the first day of Preliminary School."

Livi had finished her breakfast by now, and was waiting to make a polite escape, but the two women had barely paused for air, so entrenched in the tale of Mary Lucidon.

"Oh, Mary was so different from any of us. She was always telling these fantastic stories -- she had the wildest imagination! We just adored her. The four of us were just like sisters straight through Secondary School."

"Yes, right until the night of poor Ken's accident ..." Mathilda's voice trailed off after receiving a sharp glare from Mrs. Shaw.

The mood around the table changed instantly, which did wonders to snap Livi out of her state of stubborn disinterest. "Who's Ken?" she asked promptly. "What happened to him?"

"*Oh dear*," Jane muttered.

"Ken was a friend of ours when we were kids," Mathilda continued carefully. "Of Mary's, especially."

"Oh, it's very complicated, girls," Jane said, "very sad stuff, maybe when you're older we can-"

"Mary was a bit plain to look at, you see," Mathilda interrupted, arousing a wrathful glare from Mrs. Shaw. But with a great deal of effort, Jane suppressed her overprotective nature and allowed her friend to continue: "Oh she had a wonderful personality, but most boys don't care about that sort of thing, not when your young. Anyway, it was hard for Mary as we got older. Jane had been going hand in hand with George practically since the first day of Primary School and Anne could have had any boy she wanted – to this day I can't tell you how Peter got
her attention. I met Eddie in university and we were very happy for a very long time. But Mary -- well, the only boy she ever loved died."

"Ken?" Livi guessed.

Mathilda nodded. "Peter and Ken were best friends, as close as brothers. Anne was dating your father and Mary was dating Ken. Everyone was sure they'd get married and have some wonderful double wedding. It was very sweet -- very romantic. And then, oh it must have been twenty years ago now-" Mathilda paused and looked to Jane for confirmation, who nodded tightly, "yes twenty years ago, the boys went on a camping trip and only Peter came home."

"It was a climbing accident," continued Jane softly. "He never talked about it to either of us, but Anne said Ken died in Peter's arms. Peter never forgave himself for not being able to save him."

"And neither did Mary," said Mathilda. "Everything was different after that. We were all still friends, of course, but Mary was so distant. And then, you know, we all got married and had our families and Mary, she just got very serious about her work ... we all lost touch after that."

"But everything worked out in the end, didn't it?" added Jane quickly. "Mary wouldn't ever had made it as far as she did if she'd settled down with Ken. So you see, everyone's where they're meant to be in the end, aren't they?"

Livi wasn't sure why, but the last thing Mrs. Shaw said troubled her, and stayed with her all through the night. After all, Livi's parents weren't where they were meant to be -- at least she didn't think so. And maybe Representative Lucidon was meant to be with this boy, Ken, in a little house with a little family, back in Primareaux. Maybe her parents being executed and Ken falling off a cliff and Mary Lucidon going into politics wasn't fate, as Mrs. Shaw claimed. Maybe it was all just one giant mistake.

• • •

Over the next few weeks, Livi fell into a rigorous routine. She was in the Western Clearing, ready to start her training by dawn every morning, and every evening she stood with the Midlands Guard until well after midnight. She had never worked so hard in her life, and though she was exhausted nearly all the time, she had never felt better.

Every day she learned something new -- from scaling walls, to throwing punches -- and eventually, her blatant ineptitude was replaced with a sort of clumsy confidence. Livi's growth was visible off the training field too, and she even began to enjoy the late-night patrols with the Midlands Guard.

Though they never again encountered the strange, small creatures that were after Livi, she was on her toes each night, ready to fight if ever they did. They went out in larger groups now, and took extra precautions, checking perimeters constantly and carrying two or three or four lanterns at a time.

Tonight, however, Livi and Tess and Hickory had the rare opportunity to venture out alone, (though another patrol group was right on the other side of the field), and they took advantage of this peaceful patrol, walking and talking just like the old days:

"You know, it was smart to get out of Eaux while ya still could," said Hickory casually as he ducked beneath a fallen branch.

"What's that supposed to mean?" Livi asked, wading through a pile of damp, late autumn Garga leaves.

"Nothing -- just after the thing in Mayback, well no one really knows what it'll be like down there in a few months."

Livi scrunched up her face, confused. "What are you talking about? Mayback was a horrible accident, but-"

"Hah!" scoffed Tess. "Is that what ya think? What happened at Mayback was a lot a things, but it was no accident. Someone set that fire on purpose, Livi, and I'll give ya one guess who that was."

"You don't mean Crown Horridor?" Livi said, thinking back to the days before she left Eaux, and riot at Primareaux Castle.

"I'd bet my right eye."

"Come on, it's pretty obvious what happened there, isn't it?" said Hickory in such a matter-of-fact way that Livi felt even more ignorant than usual. "Crown Horridor knew

Saintright was going to be in Mayback all weekend; he was aiming for the First Crown -- trying to knock Saintright out."

"Ya musta heard the rumors," Tess chimed in, kicking her foot loose from a knot weeds. "About old Hubert Horridor bringin' down the crowns? Come on, don't tell me you've never heard 'em?"

"Well, of *course* I have -- they're the same rumors that've been going around forever, but they're not *true*."

"This time it's different," said Hickory. "At least that's what everyone's saying."

"I don't know," said Livi. "Crown Horridor isn't very popular, but I don't think he's capable of starting a war."

Tess laughed. "Unpopular's a real nice way of puttin' things. He's plannin' to bring down the whole Triangulation -- to reverse it and such."

"I don't believe it."

"Don't gotta believe somethin' for it to be true. Course Old Horridor's about as dumb as the sun is bright -- he'll never pull it off in the end."

"He just might start up a war, though," said Hickory. "And it's best get out before all that happens, that's all I'm saying. Now come on, we'd better get back; it's time to switch shifts."

• • •

Livi arrived back at the Petrichor exhausted. It was nearly one in the morning and she had planned to go straight to bed, but as she rounded the staircase she noticed a light flickering in the small third floor library, a usually deserted space. To her surprise, Mathilda Battlebee was sitting alone amid the stacks of books.

"Mathilda?"

"Olivia," she said, looking up from her book, "we meet yet again in the dead of night."

Were they really the same two people who met in Mrs. Shaw's kitchen just a few weeks ago? She felt so much older now.

"I should have trusted you then, Mathilda. I'm sorry."

Mathilda shook her head. "You were smart to question me after all you'd heard."

"But none of it's true. Not a single thing they say about you ... Mathilda, why don't you go back? Why don't you fight for your name?"

"So I can die trying? No thank you. Besides, everyone who matters is either long gone, or already knows who I really am."

"But I spent nearly my whole life being afraid of you. Doesn't that bother you?"

"Are you afraid of me now?"

"Of course not," Livi said.

"Good. So let's clear some things up, once and for all: I'm not a dark witch, Livi. I didn't set a whole village on fire, and didn't sacrifice one hundred newborn babies, either," she said, recounting a few of the most popular legends about her. "What people think a thousand miles away doesn't matter to me. You and I know the truth, and that's enough."

But truth was such a fickle thing. At least it had always seemed that way to Livi. When she was young the truth about her mother changed depending on the company she kept. The truth about her family, the truth about where she belonged, and to whom ... it seemed to Livi that truth was unreliable.

"Jane, can I ask you something?"

"Of course, dear. Ask me anything."

"How did it happen with you and my mother? How did she- I mean, how did it all happen?"

"Well, you know the story, don't you dear?"

Did she? She must have once, but the details had eroded over time. "Can you tell me anyway?"

Mathilda sighed loudly and massaged her temples, as if trying to recover something that was long forgotten. "Well, your mother, Anne, and I used to work together at the local courthouse, do you remember? We mainly just did filing and things like that, but one day, your mother came across some very serious information that implicated the

new Crown Horridor (Hubert had only *just* come into the
throne, then) in half a dozen infractions against the First
Crown."

"And so she tried to report it?" Livi guessed, straining
to remember a history long buried.

"We both did. We had plans to go straight to the First
Court and report it directly to them. But before we had the
chance, Crown Horridor summoned us and trumped up a
whole list of treason charges against us -- he accused *us* of
attempting to usurp the First Crown! The charges were
laughable of course, and perfectly baseless, but he still had
us sentenced to death. By then, our word was worthless and
the files had disappeared, so there was nothing we could do.

"And, well you must know this part: I ran off to the
Midlands and joined up with the Elders and your poor
mother was put to death. Then of course, your father -- well
that was truly awful..." Mathilda's voice trailed off.
Livi really did know by heart the story of her father, for it
was the only bit of honor that her family name still held: in
the weeks before her mother's execution, Livi's father never
stopped trying to prove her innocence, and on the day she
died, he was murdered trying to save her.

"None of us ever thought ... it all happened so quickly,
Livi, we all thought it would work itself out. Then when it
didn't -- well, I ran. I didn't know what else to do. I didn't
have a family keeping me here -- Eddie'd died the year before. I had nothing holding me back, so I just *ran*."

Mathilda ran her fingers through her straggly hair. "If
I could do things over I- well, I don't know what I would
do, but ... oh, well there's no use in looking backwards, now
is there?"

• • •

Livi trained through the late autumn hailstorms and
midwinter snows, through the bruises and sprained ankles,
and with the help of Hickory and Tess, it wasn't long before
her arrows met their targets and her punches grew solid.
She learned to run fast and leap high, and she could even

keep up with Tess in the obstacle course. Her instincts had been honed and her musculature refined, but there was one piece of her training that was not coming along as smoothly as the rest: the harder Livi tried to control her Luma, the more impossible the task became.

Since that day in Tiethe many weeks ago, Livi had not been able to change into her Luma-form even once. Every morning she sat down across from Quizzle in a small, closed off section of the Western Clearing. Every day she listened to him lecture about artillery and barriers and souls and tethers. And every evening, she went to bed more and more frustrated.

"The soul is like a thousand puzzle pieces," Quizzle would tell her. "Learn the pieces -- where they join and how to pull them apart -- and then you will be free."

"And what if I can't? What if what happened in Tiethe was just a fluke?"

"You've done it before, and you will do it again," said Quizzle. "Just be patient; relax and be patient."

"You've been saying that for a month. What if I really can't?"

Quizzle sighed loudly. "You have to be patient, Olivia. It might not happen today, but when the time comes, you will be ready. You're *ready* for this journey, of that I am sure. And you are going to be wonderful."

• • •

The days kept growing longer, the nights warmer, until finally, the time had come to say goodbye. Livi hadn't spoken two civil words to Benny since she the night she told him about going to Eterneaux, and things between them had only grown more insufferable. Eventually Benny's confusion developed into hot, unreasonable rage, and then finally, stony silence. But Livi was leaving in the morning, and she was determined to make things right before she did.

It took all day for her to work up enough courage to knock on his door, and when she did, Benny greeted her with his usual cold scowl.

"What do you want?" he asked, standing in the doorway, blocking her entrance.

"I'm leaving in the morning."

"I heard."

"Well, shouldn't we talk before I go?" Benny shrugged and moved out of the way to let her in, but his eyes remained unreasonably cold. "Oh, Benny, please don't be like that, not now."

"What do you *want*, Olivia?"

"Just tell me you understand."

"Listen, I don't know what you're trying to prove, but you're being really selfish, you know that? You really are selfish."

"I'm not trying to *prove* anything, Benny. And you're the one being selfish. I can't help it if you suffer from some absurd unrequited love for me, but-"

"Oh, you're delusional."

"And you're pathetic!"

"*Me?* You're the pathetic one. At least I have a family -- I have people who love me; at least no one feels sorry for me like they do for you. You know what, I'm glad you're going, Livi; now we can finally be rid of you."

"People always said you were a coward but I never saw it until today. You'd rather let your own sister die than take a risk."

At the mention of his sister, Benny's face turned nearly purple with rage. "You are a betrayer and a whore, just like your mother. And I hope you die like her too."

A violent wrath washed over her. She raised her arm above her head and slapped Benny so hard across his face that her hand felt raw for a week.

Livi left quietly the next morning. She did not look back.

13

VERLINDA

THEY HAD BEEN TRAVELING FOR NEARLY A WEEK and everyone was growing restless. All the training in the world couldn't have prepared Livi for the cramped quarters and the dizzying heights; as hard as she tried, she was simply not build for the skies. But by now, even Tess and Hickory had grown tired of life onboard, especially after a rainstorm forced them to drop anchor for two long days.

The trip was made longer and more tedious by the ancient ark Wallace insisted they take: Verlinda, as Wallace christened her, had none of the buttons or wheels or shining steel accessories that the modern arks were outfitted with. She was carved from wood and iron, and had a small but shapely body with two great propellers on either side. An old-fashioned sail kept them on due course, and the large, open-aired main deck was equipped with half-a-dozen old red hammocks, for sleeping under the stars.

The days were long and monotonous; the nights were cold and sleepless. But they were nearly there now, and excitement was building for everyone. This morning Tess and Livi hung halfway over the guardrail on the main deck, gawking at what Tess claimed was once the final battlefield of the Second Continental War:

"That's it," said Tess, pointing through the clouds. "Don'cha see it? Between all them shrubs and things."

"*That*? But it's so-"

"I'm tellin' ya, that's it. Hey, Hickory -- Hick, c'mon up here, won't ya?"

A minute later Hickory poked his head out of the hatch that led to the cabin. "What is it? What's wrong?"

"Tell Livi that there's Innamour Battlefield. She won't take just my word for it."

"Is that what you woke me up for?" With mild reluctance, Hickory leaned over the railing and took a quick look. "That's it, I'm afraid. Not much to it, but Tess is quite right. Come on now, let's all go down to the galley; breakfast'll be ready by now."

One-by-one, Livi, Tess, and Hickory, made their way down the hatch by way of a narrow ladder.

"Good morning, good morning, and good morning to you," Wallace hummed happily, nodding to each of them as they entered the dark, cramped cabin. "Breakfast is not ready but it shall be done in a few."

Livi sat down in the nearby alcove and stared absently out the dusty porthole. "How far are we now, Wallace?"

"Hm, just an evening's more, I think, I'm sure. The Noauxware River is only fifteen miles south of us now."

"Wallace, d'ya know we just flew over Innamour Battlefield?" asked Tess.

Wallace drew an invisible map out on the table with his fingertip. "Hm, oh yes, you are exactly right. And what an extraordinary bit of history that is."

Livi remembered dully, the long hours spent in history seminars back in Primareaux, and how thoroughly she'd studied the Battle of Innamour. It was the final battle of the Second Continental War -- the battle that led to the Triangulation of the Eauxian Crown. On one side was the Sovereign Nation of Eaux, and on the other was Eaux's greatest adversary, the Republic of Trilinia. The two countries had been at war for nearly a hundred years, and thousands of men lost their lives on the battlefield. Until Innamour.

At Innamour, King Astor, himself, led the charge

against the Trilinian army. King Marcous Astor had come into the throne just weeks before, when his Father, King Robert Astor was murdered on the battlefield. The previous King Astor was a bitter and power-hungry man (as was his father, and his father's father before that). But King Marcous was nothing like his father: he demanded peace, above all else.

The battle of Innamour lasted three days, and cost both sides unthinkable casualties. But as the battle drew to a close, King Astor reached a sudden and expected agreement with King Horridor, of Trilinia. A treaty was written, proclaiming the Midlands a no-mans-land, and the two countries signed it into law right in the center of the battlefield. To seal the agreement with Trilinia, King Astor married King Horridor's only daughter, Helena.

A few weeks later, when he arrived back home, King Astor split his crown in three equal parts so that no King could wreak havoc like those who came before him. King Astor made his bride, Helena Horridor, the Second Crown of Eaux, and he made his friend, Captain Salvador Lima, the Third Crown. "And Eaux hasn't spent a single day at war since," Livi concluded.

Wallace took a deep drink from his glass. "A fine story, a fine story indeed. But alas, I was referring to what happened *after* King Astor got his Queen."

According to Wallace, Marcous married Helena and they had a child together -- a boy, named Humphrey. King Astor had never been so happy in his life, but Helena was in love with another man.

Together, Helena and her lover, made a plan to murder Crown Astor and do away with the Triangulation so that they may rule the kingdom with ultimate authority. But Crown Astor was made aware of Helena's betrayal just in time. He exiled his wife and her lover to the Midlands, where they would surely be dead by winter's end, and he made his young son, Humphrey Horridor, the new Second Crown of Eaux.

Livi had never heard this version of events before, and she wasn't sure she believed it. "Who was Helena's lover?"

"Ah, his name escapes me now, but he was a good man, a well meaning man; he only lost his way for a while."

Livi was about to ask Wallace where he'd heard the story, and if it was really true, but above deck, a strong wind had just blown through, taking precedence over their history lesson. They all climbed above deck to check the sails.

"These winds are stronger than I knew; automatic steering won't well do. Man the deck; I'm taking the wheel."

"Old Verlinda here, she needs a proper captain," Hickory said, stroking the wrought iron guardrail with the same level of innocent affection most people reserved for their pets. "She's a classic, you know? She's nearing two centuries old, and acts like it too."

"Aw, don't mind him, Livi," said Tess. "He's dotes on these old ships (an' new ones too, I s'pose) like they're his natural born children. I tell him all the time he should've been born a bird, the way he carries on."

Tess had barely finished her sentence when an enormous gust of wind knocked her right off her feet. With a loud *thud*, Tess's small body smashed against one of the beams that held the sail in place.

"Tess!"

"I'm a'right, I'm a'right." But as she climbed to her feet, she winced in pain.

"You're hurt, you need to lie down."

"But there's a storm comin', there's too much to do."

"Livi can handle it, can't you?"

"Of course I can. Besides, you should rest now, because once we land there'll be no time."

"Fine, I go down below if it pleases ya so. But Hick, ya better go secure the sails right now, 'fore it gets too dangerous."

The storm came fast, and from nowhere. The sails billowed and the skies grew dark. The trees shook and the leaves turned their backs to the wind. Birds flew to shelter, and loose branches smacked wildly through the air.

Rain splattered down cooly as Livi worked quickly to batten down the hatches. Hickory tried to shut down the propellers but the lever was jammed. Then, he climbed the rigging in a too-late attempt to secure the sails.

Wallace held a tight grip on the wheel, but there was no time to drop anchor or clear the deck before Verlinda got knocked sharply and suddenly off her course. They were spinning out of control, and gaining speed as they plummeted jaggedly through the air.

• • •

Livi woke up in a meadow, draped in white. She stood up, letting her feet sink into the cool, wet grass. It turned out the meadow was really a swamp, and the large, white sheet that entangled her was actually a piece of Verlinda's sail that had come undone, and torn during the shipwreck.

She was sore, but in one piece. She must have been thrown overboard, but where was everybody else? As if in answer to her thoughts, somewhere near by, a man called her name.

Livi followed the voice to the ark, which had made a crash landing several hundred yards away, right on the river bank. The sail was shredded and the left propeller had been mangled, but the rest of the ship remained remarkably in tact. As Livi's head popped through the high-growing grass, she saw Wallace in the crow's nest, looking out. "Livi, over here, Livi!"

With the foursome reunited, and no serious injuries to report, they all got to work inspecting Verlinda's damage:

"We can fix the propeller easily enough, but the *sail* ... the tears are too big; we can't patch it," Hickory concluded.

Wallace took out his map. He hunched over the yellowing paper, muttering to himself as he studied its weathered lines. They crashed on the Eauxian side of the Noauxware River, just east of the Smetherstick Settlement -- a large and historic cluster of six Eauxian villages settled by Rudolph Smetherstick during the Ancient Times.

"I've heard of it," Hickory said eagerly, when Wallace pointed the spot out on the map. "Even back in Trilinia it's famous. Supposed to be the very first settlement on the whole Southern Continent."

Wallace nodded vaguely. "I have an old friend among the Smetherstice -- right in the village of Nourim. Allegra can get us the canvas we'll need for a new sail."

"But aren't the Smetherstice supposed to be, well, a bit vicious?"

"*Vicious*? No, no. Reclusive, perhaps. A bit wary of outsiders, maybe. But good people, once you get to know them. And resourceful as ever!"

As it turned out, Wallace had lived among the Smetherstice for nearly twenty years, and was therefore familiar with their customs, (a fact which Tess found profoundly amusing): "Figures," she said through a loud, indignant snort. "There ain't a place on that map you haven't been to. Heck, I reckon you're more a gypsy than me an' half my old caravan combined."

Everyone laughed and Hickory smiled adoringly at Tess. "It's eighty miles from here to Eterneaux. If we hustle, we can make it in two days' time. And Wallace, I expect that if you keep your pace steady, you can make it to Smetherstick and back in a just a day. That'll give you plenty of time to make the repairs on Verlinda before the rest of us return with the Emickus."

14

ETERNEAUX

WITH DAWN, CAME A BRIGHT AND CLOUDLESS DAY. Snow-bells littered the still-gray winter grass and the road in front of them was clear and firm. Wallace went west, toward the Smetherstick Settlement and the others began the journey south, to Eterneaux.

Livi started the morning cheerily, humming along as Tess and Hickory sung an old gypsy rhyme:

> We're here today, we'll be there tomorrow.
> We move, we travel, we steal, we borrow.
> Tis the gypsy way of life we lead,
> The gypsy way of life we follow.
>
> The road's our father,
> The sky's our mother,
> The creek's our sister,
> The sun's our brother.
>
> We head on far,

We soar, we fly.
We live by magic, or we die.

Tis the gypsy way of life we lead,
The gypsy way of life we follow.

Livi knew very little about Tess's life before she met
Hickory, and she suspected that was exactly how Tess
wanted it to stay. After all, over the many weeks they had
spent together training, Livi had only scraped up a few
meager facts about her new friend.

For example, Livi knew that Tess's caravan used to
travel along the souther boarder of Trilinia. She knew that
Tess's father was the caravan leader, and that Tess had sev-
en brothers and sisters in all. And of course, Livi knew the
story of how Hickory and Tess met:

It was a five years ago. Tess was thirteen and Hickory
was fifteen, and Tess had just lost her caravan. Livi didn't
know *how* she'd lost her caravan, or why Tess's family never came looking for her, but she did know what happened
after:

Hickory's village, Cappagarrif, wasn't far from where
Tess had been camping, and one day, when Hickory was out
hunting, he met a young gypsy girl in the woods. She was
all alone, surviving off what she could kill or gather, and
she held no possessions besides a filthy canvas rucksack and
the tattered clothes on her back. The way Hickory told it,
she was the most beautiful thing he had ever seen, though
Livi found that hard to imagine, since Tess was so scrawny
and plain. They fell in love and ran away together, and
they'd been wandering ever since.

Livi liked their story, but she still found them to be a
very peculiar pair. Hickory was so tall and bronze and gentle, and *Tess* -- well, Tess was as tattered and dirty and
rough around the edges as the day they met!

By sunset the singing was long abandoned and a comfortable quiet had set in. Everyone was hungry and sweaty,
and Livi (whose legs were not used to such long treks) was
so tired that singing or talking or even thinking very much,

seemed an overwhelming task.

They had walked across prairie and through forest, hiked up steep mountain trails, and passed ancient villages, but they still had a long way to go. It was the dark of night before they finally stopped to sleep, and all three fell into a deep slumber the moment they lay down.

The next day, they woke up at dawn again and walked until long past dusk. The road-system in rural Eaux was poor and undeveloped, and by the end of the second day, the rough gravel roads had completely worn down the thin souls of Livi's boots, causing painful sores to form on the bottoms of her feet. But none of that mattered because, after two days of nearly nonstop hiking, they had finally arrived at the capital city of Eterneaux.

Livi and Hickory and Tess squatted in a large thicket of brambly undergrowth a few hundred yards from the great stone wall that surrounded the city. It was getting late and Livi could have fallen asleep right there, but she knew they had a full night's work ahead of them.

Hickory sighed and stared past Livi and Tess, toward the wall. "We'll have to wait until everyone's asleep to scale the wall. Less people we cross paths with, the better, I figure. Then once we're in, the First Palace is just a clean sprint across the city; should be fairly routine, I'd say."

The evening crawled by slowly. They stayed well concealed amid the bramble, watching and waiting for an opportunity to move. Finally, around midnight, a small procession of motorcoaches came in through the main gates.

The motorcoaches were nothing like the modern, colorful coaches that frequented Primareaux's city street. Their wheels were rickety and their engines were loud, and they were built from scrap metal, with enormous silver rivets holding together the various patches of aluminum and steel and tin.

Livi was not the only one curious about the strange vehicles: Tess and Hickory watched them carefully as they approached the gate. "Look at the windows -- they got bars on 'em. Must be headin' to the prison -- a transfer or somethin'."

"Well, then this is what we've been waiting for" said Livi. "All the guards will be preoccupied checking in the prisoners."

Hickory nodded slowly. "I was hoping to wait a bit longer, but you're right, we might not get another chance like this."

There was no more time for deliberation: the trio climbed out of the bramble and sprinted down the short segment of open road, arriving half a minute later in the shadows of the great stone wall.

Tess went up first, finding the smallest of crevices in the smooth stone wall. She inserted her hands and feet into the hard vertical surface and clung on, spreading her limbs wide like a spider. At the bottom, Hickory followed Tess's every motion, spotting her in case she made a wrong move; but Tess never did. Her movements were innate, intuitive: she never hesitated -- never stopped to think or plan -- and she was crouching on the narrow rim of the wall in a few short minutes.

"Ready Livi?" whispered Hickory once Tess had situated herself safely on top of the wall. "Don't be afraid, it's just like we practiced -- easier even."

Livi's stomach was doing somersaults and her hands shook uncontrollably as she placed them on the cold stone. Hickory was wrong: this was nothing like they had practiced. This was not a game or a test, and Quizzle wasn't right beside her, ready to rescue her the second she misstepped.

Suddenly, she forgot every lesson she ever had. She was mute and her limbs felt frozen and heavy. For a moment she was absolutely certain that this was all a terrible nightmare: Violet wasn't really sick, and she and Benny and the others had never left the safety and comfort of Primareaux. And in that moment, she felt happy.

Perhaps it was the jolt of happiness that ripped Livi out of her self-pitying daze, or perhaps it was the cold breeze that blew against her back as she remained plastered against the wall. Livi didn't care why or how she began to move; all she knew was that she was no longer frozen.

Slowly, she inched her way up the great wall.

Soon her nerves subsided completely and she remembered how to climb. This wall was different from the one she had practiced on: it was easier, just as Hickory had promised. The rock felt coarse beneath her palms and there were plenty of imperfections in the sleek facade -- countless nicks and cracks and holes and notches -- in which she could insert her hands and feet.

Livi reached the top nearly as quickly as Tess had. She was feeling very pleased with herself and was thinking about the hearty congratulations she would surely receive, when she lost her footing and found herself dangling precariously off the edge of the wall, hanging on by just her fingertips; an audible gasp escaped her lips.

Tess crawled over and hauled Livi unceremoniously back onto the ledge. "Be careful won'cha? Jus' sit on down."

"Who's there?" called a gatekeeper.

"Quick Tessi," whispered Hickory, who had scaled the wall in about ten-seconds flat, and was now leaning casually on the shoulder a large stone gargoyle (one of many stationed on the rim of the wall).

Almost too quickly for Livi's eyes to follow, Tess slithered over to the gatehouse, whipped out a tiny blowpipe, and shot the complaining officer in his neck. There was a light hissing sound and soon the entire gate-
-house was smothered in a thick layer of fog.

"Better get the other one too, while you're at it," Hickory advised.

Tess nodded and crept over to the other unsuspecting guard. She shot her blowpipe again, causing another heavy fog to fill the second gatehouse. By now, however, the fog had settled in the first gatehouse and Livi could just make out the lines of a man, looking deadly still, slumped in the corner of the small square building.

"What was that stuff?" Livi asked when Tess returned.

"Huh? Oh, just some powdered foggin' flower. Puts whoever it lands on in a nice daze."

One after another they descended, until all three pairs

of feet landed safely on the others side of the wall. "Welcome to Eterneaux," Hickory muttered, sounding highly satisfied, as their backs pressed against the concaving inner wall. The wall was set slightly away from the city, and Livi guessed they were around a quarter of a mile from where Eterneaux really began. From here, they could see everything, and the sight before them was tremendous.

The whole city was lit by a soft golden light, filling the windows, rising up from the streets, and lighting the rooftops of the tallest towers. The public roads, some skinny, some quite broad, stretched in and out, winding and crisscrossing, accessing every cavity of the city with ease.

Steps away were the motorcoaches that they had watched enter a few minutes earlier. Just as Livi had predicted, all the officers on duty (she counted seven) flocked around the vehicles, preparing to take inventory.

With Hickory in the lead, then Tess, and finally Livi, they crept in single file down the hill toward the city center. The road was slick beneath her feet and it was hard to keep balance as they moved in swift decent.

Livi only turned back for a moment, to make sure they weren't being followed, when she saw him: A boy, about her age, standing by the carriages.

She turned right around, insisting she'd seen nothing, but his eyes bore into the back of her skull and she had to look again. She was already halfway into the quarter-mile that separated the wall from the city, and she couldn't see him well from here; still, she was able to gather general evidence to how he looked: his hair was cropped short and he looked tall, despite the way he was hunching over, and he was wearing a dark blue prison jumpsuit. With his hands bound tightly behind his back, he crept past the line of prisoners and snuck around the front of the coaches, ducking for cover as three more officers arrived to help with the transfer.

He was running toward the city -- toward *her* -- still hunched over, his face well-hidden in the shadows, inching closer with every awkward, pained step. *He must be escaping*, Livi thought anxiously. Then, all of a sudden, his head jerked up and she caught his eyes.

For a moment she froze, uncertain he had seen her. Tess and Hickory were a dozen yards ahead already. They hadn't noticed the boy, Livi was sure. If they had, Tess would have pulled her out of sight at once. She ran to catch up -- turning back just for a second. The boy was still there, staring at her, and as she turned, a fleeting grin crossed his lips.

There was no more room to wonder, she knew he had seen her. But she had also seen him, and it was perfectly clear from his blue prison jumpsuit and bound hands, and from the way he ducked behind the motorcoaches and lurked in the shadows, that he wanted to remain hidden as badly as she did. Her breath returning, Livi ran to catch up with the others, trying very hard to forget the strange boy in the blue prison jumpsuit.

. . .

There were three grand palaces inside the walls of Eterneaux, one for each of the three crowns of Eaux. To the West, a black stone road led to the gates of Horridor Castle. Carved from onyx, and decorated with tormented bronze sculptures, the castle was as dark and mysterious as the family who had been occupying it for centuries.

To the East, the Third Castle lay at the end of a sweet and winding path. Simpler than the others, and perhaps more refined, Livi visited the Third Castle once on a school trip, a very long time ago. Now home to the famously reclusive Petterina Wispen, the castle looked dead and unoccupied, and its renowned rose gardens appeared abandoned.

Finally, due north, and suspended in mid air at the top of Winniwill Hill, was the First Palace of Eaux. Made up exclusively of turrets, the First Palace was an extraordinary sight. Some turrets simply hovered inches from the ground; others were raised high in the air, parallel with the clouds; still others were even higher than that, shooting far into the sky, mingling with the stars. The turrets were connected by a series of bridges, which, as legend warned, were quite unsteady and likely bewitched.

Their ultimate destination was the Royal Greenhouse, which sat on the grounds of the First Palace. Livi did not yet know how they were going to get in, since the grounds were surrounded on all sides by a large iron fence, but she was sure Hickory and Tess has a plan. After all, they were so fearless and eager and bold, and though she wasn't sure if she'd ever feel like she belonged among such brave, agile creatures, she was enjoying being included.

As they led Livi toward the First Palace, they seemed perfectly unconcerned with being seen or caught. They leapt over bridges and took flights of stairs three at a time; they clambered up empty streets and smiled broadly as they went.

The fun was stalled, however, when, out of nowhere, three men -- each wearing the crisp plum-colored uniform of the Royal Guard -- came charging from the shadows. "Hold it right there," bellowed the first guard, aiming a long spear at Hickory's exposed neck. The officer was rounder than he was tall, and the point of his spear (which was not unlike the ones Livi had practiced with back in the Befallen Forest) towered over him almost comically. "What d'ya think you're doing out this time of night?"

"Aw calm down there, Murdoch," said the tall, muscly looking guard standing in the middle, "they're just kids, they are."

"Kids or not, they're up to no good, Fred, I can-" but Murdoch was cut short when an official sounding voice came booming over the large square radio fastened around his enormous waist; the voice was issuing a warning about an escaped prisoner. *The boy from the gate*, Livi thought, suddenly sure she'd made a big mistake by not warning Tess and Hickory about him.

Upon hearing the warning, all three guards became fiercely alert, standing up straighter and scowling deeper than they had just moments ago.

Hickory must have noticed the change as well because he put on his most serious voice and his most menacing glare, and looking down to meet the short, round officer's stare, he said, "You should keep walking."

"Shut your trap, boy. And stay right where you are -- hands where I can see 'em, understand?" All three guards had their weapons drawn now.

"Guess we gotta bring them in, huh, Murdoch?" said the third guard sullenly. The third guard was slack-jawed and wide-eyed and wielding an enormous crossbow, which he aimed directly at Livi's forehead. Livi found it difficult to take him seriously, however, as his crossbow was *so* enormous, that it looked as though the exceedingly gangly man would topple over at any moment.

"Listen, we don't wanna have to hurt ya fellas," said Tess, sounding perfectly calm. "Jus' move along now."

Murdoch sneered. "Oh, now the little street rat's got somethin' to say."

"What did ya call me?"

"Tess no," cried Hickory. But he was too late: Tess was already lunging at Murdoch, and before anybody knew what was happening, his spear had clattered to the ground and Tess had her hands wrapped around his stubby neck.

"This is not according to plan, Tessajune."

"Oh he deserves it. And *you*," Tess howled at the muscly second guard, whose spear was jutting out in her direction. "Would ya stop pointing that thing at me already? I said put it down."

Then things began to happen very fast: First Tess, (who had left Murdoch cowering on the ground) walked straight up to the officer called Fred, pried the spear from his hands, and punched him so hard in the gut that he toppled over in pain. He recovered quickly, however, and lunged back at her, fists clenched and teeth bared. Tess dodged his first two punches. She pivoted left and pushed her right leg up and out, kicking him right beneath the sternum.

At the same time, Hickory ripped the slack-jawed guard's crossbow from his hands and snapped the arrow over his knee in one fluid motion. The guard then responded by smashing his fist into Hickory's hard jaw.

Though her mind was frozen in fear, Livi's muscles

remembered their training, and somehow she knew exactly what to do: she hurled herself at Murdoch, who had scraped himself off the ground and was looking around wildly for an available weapon. Murdoch turned out to be surprisingly spry, despite his enormous girth, and managed to dodge several punches before Livi's fist finally met his face with a loud *crack*.

Whether it was the sound of his jawbone snapping or his nose breaking, or Livi's *own* hand shattering against the pressure, she didn't know, and she didn't care. She was so amazed at the force with which she punched, that she forgot for an instant where she was and what she was doing, and in that half of a second's hesitation, Murdoch came back strong, landing several impressive hits before Livi had the chance to realize what was happening.

Murdoch ripped Livi's bow and her sheath of arrows from her back and threw them out of reach. Then he grabbed her by the back of her shoulders and tried to force her to the ground. She jabbed him in the groin with her elbow and made him to lose his grip around her; he was still recovering when Livi landed an impressive right hook. Murdoch looked so enraged by the idea that the small, unarmed girl was beating him senseless that Livi doubted he had even noticed the gushing red stream coming from his nose. But he was still not down.

The short, stout guard limped toward her, fists clenched and blood dripping from his face. She had done at least as much damage to him as he'd done to her. *At least that's something*, Livi thought as he inched closer.

She considered grabbing for the knife she had concealed at her waist, but before she could, Murdoch had her by the neck and slammed her down against the green marble road. Livi's hand was throbbing and her face was swollen; her body was worn, it was beaten.

Murdoch leered over her and was about to attack when Tess came out of nowhere and threw herself on top of the guard, knocking him off Livi, and kicking him until he crumpled to the ground.

Tess grinned at the defeated man. She drew an arrow

from her sheath and aimed for the guard's fat chest. "Hey Livi, how 'bout some target practice?" she called through a hearty laugh. Then, noticing Livi's wounded expression, "Aw, *gosh* now, I'm only kiddin'. Only cowards aim ta kill."

Livi sighed in relief.

Tess dug around in her rucksack and pulled out a length of rope. "Here, help me tie 'em up." They went to work tying up the slack-jawed guard, but before they could finish, Murdoch reached weakly across his large, bruised body and found his radio. By the time Tess had pried it from his hand, he had already called in backup.

"Gosh now, why'd ya go and do that?" Tess muttered, more to herself, than to Murdoch. "Well, hurry then, Livi; we don't have much time."

Hickory was still fighting the second guard, Fred, but when he heard Murdoch call for backup, he removed himself from the fight and left Fred half-standing in the middle of the street. "We gotta go," he yelled to the girls, who were still fumbling with the rope. Several pairs of footsteps were coming from around the corner. In another minute they would be outnumbered. "Forget the rope, we gotta go now!"

They ran until they were sure they had lost the guards, and then collapsed exhaustively at the top of a short flight of stone steps in the center of the city. Hickory pulled out his map to see where they had ended up and let out an exaggerated sigh. "We've gone almost three miles out of the way. Damn guards -- if it wasn't for them, we'd nearly be there by now."

"Well, no use cryin' bout it. Let's jus' get goin'. Maybe we can make up some time."

Now they moved quickly and with purpose -- their flighty, excited wanderings, long gone. It was still the middle of the night, but the deep gray sky warned that dawn wasn't so far off, and everybody was tense and hurried. Hickory kept his map open now, for fear of losing their way again, and Tess checked behind her at every bend. The game was over now; they had a mission, and it was time to see it through.

"Hey, come this way," called Hickory, turning down a narrow side-street. "Yeah right here, I think it's a short cut."

But they had not gone three feet down the street when a terrible blankness overtook them. *"No,"* Livi hissed, trying desperately to cling on to herself as a waft of shadows came alive and inched toward them.

Hickory and Tess already looked glazed over and empty; they began moving away from Livi and toward the herd of Unthinkers. "Tess -- Hickory!" Livi called, but it was hopeless. They had already succumbed to the Unthinkers, and Livi would be next.

It was now or never. Everything that had been holding her back didn't matter anymore; she *had* to turn into her Luma. Livi squeezed her eyes closed and thought back her many weeks' training: *"Your soul and your body must work together ... find your soul within your body and learn how it breaks down ... it's a puzzle, Livi, just focus on the pieces..."*

With a cry of pain, she burst out of herself and into an enormous blast of pearly, effervescent light. Her body collapsed to the ground and she watched from above as the Unthinkers fled, letting out shrill squeals as they galloped back into the darkness.

"Tess, Hickory, are you all right? Did they get you?" Without the slightest hesitation -- without a thought of failure, or the tiniest of doubts -- Livi transitioned back into her body and ran to her friends' sides. *What if I was too late,* she thought, shaking Tess. "Are you okay? Say something!"

"Well darn, Livi," Tess said suddenly, bursting out of her daze. "Took your sweet time, now didn't ya?"

Livi ignored her friend's slight and hugged Tess's small, dark frame so tightly that she feared she'd broken a rib. A minute after that Hickory snapped awake too. Soon his nose was buried in his map again and he was shouting out directions as if nothing had ever happened.

• • •

By the time Livi, Tess, and Hickory arrived in front of the First Palace, the protection of the night was gone and the dawn of a new day danced on the horizon. The trio slunk behind a series of large topiaries and took inventory of their surroundings: there were four men standing at the front gate and dozen more waiting for them on the other side. Their original plan had relied heavily on the dark of night for camouflage, but now getting in unnoticed was going to be nearly impossible.

"Well, we're not going to be able to just dance on in there, that's for sure," hissed Tess.

"If we can just get past those front guards without making a fuss," whispered Livi. "Once we're inside it'll be easy."

"And how d'ya propose we do that? We could fight 'em I guess, but that'd cause one heck of a rustlin'. Hick, what do you think?" Tess cast an impatient glance toward Hickory, but he didn't seem to be listening: his eyes were locked on the Royal Guards and he was muttering intensely under his breath.

Then, all of a sudden, something very strange happened to the guards: mouths were left gaping and eyes were stuck mid-blink; fingers were clenched stonily around spears, and men were stuck in mid-salute. The Royal Guard had been frozen in place.

"It worked!" Hickory exclaimed a little too loudly for comfort. He jumped out from behind the topiary trees and marched proudly through the main gates of the palace. "Come on girls, whatcha waiting for?"

"How'd you do that?" Livi asked excitedly, as she followed him into the palace.

"I used this stunning spell that Emelda taught me ages ago. I didn't think it'd work but, well, look at them."

"*Oh no*," Tess groaned -- a response that Livi found extremely odd.

"What's wrong?"

"Ya know you're no good with magic, Hick."

"They're *stunned*, now aren't they?"

"Oh for Lord's sake, Hickory -- they're a'ready

startin' ta wake!" Tess smashed her fist frustratedly against a nearby bronze statue. Down the line a guard started to blink awake, and then another.

"You can fix this, right Tess?" Livi said, a tinge of urgency coloring her restrained tone. They were trespassing on the private property of the First Crown of Eaux, and the guards outnumbered them ten-to-one.

Tess looked over the mess of guards. They looked like they were going to burst free from the spell at any second. She reached into her satchel and sifted through a variety of pouches and tins and jars. "I'm sure I have somethin' -- hm, 'fraid foggin' flower won' do the trick, not in their state. I could try some sqaushweed but I'm not sure I got enough. Oh, look here -- jarred flummox."

The large glass jar opened with a pop. Inside were what looked like a hundred or more slimy, squiggling snails, black as night. Tess reached in and took one of the snail-like creatures into her hand, letting it wriggle around in her palm. "Go on, take a few an' help me get all the guards. Just plop 'em right on the ear an' they'll do the rest."

Livi cringed as Tess placed one in her hand. "What are they?"

"Don't be afraid," said Hickory. "Flummox are perfectly harmless. They're primitive magical creatures, you see -- parasites, really. They feed off human memories."

"So it won't hurt them, then?"

"Naw, but it'll confuse the heck outta them."

They went around to each of the guards' ears until every one of them was home to a flummox. "There now, all done. Now, let's get on with it before anyone else comes around."

"Wait -- just hold on a second," said Livi. "Hickory, Tess, go around and take off a couple of the guards' overcoats. And maybe some of their caps too."

"That's real good, Livi," Tess exclaimed, catching on to Livi's plan. "We stick out like a couple a cacklin' witches on Sunday mornin' lookin' the way we do."

It was true: they were still wearing the same old, grimy clothes that they had on when they left the ark, and every bit of them was caked in mud and dirt and dried up blood from their long journey. If they tried to walk across the grounds now, in the daylight, they'd be spotted instantaneously.

They got to work stripping the guards of their clothes, and dressing themselves in their new, less conspicuous garments. Naturally, they still looked completely out of place -- Tess and Livi with enormous bows flung across their small backs, the tails of their coats reaching well past their knees, and Hickory standing about a foot taller than anybody else in the kingdom, his broad shoulders pulling against the regal purple fabric. Still, with the plum-colored coats of the Royal Guard swarming around every corner, these poor disguises were better than none at all.

15

WHEN SHEEP
MINCE WORDS

IT WAS MIDMORNING by the time they reached the Royal
Greenhouse. They had been very lucky the rest of the way,
sneaking by quietly or knocking out swiftly, those who
crossed their path; and so far, it seemed that nobody realized
there were intruders on palace grounds.

The greenhouse was tucked neatly away, between the
First Palace's northernmost turrets and the redbrick serv-
ants' cottages that lay at the bottom of Winniwill Hill. It
was large and round and old-fashioned, and though it connected seamlessly to the rear of the palace, by way of an old
iron footbridge, the dome of paneled glass still stood out
against its harsh stone exterior.

Tess tugged on the enormous glass doors. "Locked."

"You've got a spell or something, don't ya, Tess?"

"No, wait," said Livi. "I have an idea."

Livi exploded from her body and burst seamlessly into
her Luma. She blocked out all noise and commotion and
focused entirely on the large brass keyhole, melting in slowly. She filled the negative space, conforming to the tiniest
nook and crevice within the mechanism. Ever so carefully,
she rotated left, then right, becoming the key. She pushed

harder, turning the lock as she shifted. Finally, she heard the click of a bolt, then another. The door swung ajar.

Livi was ecstatic. No longer limited by her body -- no longer bound by space or size, Livi now moved in ways she never thought possible. And it was not just her movements that had changed: once Livi understood that she heard, not from her ears, but from somewhere else, somewhere deep inside, layers of sound flowed through her in octaves she never imagined existed. Once she recognized that she no longer used her eyes to see or her fingers to touch, and that she spoke from some visceral part of her soul, having nothing to do with her vocal cords or her lips or mouth, moving and tasting and touching and seeing all became second nature.

It was like tying her shoelaces or riding a bicycle: at first, everything required practice, but the moment she learned, there was no unlearning, no considering, no thinking twice. Now she felt as natural floating inside a keyhole as she did when she had two feet firmly on the ground.

Livi slipped carefully out of the keyhole and back into her body. Together, the three friends walked freely through the large glass doors.

The greenhouse looked even more enormous from the inside. Thousands of plants clogged the floors and tables and walls, and rows of greenery stretched on endlessly, winding their way around the glass dome. Livi pulled out a charcoal drawing of the Emickus plant that Wren gave her before they left. "How are we ever going to find one tiny plant in all this?"

"Emickus will be in the medicinal section," said Hickory, as if it was the most obvious thing in the world. "We just have to figure out the layout."

"But nothing's labeled."

"Oh, quit whining, will ya now, Livi? It'll turn up; we only gotta do some lookin'."

Livi would have been very annoyed with Tess had she heard her; however, at the exact moment that Tess began to speak, Livi caught sight of a slim, redheaded figure ascending the small hill and moving toward the greenhouse. A surge of anxiety swelled through her.   "Whatever we do, we'll have to do it fast. Crown Saintright's just around the corner!"

"Come on, down here."

They situated themselves behind a large display of cacti just as Crown Saintright entered the greenhouse.

Even beneath the hard artificial light, Livi had never seen such a beautiful creature. In portraits, the First Crown had always appeared serious and brazen and full of sharp edges, but here, with a blue ribbon keeping her loose copper curls tucked neatly behind her ears, she looked almost sweet, almost childish.

Following a few steps behind, was Saintright's most trusted assistant, Miss Delilah Anthrope. Delilah looked only a little older than Livi. She was wide-eyed and fair haired and might have been pretty, if it weren't for the deep gray circles under her eyes, and the lines of worry that rose up prematurely on her nicely aligned face.

"Delilah, what happened to my lilies?" growled Crown Saintright. All the innocence and gentleness Livi saw in her face just a few seconds ago was gone now, and deep contempt colored her plump lips. "Who's their care-taker? Someone should be tending to them at all hours." The patch of lilies looked wilted and close to death, though everything around them was in full bloom.

"The caretaker on duty is called-"

"I don't care what his *name* is, Delilah; just find him and *rep*rimand him."

Delilah bowed, sinking low and deep, and then walked hurriedly out of the greenhouse and down the hill, toward the small family of cottages where the caretakers lived.

"Oh you poor creatures," Crown Saintright cooed, cupping one of the dying lilies in her hands. "I'll find who hurt you."

"Sometimes things die, Mavis. And for no reason at all."

Crown Saintright snapped around to face her intruder. "What are you doing here, Hubert?"

Crown Hubert Horridor was old and gray, and in his

brightly colored robes, his hair looked as white as fresh snow. But his posture was that of a man half his age, and his eyes were calculating. "Oh, I'm only here to pay a friendly visit."

"*You* did this, didn't you?" Saintright asked shrilly, pointing at her wilted flowers.

"I haven't the faintest idea what you're talking about, Mavis. It sounds like you could use some proper rest."

"I know you killed my flowers, and I know what you're up to. You won't intimidate me by poisoning my lilies or by ransacking my library or with any with others tricks you have planned."

"Oh, you're even madder than I thought. I didn't touch your flowers, and as for the library, I've got plenty of books of my own; I have no need to trounce through that dusty old place."

Horridor strode across the enormous dome, passing right by the table of cacti beneath which Livi, Tess, and Hickory hid, and stopping at a glass shelf that was home to several strange, snapping plants.

"The Red Dragon," he said ominously, lifting one of the peculiar plants from its shelf. Long, yellow needles enveloped its budding center, protecting the precious crimson flower at all angles. "A single prick from its spiny shell and you're dead -- no exceptions. Yet its flower can cure even the most venomous of bites. One must be careful when handling such a delicate creature; even the smallest misstep can end you."

Saintright, who didn't seem the least bit intimidated by Horridor's horticulture lesson, glowered deeply at the Second Crown. "I grew that flower myself, from just a seed. That one, and each of its brothers." She yanked the Red Dragon out Horridor's hand and stroked the length of its spiny exterior. At her touch, the spines miraculously recoiled, leaving a smooth, almost plastic surface in their wake. "It know's not to bite the hand that feeds it."

Saintright glared bitterly at the old man. "I know what you're planning, Hubert, and I'll take this entire kingdom down before I let anyone remove me from my throne.

You made a big mistake with Mayback-"

"Mayback was a tragic accident."

"Mayback was a massacre! It was a coup, and it failed. You're pathetic, and if you ever try a stunt like that again, I'll kill you myself."

"You poor creature," Horridor said, his voice cloying, "you are sick with delusions. Everyone knows I was a thousand miles away when Mayback fell asunder. It was a tragedy, certainly, but my hands are clean."

"It was your Minister that slew my own. It was your men that lit the flames, your orders."

"*Prove it.*"

"I don't need to. The people are coming for you, Hubert. They know what you did to me ... what you've been doing to *them.*"

"The people know nothing."

"They know enough," Saintright countered. "And they don't need anything as banal as *proof* to make you pay. They're going to rebel, and they won't be after me, or Mary, or poor Petterina. They'll go after you, and they'll rip you to pieces."

Horridor scoffed. "The people are sheep, Mavis; they will go where they're told."

"Ah, but it is the sheep you must beware, Hubert, for in herds they are mighty."

Something flickered behind Horridor's eyes. Was it fear? Contempt? There was no chance to find out; Saintright's assistant, Miss Anthrope had just appeared, announcing her arrival with a well-timed cough.

"Delilah," Saintright shrieked, "where *were* you?"

"I was dismissing the caretaker, ma'am, just as you-"

"I don't *care*, Delilah; I needed you here. Finish this up, and don't forget to turn off the hoses when you're done."

Livi didn't know who she hated more: the conniving Crown Horridor, or the bluntly abusive Saintright. But either way, she was pleased when the latter escorted the former out of the greenhouse, followed a few minutes later by Delilah Anthrope, who left the hoses dripping.

Finally the greenhouse was empty again. When they were certain it was safe, the trio popped out of hiding and took to separate corners, each in search of the Emickus plant. Livi was stationed between Crown Saintright's wilted lilies and a table of miniature trees that had been carefully pruned to look like leafy, green cottontails. She had hardly started to search, however, when a strange voice interrupted her:

"Looking for *this*?"

Livi whipped around and shrieked in surprise when she recognized the strange boy who faced her. "It's you! You're the prisoner from the gate -- the one that escaped."

"Name's Kip Crowley," he said brightly, extending his hand in greeting. The boy looked perfectly unconcerned that Livi saw him escape; in-fact, he seemed rather pleased to hear that she remembered him. Tall and sinewy, his blue prison jumpsuit had been replaced by neutral layers, but he was wearing the same fleeting grin. And in his large, calloused hands, he held the Emickus plant.

Livi couldn't believe it. Had they really found the Emickus? She realized then, that a large part of her never fully believed they could do it. But here she was, standing in front of Violet's cure! Now all she had to do was get home in one piece, and Violet might actually have a chance.

"You followed us didn't you?" Livi asked Kip Crowley, trying very hard to suppress her excitement. "You shouldn't have done that."

"Eh, it was no trouble, really."

Tess and Hickory (who came running over the moment Kip revealed himself) were now hovering protectively around Livi. "Maybe ya need me to knock the trouble into ya then?" said Tess, fists clenched.

"No need for that," Kip said. Then, turning to Livi, "So what's your name anyway?"

Livi hesitated. "I'm Livi. And this is Tess and Hickory."

Kip grinned broadly at each of them. "I'm happy to make your acquaintance."

"Wish I could say the same," Tess said.

Kip held the Emickus plant out to Livi. "Well, so do you want it or not?"

She snatched the flowerless brown plant from Kip without meeting his eye; she couldn't let him know how grateful she was. "We would have found it on our own."

"I think what you mean to say is, 'thank you.' And you're quite welcome."

"I'm not going to *thank* you for following us."

"Well, anyway, I've got a way you can repay me."

"*Repay* you?" Tess and Hickory said in unison.

"That is the Emickus plant you're holding after all."

"We *would* have found it," Livi repeated, more shrilly this time.

"Sure, but it would have taken days, the way you three clank around."

"How about I knock your two front teeth out?" Tess snarled, lunging toward Kip Crowley. "How's that for a thank you?"

Hickory jumped forward and caught Tess by the back of her shirt, restraining her just in time. "Don't Tessi -- he's not worth the trouble."

Tess thought for a moment, then exhaled loudly and turned to leave, signaling for Hickory and Livi to follow.

"Wait, listen, don't go." All the confidence had drained from Kip's voice and now his tone was almost pleading. "Just hear me out for a second, will ya? You're right, I'm sorry, I shouldn't've followed you. But I was thinking we could help each other."

"I told you, we don't need your help."

"I saw you sneaking in over the city wall -- you're not from here, you don't know how this place works. But me -- I know this city like a porcupine knows his quills; I can help you get out."

"We got in just fine; what makes you think we'll have trouble on the way out?"

The boy laughed and some of the confidence returned to his face. "You *fought* your way in. You can't be doing that now, not in the daylight. Or the whole Royal Guard will be on ya before you can say Astor is my King. And trust me, those disguises aren't fooling anyone. But stick with me and I'll slip ya right out."

Tess and Hickory stared at each other for several seconds. "An' just what'll we need to give you?" Tess said finally.

"Just a lift, that's all. A ride outta this place; don't care where, as long as it's on the other side."

"If you know your way around here so well, why do you need our help?"

"Eterneaux's not the problem -- I've hopped that wall half a dozen times, at least. But I need *all* the way out. Out of Eaux. And the only way to do that is by sea or sky. You've got an ark, don't ya? Waiting out by the river?"

"How'd ya know that?"

"You should learn to keep your voices down if you don't want people knowing your business."

"Yes, we have an ark," Hickory admitted begrudgingly. "But we're not taking a complete stranger aboard."

"Well, you think about it, but in the mean time, I suggest ya hide; someone's coming."

"What're ya talkin-" Tess stopped short, as the door to the greenhouse flung open again, leaving them barely enough time to duck out of sight.

"Why *here*, Mary? Of all places, why do you insist on meeting *here*?" It was Hubert Horridor again, and he was angry.

Livi's heart pounded. *The greenhouse was supposed to be empty*, she thought irritably as she watched a second person enter behind Horridor. It was a woman, gray haired and bespectacled, with the look of fierce superiority blasted across her plain face.

"I have business here," said Representative Mary Lucidon matter-of-factly. Then, finding her way to Saintright's lilies, "I have to check on a project I've been working on."

"You, reckless, *stupid* woman," began Horridor viciously. "You poisoned her flowers, didn't you?" Mary did not respond, but smiled coyly, which was enough of an answer for Horridor, as well as for Livi, who was watching breathlessly from beneath a nearby table. "She's on to us, Mary. Now is not the time for you childish games."

"She's on to *you*," Representative Lucidon corrected.

"And why is that?" Horridor spat. "I knew Mayback would backfire, but you wouldn't listen! Now Mavis knows exactly what we're up to. If the Shepherd finds out about this-"

"Oh Hubert, you worry too much. I admit Mayback was a blunder, but none of that matters now. Crown Saintright is overruled. Outnumbered."

"Is she? The people's allegiance is to *her*, Mary, not us. They have been uneasy for months, ever since the Unthinkers arrived in Eterneaux. How long did you think we could explain away all those disappearances? How long did you think the people would remain silent? And then you went and murdered the First Minister! The only man in the entire country who's been publicly acknowledging the disappearances! Nothing could have made us look more guilty. There's a lot more of them than there are of us."

"You're getting hysterical, Hubert," the Representative said blithely. "You know I can't stand it when you're hysterical. Anyway, the people do not matter, not now. Not anymore."

Livi's knees pressed painfully against the rough greenhouse floor, but she dared not move; she dared not even breathe. Was this really the same Mary Lucidon who was best friends with her mother? The Mary Lucidon who was Primareaux's most prized export? The secrets in this greenhouse were too many to count, and she suddenly felt like she was suffocating. This was the sort of eavesdropping that could get her killed.

"Let the people come for us," Mary continued. "Let them rebel, I dare them to try. They don't have a chance against us now, not when the Shepherd-"

"Do not speak that name! You have no right, is that understood?"

"And what right do you have?" Representative Lucidon countered. "It's time you kneel at the feet of a true leader."

Horridor's withering, wrinkled face turned so purple with rage that Livi thought that he must be having some sort of fit. For a moment, he and Lucidon stood across from each other, both perfectly silent. Lucidon looked as though she was bracing for him to go into a rage, but a few seconds later, Horridor regained his composer and his complexion returned to the usual pasty white.

"I kneel to only one, the only *true* Crown of Eaux: the Shepherd. Feel free to keep this up, Mary; you won't be laughing when the Shepherd dissolves the Triangulation, and you with it."

"Watch your words, Hubert. You might have bought my allegiance for today, but who knows what will happen tomorrow?"

Horridor laughed. "You *are* ruthless, aren't you? It's why you were chosen for this job, after-all."

"I was chosen because I was valuable-"

"You were nothing!" Horridor roared. Then, steadying his voice, "Now, don't get me wrong -- I think you've done your job marvelously. But you're replaceable, you mustn't forget that. Stay out of trouble, Mary -- keep your nose clean, your feet steady -- and there just might be a place for you later on."

"*Later on?*" Livi mouthed to the others, but all three of them shook their heads, looking just as confused as Livi felt.

"What were you doing in Mavis's library?" snapped Horridor.

"You know perfectly well what I was doing: that library has access to the Back Corridors. And you can imagine what a disaster it would be if she found the entrance, so I was sealing it off."

Right away, Kip leaned in close and whispered the answer to Livi's unasked question: "They're a network of passages that connect the First Palace to the rest of Eterneaux. Legend says they've been around since Ancient Times -- that Eterneaux was built around *them*, not the other way around."

Livi was just thinking that Kip might be useful after-all, when Tess let out a roaring sigh, followed by a very loud "*a-chu!*".

"What was that?" said Representative Lucidon, looking around suspiciously. "Someone's here, Hubert; someone's been spying."

"Whoever you are, show yourself," demanded Crown Horridor, glancing nervously around the large glass room.

Tess, who had flushed bright pink after her blunder, drew a sharp blade from the sheath attached at her waist, preparing for a fight. But Kip shook his head and pressed his finger to his lips. Then he pointed toward the back door, motioning for them to follow.

"They'll see us," Livi hissed.

But Kip shook his head again and mouthed something that Livi couldn't understand. Then he pointed at Livi's bow and quiver and motioned for her to give them to him.

Livi still wasn't sure if she could trust him, but right now, she saw no alternative. Tess and Hickory must have come to a similar conclusion, because they both shrugged and gave Livi conceding looks. With some reluctance, Livi handed her bow and a single arrow to Kip.

"Get ready to move," he whispered fervently. Without waiting for a response, he shot an arrow clean across the greenhouse, hitting a large ceramic pot. The pot crashed dutifully to the ground, monopolizing Crown Horridor and Representative Lucidon's attention long enough for Kip, Livi, Tess, and Hickory to crawl out through the back door. And before Horridor or Lucidon realized what had happened, the four were already halfway down the hill, running wildly for the cottages.

16

MRS. PITTER

KIP GUIDED LIVI and the others to one of the furthest away cottages and rapped loudly on the front door. "Eddie, it's me -- open up! So do we have a deal or what?" he said, turning from the still-closed door, to face Livi, Tess, and Hickory. In the distance Livi could hear shouts and the clamoring of spears. The game was up: the guards would be here any minute.

"Yes -- yes, fine," she said. "We'll take you on our ark, but you've got to get all three of us out of Eterneaux safely or the deal's off."

Kip nodded in agreement and he banged again on the front door. A second later the door swung ajar and a small, frizzy-haired woman popped her head out. "What in the Good King's name are you doing here, Kipper? Weren't ya s'posed to be locked up out in Teleteaux or somewhere?"

"Just let us in, won't ya?" Kip shoved by the woman and signaled for the rest follow. Eddie's cottage was shabby and small but it had a large redbrick fireplace and a bed and a nice old kitchen stove. It was a fine sized home for one little woman, but the space grew increasingly cramped as Livi, Tess, and Hickory all filed in behind Kip.

"You're running again, aren't ya Kip? Why can't ya just serve out your sentence like every other fool on the block, huh? And who are *they*? Why are ya bringing strangers around, Kipper? I've told ya a hundred times-"

"Don't worry, Eddie, we're friends of Kip's," said Hickory, smiling.

"It's *Edith* to you, sir, Edith Pitter. And I don't care who you are, you're causin' trouble and I don't like it."

Livi, who had been working very hard at being a good houseguest, was somewhat put off by the old woman addressing them with such disdain, and her face must have shown it because Eddie stopped talking and focused her glare on Livi. "Got a problem there, little miss?"

"Aw don't mind her, Eddie," Kip cut in. "Anyway, you're not gonna see her again, or me, for that matter; this is the last time Old Eddie, I promise."

"*Sure*. Sure it is, Kipper. Tha's what ya said last month, when you were runnin' from that old fool from the Third Court. And it was what ya said the time before that, when ya needed a place to hide from that sweet little thing that was all hung up on ya. What was she called again? Elizabeth? Marjory?"

"Her name was Melanie, and she was a downright *maniac* -- you'd've hidden too. But anyway, that doesn't matter; this time really is different. I'm getting outta this place once and for-all, and these folks here are gonna help me."

"As if this is the worst place in the world to be," Eddie grumbled, more to herself than to anybody else. "Some people would consider themselves downright lucky to be from a fine city like Eterneaux. Not you though, boy; you've always gotta find something new. Something *different*."

"I know, I know, I'm a walking sin. Now listen, we don't have alotta time. Please, just let us go through."

Eddie shook her head and glowered vaguely in Livi's direction. Then, just when it looked like she was about to protest further, there was a loud banging at the door. "Mrs.

Pitter? Come on now, Mrs. Pitter -- open up!"

"Quick Eddie -- if they catch us in here, we'll all be in for it."

Eddie, who didn't seem the least bit concerned about the very official sounding voice shouting at her from the other side of the door, grunted loudly and shuffled across the small room, to the fireplace. She moved an old silver picture frame off the mantle and then pushed. Slowly, the fireplace began to dislodge and soon the whole thing had shifted left, revealing a stone aperture built into the floorboards.

"Go on, kids, get outta here."

One-by-one, they shinnied down the hole and landed in a dark, cylindrical tunnel.

From just above their heads they could hear two -- no *three* -- pairs of boots clomping in to Edith Pitter's cottage. The guards' voices were muffled but they were definitely arguing.

"Don't worry about Old Eddie," said Kip, as if reading Livi's mind. "She's been in way worse jams than this; she'll be just fine."

"So these are the Back Corridors, eh?" said Hickory coughing loudly as a wave of dust made its way into his lungs.

"Not as glamorous as they sounded?" Kip said. "Anyway I usually leave a torch down here, just in case ... should be around here somewhere ... ah, here it is."

Kip fumbled around in the dark for another few moments before striking a match and lighting the torch. The tunnel in which they stood formed a perfect circle, like a giant stone pipe. It was clearly man-made, and very, very old.

"How do you know about this place?" Livi asked, her voice echoing off the round walls. "I've lived in Eaux all my life and I've never even heard the Back Corridors mentioned until today."

"I used to work down in the salt mines. There's a tunnel down there just like this one. At first I thought it was part of the mine, some weird stone annex or something.

Anyway, one day I followed it. Took me all around Eterneaux, and even a little ways beyond. Got passages linking
to all *three* of the castles, ya know that? Granted, most of
the entrances and exits are block off nowadays, but if ya
know where you're going, you can get practically anywhere."

"And you know where you're going, then?" Hickory
asked skeptically.

"Course I do. I've spent ages wandering these tunnels
-- heck, that's how I met old Eddie: One day when I was
down here exploring, I poked my head up out a the tunnel
and found myself staring straight into Eddie's kitchen. Bit
rough around the edges, I'll give ya that, but she's good lady, that's for sure. Helped me outta trouble loads a times."

As the Back Corridors wound on, Kip proved compe-
tent and unreserved. Livi was amazed at the speed and ac-
curacy with which he could simultaneously walk and talk.
In a strange way he reminded her of Violet, only he didn't
babble like Violet did; he spoke pointedly, and with purpose. All his stories and questions seemed overtly fascinating, and even necessary, to Livi who listened wide-eyed to
the strange, handsome boy who lead her through the darkness.

"So what do you all think about that stuff Crown Horridor was saying?" Livi asked after they'd been traipsing
down the tunnels for more half of an hour. "Do you really
think he's working with the Shepherd?"

Tess shrugged. "Dunno, but he sounded pretty serious
to me."

"Aw please, the Horridors are always up to somethin'
shady, but it's all talk," Kip said nonchalantly. "But tell me
something else, will ya? Who's this Shepherd you all are
going on about?"

Livi exhaled thoughtfully. Should they tell him?
Could they trust him? Did it even matter? She decided it
didn't, and after catching reassuring glances from Tess and
Hickory, Livi explained to Kip everything she knew about
the Shepherd, which only took a minute or two, since she
knew so little.

"Well that explains a lot," Kip said once she was done.

Livi couldn't tell whether he was being sarcastic or not, and she didn't particularly care. Horridor had explained the disappearances in Eterneaux, at least: Unthinkers had been hanging around, taking people and turning them into more Unthinkers. *But why?*

Livi was about to ask out loud the question she'd been pondering in her head when the torch Kip had been carrying blew out.

"*What the* -- hold on, lemme just find another match." In the perfect darkness, Livi could hear Kip looking through his pockets, searching for the matchbook, but he wasn't quick enough.   Something small dropped from the ceiling. Then something else. Again and again bodies dropped, surrounding the four travelers. Six *no* eight *no* ten new bodies were among them now.

A high pitched cackle echoed down the corridors. "GET THE GIRL."

17

THE HORSE THIEF'S GREAT ESCAPE

THE FOUR FRIENDS WERE SURROUNDED and blind in the perfect darkness of the Back Corridors. They were outnumbered more than two-to-one by the same strange, small creatures that had cornered them in the Befallen Forest last autumn. The beasts' mode of attack was the same, too: dirty and brutal and in total darkness.

The fighting was immediate and intense. Livi pulled her knife close to her body, exactly as she'd done months before, only this time her movements were practiced, refined. When they reached for her, she was ready. She didn't rely on sight, swiveling her blade toward the sound of their clumping feet, making elegant thrashes through scaly skin, warding them off just well enough to keep her feet planted on the ground.

There was something off-putting about fighting in the dark, something shameful about wounding another when you cannot see their face. The anonymity felt cowardly to Livi, and it threw her off her game. She was hesitating when she should have been swinging, freezing up when she should have ducked.

Livi was holding her own, but just barely. Nearby Tess and Hickory and Kip were fighting them off two at a time, but by the sound of it, they were having as much trouble as she was. They needed to relight to torch; they needed to gain an advantage.

"Forget about the others -- just get me the girl!" the leader ordered just as he had before. At his command more bodies turned their attention to Livi, more claws thrashed against her skin.

It was impossible to fight them off now; they restrained her in seconds.

Livi screamed and cried and bit and scratched as they pulled her down the tunnel. Nearby, she was vaguely aware that Hickory and Kip were trying to pry her loose, but the creatures that had her were too strong.

But then came a blast of light so bright that it made Livi see stars. For a moment, in the middle of all the chaos, Livi thought she'd managed to transition into her Luma, for she'd never seen light so bright before except when it came from her. But that wasn't it. The light was coming from somewhere else: it was coming from Tess.

Everyone, the beast included, had frozen in place, stunned by the bright light. Then started whispering, repeating something over and over, and as her words got louder, the light became brighter:

"Revolt, Rebuff, Repel, Repulse.
Sicken, slower, weaken, lower.

Anger twice the mouse's tail.
Penance thrice the critter's nail.
A quarter turn round the lion's mane
Leave now, sweet foe, or take this pain."

And then, as quickly as they'd appeared, the beasts were gone. None of them caught a glimpse of their mysterious attackers, and thanks to Tess's spell, none were seriously injured either. The group was visibly shaken, howev-

er, especially Livi, who did not like the idea of being followed or chased, and liked being nearly captured even less.

"Wallace will want to hear about this," said Hickory
seriously once the foursome began moving again. "Whatever's after Livi clearly hasn't given up."

"So those things have tried this before?" Kip asked.

"Once, a few months back," said Livi. "Hey Tess,
you were great back there. What was that?"

Tess blushed slightly. "Just a basic repelling spell --
not even gypsy, jus' one a Emelda's ."

"So can anybody do it?" Livi asked, imagining all the
ways a trick like that could come in useful.

I s'pose so, sure. Jus' requires a bit a practice, like
anythin' else. An' some skedaddleweed, a course."

"Some *what*?"

"Skedaddleweed. Ya gotta chew up a bit right before
ya say the spell. Don't swallow it, jus' hold it in your cheek
an' say the rhyme and in with any luck, whatever's buggin'
ya will skedaddle on-"

"Hey so we're comin' up on an exit," Kip interrupted
sounding slightly strained. "I was gonna take you on a little
further and exit through the salt mines, but I figure we'd
better just get on out of these tunnels in case those things
come back." Everyone nodded in hearty agreement. "So
this here will take us out around Eaura's Circle. It's a bit
more risky, but we should be fine -- it's usually so crowded
no one'll notice a couple extra faces popping up outta nowhere."

"And what do we do once we're out on the street?"
said Hickory. "We can't exactly walk around in these uniforms all day, can we? And then there's the small matter of
getting us out past the gates."

"Don't worry, I've got all that covered. Just put these
on, will ya?" Kip threw a long gray cloak to each of them.
"You'll blend in just fine with these -- though you girls had
better ditch those crossbows."

"Talk about coming prepared," Livi said, staring at the
beat-up canvas backpack from which Kip pulled the cloaks.
"What else do you have crammed in there?"

"Oh just the standard ... a couple days rations, some clean socks ... a guy never knows when he'll need to make a getaway."

They exited the Back Corridors via an abandoned manhole on a dead-end a block and a half from Eaura's Circle. The alleyway was deserted, and just as Kip had promised, they transition smoothly into the crowded main road one block over.

Livi tried to match her pace to Kip's, who moved nonchalantly through the crowd, but she couldn't emulate his composure, maintaining a nervous, uneven stride, and looking over her shoulder at every turn.

"Loosen up, will ya?" Kip whispered, taking hold of her arm. "No one's following us, so just relax. We're almost there, anyhow. This way."

They followed Kip out of the city center, and headed into what Livi thought must be Eterneaux's version of the Old Town: the streets were quieter here, the houses were older, and the shops were more quaint. Soon, the foursome arrived in front of a large, shabby house on the corner of a tree-lined street.

"This is Mick's place. Great isn't it?"

"It's, um -- well, who's Mick, anyway?" asked Livi.

"Mick owns Clarren Orchards, out by the mountains. The man's got a boat-ton of money, though you'd never know it, the way he lives."

Kip tapped on a window pane that looked into the kitchen; a second later the ramshackle front door swung open so quickly that Livi was sure it would fall straight off its hinges. A tall, broad-shouldered man in beat-up blue overalls appeared in the doorway. He had straggly blond hair, and though Livi suspected he was only about forty or fifty, a life in the sun had aged him dramatically.   "Why, if it isn't Kip Crowley. Where've ya been, son? You haven't come round in at least three weeks now."

"Yeah, sorry about that," Kip answered vaguely, scratching the back of his head. "Anyway, I've got some friends I want to introduce."

The man nodded pleasantly as Kip introduced everyone. "Well, any friend a Kip's. Anyway, I'd invite ya in but I'm just about to make my deliveries. Come round later, though. The misses is cooking up a nice stew; there'll be more than enough to go round."

"Actually, Mick, I was hoping you could help us out. Do ya think you could give us a lift out of Eterneaux in your truck? We're heading north, ya see."

"Aw come on now, Kip. I've got at least a dozen more deliveries to make before the day's over. Come back tomorrow, bright-and-early; I'll take ya on my way to the orchards."

"It has to be today; it has to be now."

Mick folded his arms. "What sort of trouble are ya in this time?"

"It's nothing, my friends here just need to get on out of Eterneaux without making a fuss, that's all, and I thought I could help."

"You mean you thought *I* could help?"

"Come on Mickie, you owe me."

The man sighed. "All right, all right. Meet me round back in five minutes."

A quarter of an hour later Livi, Tess, Hickory, and Kip were squeezed together under a tarp in the bed of Mick's old red pick-up truck, well-hidden amid fifteen or twenty large sacks of apples.

"You sure have a lot of friends," whispered Hickory.

Kip grinned. "Well, what's life without 'em?"

It was at least a half-hour's drive from Mick's house to the enormous gates of Eterneaux, and Livi couldn't keep her eyes open as the old truck bounced gently down the cobbled streets. She must have dozed off, because the next thing she knew, the truck was stopped, and she heard voices arguing nearby:

"Aw, I don't have time for this," Mick was grumbling. "I have a delivery all the way out in Green Acres. I've gotta get moving."

"*Green Acres*?" said a second man's voice, skeptically. "Why would anyone in Green Acres order from Clarrens? They've got half-a-dozen nice sized farms out that way."

"Well, hell Steve, I don't know. How bout ya come along and ask them yourself? Now let me through already."

"Sorry Mick, orders are clear. We've got to search every vehicle that crosses the gate."

Livi heard the door to the truck swing open and Mick step out. "Come on then, let's get this over with."

Two pairs of boots clomped around the truck. Half a minute later the truck bed clanked open. "See there, Stevie. Nothing but apples." The two men laughed. Livi stayed motionless beneath the thin black tarp, praying that the gatekeeper didn't decide to search more thoroughly.

"All right then, Mick. Sorry for the trouble." He slammed the truck bed closed. "Just with the break-in at the greenhouse, and then the escape and all, earlier this morning -- well, ya can never be too careful."

"*Escape?*" said Mick, sounding surprised.

"You didn't hear? Last night there was a big prison transfer: two full coaches of detainees heading to the local jail. Well, one of those guys escaped somehow and it's been crazy ever since. And then, just a little while ago intruders were spotted inside the First Palace. Crowns' are in an uproar. Course the guards are the ones who get it -- said we weren't paying attention, which I can tell ya right now wasn't the case."

"You don't say?" said Mick. "Who was it that escaped, anyhow? No one dangerous I hope?"

"Nah, nobody dangerous. Just some scoundrel thief -- Crowley I think his name was."

"Crowley, huh? Well, Steve, I'm sorry for your troubles, but you fellas'll catch him. Anyway, like I said, I've got deliveries."

"Sure, sure. You go right on through."

Livi couldn't remember a time when she felt more relieved. The attack in the Back Corridors already felt a thousand miles away, and the further they drove from the walls of Eterneaux, the safer she felt. They stayed under the tarp until they were sure the coast was clear, and then Mick ordered Kip to come up front with him.

Kip looked genuinely worried as he slipped into the truck's cab through the large rear window.

"You're running from the state again, aren't ya boy? You just never learn, do ya?"

Kip let out an exaggerated sigh. "It's not like that, Mick."

"Oh really? What's it like, then, huh?"

"You wouldn't understand ... All right, all right, I'll tell ya. You know Ellie Franklin? She's a few years younger than me -- still in school, I think."

"I know her. Nice girl, good family. What's she got to do with this?"

"Well, I made a deal with my friend, Winston, a few months back. You see, me and Ellie, we've known each other forever, and so Winston figure that if I liked him, she would too. He said I could borrow his horse any time I wanted, and all I had to do was talk him up a bit to Ellie Franklin. Well, it turns out Ellie already had a boyfriend and they were going to get married right after she graduated. But I did my part -- I was still entitled to his horse, wasn't I?" Kip stared expectantly at Mick, but when no hardy agreement came, the boy continued: "Well, anyway, I guess Winston didn't think so, because a few days later, when I took his horse out for a ride, he called the Royal Guard on me. Can you believe that, Mick? That *Royal Guard* over me borrowing a damn horse!"

By now, the others had given up all pretenses, and were staring shamelessly through the back window, watching the two men argue.

"It was *you* that stole that poor boy's horse?" Mick bellowed. "That was all over the city! I was locking my livestock up at night because of you."

"It was an honest misunderstanding, Mickie. Come on now, you're no saint."

"Well compared to you I goddamn am. You'll just never learn, will ya Kipper?"

Kip and Mr. Clarren argued for the better part of an hour, but the conversation grew progressively lighter as they went. Mr. Clarren drove far beyond Eterneaux, and didn't

stop until they were nearly halfway to the river, letting them
out on a deserted country road. By now, they had long
made up, and Mr. Clarren looked genuinely sad to see the
boy go.

"You're really leaving this time, then?"

"It's time, Mick."

"But where ya gonna go?"

Kip shrugged. "I'll figure it out -- I always do."

* * *

A chill had set in, and though it was barely dusk, Livi,
Kip, Tess, and Hickory decided to set up camp for the night
in a large field by the side of the road. It was as good a
place as any for a camp: the land was flat and relatively soft,
and the forest was still at least a half-mile ahead. Hickory
pulled out the old olive-colored tent and Tess started on the
fire.

The pair worked in quiet harmony and it was clear to
anyone watching that they had done this hundreds of times
before. There was a rhythm between them -- a sort of inti-
macy that Livi herself had never experienced. It was an in-
timacy that she deeply envied, and she could not help but
feel like an intruder as she sat on the sidelines, searching for
a way to make herself useful.

"Do you hunt, Kip?" she asked abruptly.

"Course I hunt."

"Good, come with me."

A few minutes later, the pair was marching across the
flat country plain with bows flung across their backs. They
agreed not to waste time searching the prairie, and to head
straight into the forest, where there was sure to be game. It
was the better part of a mile out to the tree-line, but they had
more than an hour of daylight left, so it seemed like a fair
bargain.

"So who's sick?" Kip asked once they'd been walking
for a while.

"How did you know?"

"The Emickus, remember? It's the ugliest plant I've

ever seen but it's good for all sorts of ailments."

"It's a friend of mine, I think she's dying."

"That's too bad. You know her well?"

Livi had been trying very hard not to think about Violet ever since she left the Petrichor. Violet was the closest thing to family that Livi had, and the idea of losing her -- *well, there's no need to think that way, because she's going to be fine* -- Livi thought sharply. Eager to change the subject, she directed the conversation onto Kip: "Why are you in such a rush to leave Eaux? It's not just because of that silly thing about the horse, is it?"

"Nah, it's not about the horse. If I'd stayed put, that would have been cleared up in a week, anyway."

"So why, then?"

"It's just been a long time coming. And I guess it was just time for a change." Livi watched Kip, expecting him to say more, but he stayed determinately silent. Though she was very curious about the strange boy, and had at least a dozen more questions for him, the pair had just arrived at the edge of the North Forest and the time for talking was over.

Just beyond the North Forest was the Noauxware River. Tomorrow they would trek all the way across it to get back to the riverbank where Wallace was waiting. But for tonight, they stayed along the tree-line, dipping only slightly beneath the dense green canopy in search of their dinner.

They had been crouching together behind a large spruce tree for quarter of an hour when Kip removed his heavy green jacket and tossed it to Livi. "Take it."

"No thanks."

"I can hear your teeth chattering from all the way over here, and it's annoying, quite frankly; just take it."

As she shrugged into Kip's jacket, two deer crept into view. Immediately, they both took aim at the grazing creatures. "Put that thing down!" Livi hissed. "It's a waste to kill them both, there's only four of us." Kip rolled his eyes, but complied. She shot her arrow straight into the heart of a large, proud doe. It died instantly.

Livi was relieved when Kip offered to carry their

bounty back to the campsite. Her months of training back at the Petrichor made her as good a shot as anybody, and she was fiercely proud of her newly enquired skills; Livi could have hauled the dear back if she'd wanted to, but she was just as happy to be free from the burden.

That night, Livi ate better than she had in weeks. The fresh venison cooked nicely over Tess's fire, and everyone was happy to be free from the canned beans and dried meats that had been their main forms of sustenance since leaving the Petrichor.

Livi was full and happy and, most of all, exhausted. She was seconds away from saying goodnight, when Hickory and Kip started talking: "So what are your plans once we get out of Eaux? Do you have family out in the Midlands?" It was a question at the forefront of Livi's mind, and suddenly her fatigue evaporated.

"Nope, no plans -- just nothing worth staying for. And no family either. I mean, I had parents once, obviously, but I never knew 'em. Anyway, I just figured it was time for an adventure."

Hickory beamed brightly at this last admission. "If it's adventure you're after, why don't you come with us, back to the Petrichor?"

"The what?"

Suddenly everyone was trying to talk at once. Tess, who just moments ago, had been actively ignoring the conversation, began by regaling Kip with a story about the time she snuck into Emelda's kitchen and put a spell on all the food to turn it purple; Livi was gushing about Wallace and Quizzle and Wren, and Hickory went on a ten minute rant about what he called the "*mission* of the Elders." Then Tess followed that up by assuring Kip that the Petrichor wasn't nearly as serious a place as Hickory made it sound.

They took turns explaining about the Elders and the Befallen Forest, and then Tess and Hickory told Kip the story of how they met. They went to sleep a little while later, but Livi -- her exhaustion long forgotten -- stayed out with Kip, watching the stars.

"I'm from Eaux, too, you know. From a city called

Primareaux."

"That's back east, isn't it?"

"It's the largest city on the coast -- which isn't saying much, I guess, considering its competition." Livi picked up a nearby stick and used it to trace a map in the dirt. "You've got Teleteaux a couple hundred miles to the South. The city itself isn't much, but their university attracts lots of different people. And then there's Lilaeaux-"

"I know Lilaeaux. I spent some time in the area a few years back -- in a little town called Brewster."

"What were you doing in Brewster? There's nothing up there but a couple of stop lights and that old fish market."

"Oh, just tracking something down. I wasn't there long, maybe a month or two. It's a nice place, though, nice and quiet ... hey, can I ask you something?" Livi nodded. "Back at the greenhouse, you -- well, you sort of fainted and then the door opened. You did something, didn't you?"

"You saw that? *Right*, well, it's sort of hard to explain."

Livi started out by telling Kip only the barest version of events, but she soon found herself relating the whole story to him: Tiethe and the Unthinkers, how it felt when she was in her Luma-form, and how hard it was at first. They stayed up half the night talking and by the end of it, Kip knew practically everything.

Livi was surprised by how relieved she felt after telling Kip her story. It was the first time she'd said it all out loud, from beginning to end, and she found the experience strangely helpful. She slept more soundly that night then she had since leaving Primareaux.

• • •

The next day, they were back on the swampy banks of the Noauxware River, and they found Verlinda, exactly where they had left her one week ago. Only, the ark was *too* much the same: the sail was still in tatters, the propeller was still mangled, and most disturbingly of all, Wallace was nowhere in sight.

18

ABANDON SHIP

THEY SEARCHED EVERY INCH of Verlinda, and the surrounding forest, but there was no sign of Wallace. He left no note. There were no scratches, or signs of a struggle. It was as if Wallace had never existed.

"And you're sure he said to meet back here?" asked Kip.

"Course we're sure."

"He probably just got held up at the Smetherstick Settlement. He's got old friends there, doesn't he? Probably just lost track a time."

"Maybe," said Livi. "But wouldn't he have found a way to let us know?"

"We've got to go to Nourim," said Hickory. "It's our only lead. We'll track down that woman, Allegra, and see what she knows ... unless anyone's got a better idea? Good, then it's agreed. But we'll have to wait until tomorrow; it'll be dark soon enough and there's no proper path heading west."

Hickory spent the rest of the afternoon reviewing his maps, trying to decide the best route to take to the Settlement; Tess got to work fixing the broken propeller, and Kip was recruited to assist. Feeling useless, Livi took a walk down the riverbank, hoping to stumble upon something -- *anything* -- that would help explain Wallace's disappearance. But when she found nothing unusual hiding in the swampy undergrowth, she decided to turn back.

It was nearly dark now and there was no moon to guide her. She hadn't realize how far she'd strayed and everything looked different in the shadows. The croaking of frogs felt louder, the cawing of birds, more dangerous. The grass began to rustle behind her; the trees nearby were shaking.

Something grazed her shoulder and a shiver leapt sharply down her spine. Then a voice called her named: "Livi! There you are."

Livi's fists unclenched. "*Kip*. It's only you."

"Scared ya, huh? Well, you shouldn't have come out this far by yourself; it's not safe."

"I'm tougher than I look."

"I'll bet you are," he said, grinning. "Anyway, let head on back, okay?"

Livi was too relieved by the sight of her new friend to pretend she didn't need his help, and she followed Kip back toward the ark without protest.

"Hey, ya know, I'm sorry about Wallace," Kip said as the pair stomped through the high, wet grass.

"Oh, I'm sure he's fine; I'm sure it's just some sort of misunderstanding. The one I'm really worried about is Violet."

"Violet?"

"She's the one who's sick, back at the Petrichor. She really needs the medicine we stole from the greenhouse; I don't know how much longer she can wait."

"Well, you never leave a man behind, Livi."

"I didn't mean -- I wasn't suggesting that we shouldn't go looking for Wallace."

"I know," said Kip. "I'm just saying, Violet'll understand."

Livi nodded. They were nearly back now and she could hear Tess and Hickory arguing a little ways ahead. "Hey, you know, you don't have to come with us to Nourim if you don't want to."

"Am I really so much of a nuisance?"

"It's not that. It's just, you've never even met Wallace -- I don't want you to feel obligated."

"Well, sorry to disappoint ya, but I'm coming. I didn't leave Eterneaux just so I could hang around in the woods, after all."

"Why *did* you leave?"

"I already told you," said Kip, "to have an adventure."

"That's not a real reason."

"Is for me. And anyway, I'm too much of a free spirit for that place, or at least that's what Eddie's always saying."

Livi laughed. "A free spirit is just a nice thing to call someone who doesn't fit in."

"Maybe, but I think I'd rather not fit in."

"You're really strange," she said.

"Oh yeah? Well, me and you aren't so different."

Liv scoffed loudly; she didn't know much these days, but she was certain that she and Kip were nothing alike.

"Don't believe me, huh?" he said. "Well, let's see, for a start, I'd bet ya ten-to-one you're an orphan, same as me ... yup thought as much. And now you're wondering how I knew that. Well, it's just one of the perks of growing up the way I did: I can spot a kid like us from miles away."

"I'm not like you."

"Oh yeah?"

"*Yeah.* I'm no criminal, for one thing."

"Sure, maybe the details are different, but we're the same deep down, I can tell. Only *I* don't waste my time trying to be something I'm not."

"I don't do that."

Kip shrugged. "If you say so. Anyway, we'd better hurry up and get back. Long day tomorrow."

• • •

First thing the next morning, they began the hike west, toward the Smetherstick Settlement. They marched along in a stony silence, worry and exhaustion baring heavily on their backs. No one wanted to admit just how strange Wallace's disappearance was, but Livi couldn't dispel the nagging feeling in her chest, warning her that something wasn't right. And the farther they walked, the louder that nagging became.

It was hours into their hike before the uncomfortable quiet was finally broken by a suspicious rustling coming from the trees just behind them. Arrows were drawn from their sheaths and daggers were eagerly wielded, taking at aim at whatever might emerge from the dense greenery. Livi stood still and held her breath, part from fear, and part because some tiny piece of her was expecting Wallace to emerge from the trees.

And though, it was not Wallace who appeared, it was something nearly as hopeful: through the brush, a baby mooncalf -- glittering opal beneath the blinding sun -- approached timidly on his four wobbly, newborn legs.

"Well, would you look at that," Hickory said, laughing. Since Wallace had gone missing, Hickory's mood had been unpredictable to say the very least, and so the sound of his laughter was especially pleasing.

"What is *that?*" said Kip. "What's wrong with that cow's skin?"

"That there's no cow, Kip," Tess said, grinning. "That there's a mooncalf."

"A *what?*"

"A mooncalf," said Hickory. "They're really common in the Midlands, and we've even spotted a few in Trilinia. But in *Eaux* -- well, it's pretty daring of the little guy to show up here."

"How come?" Livi asked, inching closer and sticking

out her hand so that the young creature could smell her.

"Poachers. Tanneries around here will pay top dollar for mooncalf hide. And the horns on the males fetch as much as ten-thousand pieces if ya know where to take 'em."

Livi observed the small, glistening horns protruding from the top of the bull-calf's head and shivered.

"Hunting Mooncalves is outlawed practically every-where in else the world," Hickory continued. "Even most parts of the Midlands have written up some laws about it -- unofficially of course."

Tess reached out to pet him. "Where'd ya come from, lil one? Where's your mama?" The mooncalf jumped back in surprise, all four of his hooves leaving the ground at once. "Don't be afraid now, I'm not gonna hurt ya."

The calf was very young and clearly unsteady on his long, thin legs. His golden brown eyes peered curiously from either side of his oblong head, and in the daylight his skin looked almost prismatic, taking on a different color with every step.

"I've never seen a mooncalf in the daytime," Livi said.

"That's because they almost never come out in the day. Probably got left behind when the rest of the flock headed home last night."

"Poor thing, let's bring him along."

"I don't know," Kip said, staring uncertainly at the strange creature. "Her mother's probably looking for her; we should just leave her right here so they can find each other."

Tess shook her head irritably. "Damn, you city kids are all the same. That right there's a *bull*, and a fine one, too."

"What's the difference?"

"*The difference?* Well, how would ya like it if I went round callin' ya 'miss,' huh? You can stay here if ya like, and wait for his mama all by yourself, but this little guy's comin' with us."

And so, four became five as they trudged on through the forest. The mooncalf lifted everyone's spirits, and even

Kip, who was hesitant at first, grew appreciative of the young bull's carefree demeanor.

Though Wallace's disappearance still weighed heavily on the group, by the middle of the day, they were nearly at the Settlement and morale was way up. Livi was about to suggest that they take a break for a picnic lunch, when she something made her stop dead in her tracks, her wide blue eyes locked on the red horizon: a forest fire had erupted several hundred yards ahead of them and was moving quickly in their direction. The others stopped too, their gazes following Livi's; a wave of fear swept through the group.

"Well, we've just got to change course," said Kip. "The fire won't be able to catch up with us *that* fast."

"But that's no ordinary fire," Hickory said, keeping his voice low. "That's an Inferno." He backed away slowly and signaled the others to do the same. "Run -- we gotta run!"

"Wait jus' a second now," Tess said. "An Inferno? Out *here*? Naw, no way, Hick. Not a chance."

"Look at how it travels," Hickory said, with forced restraint in his voice. "An ordinary forest fire swallows up what's in its path; *these* flames are expanding, *strengthening* the forest as they burn." What Hickory said was true: the trees were not on fire, the trees were *infused* with fire. It was as if every branch and tree trunk and early spring bud was carved from flame. "I'm telling ya, we've got to go. Now, *please*, we've got to run!"

This time, nobody questioned his order, for even as he spoke, the flames travelled significantly closer. They took off in a sprint, racing back the way they came. Even the little mooncalf ran, going as fast he his four gangly legs could carry him.

But they hadn't gotten half a mile when it became painfully apparent that there was no outrunning these flames: as fast as they were, the fire was faster, and everyone could see it. The group came to a sudden and defeated halt.

"We need a plan," said Hickory. Then, motioning to Tess's rucksack, "Tess, you've got to have something in there that'll help." He didn't wait for her to answer, ripping the bag from her shoulder and emptying it onto the forest floor. Out spilled countless glass jars and colorful vials, several tin canisters, and half-a-dozen brown velvet pouches.

Tess got to her knees and started picking up the contents of her bag. "Nothin's in here, Hick. There ain't nothin' on this planet that can put out an Inferno, and I say it's time we faced facts."

A weighted silence fell upon the group. *Could that really be true?* Livi thought. *After all they'd been through, was* this *the way things would end?* *No*, she decided determinately. *No, they would not die today.*

"What about just water?" she suggested, hopefully. "I could transition and fly back to the river and-"

"*Water*? Gee, Olivia, no one's ever thought of *that* before," Hickory said, his voice bursting with contempt.

"Hey watch it, will ya?" Kip said, glaring. "She's only trying to help."

Hickory grunted vaguely and rolled his eyes, but when he spoke again his voice had softened slightly: "Water won't do a thing to stop an Inferno, Livi. And besides, you'd never have time to get to the river and back again, not even by flying."

The Inferno, as Hickory explained it, was not really fire at all, at least not the type Livi was used to. It didn't feed from wood, or leave ash where villages once stood. The flames came from the trees themselves, beginning in the roots and growing outward. The fire could not be drowned out with water or suffocated in dirt. Its properties were different, stronger: It was the defense mechanism of an ancient and extremely rare type of tree, the *Infernious Arborous.*

"Well, so what, then? What are we going to do?"

"There's nothin' *to* do," snapped Tess. "In a few minutes we'll all be fryin' up like old Emelda's bacon grits."

"But that can't be it! No -- no, there must be something we can do."

"There *isn't*. Now listen here, we've got two choices, and *only* two: burn up cryin' out for our mamas, like damn fools, or burn up with pride. There ain't nothin' we can do to stop this thing from scorchin' us alive, so shut the hell up a'ready and get ready to die the way God intended: brave an' with glory."

When Tess got angry, or talked fast, or worst of all, when she was scared, her thick gypsy accent grew even thicker, and it had never been as prominent as it was right now. Though she would never admit it, Tess was terrified.

"If you're ready to give up, fine by me. But I'm sure not," Kip said. "I am *not* going to die, not now, and *not* like this."

"Kip's right, we need to think. There must be a way to put out the fire."

"There isn't, Livi!" Hickory roared. "Listen here, Tess and me have been in enough tight spots to known when we've been beat. It's over -- it's the end of the road. So just shut up already."

"Hey what's your problem?" Kip growled.

People were growing tenser and words were getting nastier with every second that went by. And in the few short minutes since they had stopped running, the fire had expanded tenfold. As if flipping a light switch, every tree in sight had turned the color of hot ember.

Kip's muscles were tight and sweat poured from his forehead, but when he spoke, his voice was calm: "Okay, so we can't put the fire out. What if we moved *between* the flames. Some of the trees are far enough apart. If we move carefully enough, we might just be able to slip through."

"You don't know anything, do you?" said Hickory cruelly. "The Inferno isn't just flames, it's energy. It's created a forcefield -- there's no crossing the lines of an Inferno, no matter how *careful* you are."

"So *what*? What then? You want to just give up? You're okay with just *dying* out here?"

"Yeah, we are. So get used to it." Hickory kicked the dirt violently.

Perhaps it was because Hickory and Tess so rarely felt

true fear, that they both reacted so poorly to it: Tess becoming impossibly negative, and Hickory bursting with rage at every turn. For years the pair met enormous obstacles, and they always came out victorious. *They must have been waiting for the thing they could not defeat,* thought Livi. *Why else would they be so willing to accept it?*

But Livi, on the other hand, was afraid *all* the time, and maybe Kip was too, because together their spirits only grew stronger, their voices only grew steadier, and within them, hope did not die -- it bloomed in the face of death.

The entire forest, as far as the eye could see, was engulfed in the incredible heat of the Inferno. A gentle breeze whipped the air, rousing the fiery buds and tugging the flaming branches this way and that. The Inferno's red-hot blaze and its pulsating energy kept the group smashed together in a tight circle, locked in on all sides by sweltering, throbbing heat.

"*Ahh!*" Livi shrieked as a flaming leaf wriggled loose from its branch and dropped onto her arm, leaving a welt in the shape of a perfect, four pointed leaf on her forearm. The pain was fierce and sudden. Her whole body burned as she fought to hold back tears.

The mood was grievous and even Livi was beginning to feel the searing pain of defeat. But while the rest of the party fell deeper into a hole of despondence and despair, the mooncalf was growing increasingly restless in the con--fined space, wiggling nervously around the tiny area that was still free from the flames.

It seemed that he either did not understand the danger, or didn't care about it, because as the seconds ticked away, the mooncalf grew more daring. First he let his hoof slip out of the circle, then he wiggled his tail, letting it fly inches from the flames. And then: "*No!*" Tess shouted. The mooncalf finally let his instincts prevail, running straight through the flaming forcefield of the Inferno. "No!" Tess shouted again. "No, please, no!"

And all of a sudden Livi wanted to laugh. Tess's frantic response seemed sort of silly to her, since Tess had already accepted the inevitability of their deaths. Had she not realized that it meant the young bull would die with them?

The mooncalf ignored Tess's pleas and trotted effortlessly among the flames, weaving playfully between the trees. It took a few moments for everyone to realize what their eyes were seeing: the mooncalf was not being burned alive; in-fact, quite the opposite: he was leaving a clear trail where fire once raged.

"But I though you said..." muttered Kip, letting his voice trail away as he watched the mooncalf dance unscathed through the burning forest. "Shouldn't he be...?"

"How is this possible?" Hickory whispered, almost too quietly for anybody to hear.

Livi followed the mooncalf with her eyes as he moved easily through the fiery wood. With every step the creature took, he left behind a cool, iridescent hoof-print where there once was fire. Around them, the pulsating had become weaker, as the forcefield was compromised by the mooncalf's game.

Silently -- as if afraid to scare off their good fortune -- Hickory reached into his rucksack and retrieved the map. In a few deliberate gestures, a plan was formed, and the group slowly began to cross the once impenetrable lines of fire.

The quartet moved carefully behind their mooncalf as his silvery hoof-prints created a disorganized path through the trees. They corralled him this way and that, guiding the young creature across the Inferno, and toward the Smetherstick Settlement.

Hope swelled with every step they took until finally, the blazing forest ended, leaving the gang on a thin grassy trail. Thrill washed over them: they were alive; the danger had passed, and they were alive.

Tess and Hickory embraced, the mooncalf danced, and Livi ran straight into Kip's arms. Sometime amid the flames an alliance was born between them, and as he wrapped his arms around her, she felt sure the partnership would only grow stronger.

"You don't suppose that explains where Wallace went, do ya?" Kip said, grimacing, as he and Livi broke apart.

Hickory shook his head. "I doubt it. Wallace had a different route marked on the map. He must've known this was here. I was just an idiot; I thought I'd found a shortcut."

Livi examined the large welt on her forearm, wincing at the sight. Then, as if reading her mind, Tess handed her a tin canister. "Ground hydra. The stuff won't heal ya up completely, but it should ease up the pain at least."

Livi accepted the medicine gratefully and slathered the strange blueish-gray power onto her arm. The pain dulled immediately and just like that, all the harsh words she and Tess had exchanged in the Inferno were forgotten. Hickory and Kip appeared to have reconciled as well, because the pair was chatting amicably as they bent themselves over Hickory's map:

"We're just about there, then, huh?" Kip was saying.

Hickory nodded and then pointed to the large field that lay on the other side of the thin road. "I think those are the Nourim Outfields, which means it's just a half-mile or so to the village."

Nourim was not only the westernmost point of the Settlement, it was also their primary agricultural community, and the large, well tended fields that spread out across the road provided food for all six of the villages that made up the Settlement. All they had to do now was follow the road north and the would reach the village.

Behind them, the trail of silvery hoof-prints was beginning to fade. Everyone was ready to get going -- everyone except for the mooncalf. Hickory tried calling for him and Tess tried pulling him along, but the stubborn creature would not budge. They were beginning to wonder if they should just leave him behind when he began turning in tight excited circles: a few steps in front of them a large female mooncalf stood proudly in the middle of the narrow road. The young bull bounced toward his mother and the pair trotted off together, up and up and up, into the setting sun.

The four friends were alone again. They walked the path in near silence, too relieved and happy to be alive, to make even small conversations with each other. Insistent on reaching the village before sundown, they pushed on.

Exhausted, the grassy trail wound on, and despite their many diversions, they arrived in the village of Nourim just as the sun was settling into the Great Valley, between the twin peaks of the Nexus Mountains.

19

ALLEGRA

NOURIM WAS A TINY VILLAGE. Along the flat dirt road, raw wooden cabins existed in nestlike clusters, and sheep roamed freely in the street. The village appeared free from inhabitants and Livi was beginning to wonder if perhaps Nourim had been abandoned, when she arrived in Nourim Central Market.

Nourim Market was vast and plentiful. Hundreds of vendors lined the square, selling fresh breads and sweet ciders, fruits shaped like stars, and vegetables the color of the sea. Slabs of meat hung red and bloody, and sacks of spices enlivened the senses.

The market was as thick with customers as it was with produce. Grocers were shouting numbers at each other; women were buying flowers; men were hurling fish; children ran around unsupervised, weaving in between carts, and stealing strawberries from fruit stands. In a way it reminded Livi of Tiethe, the Oracian village she'd visited a few months ago: they were both small and picturesque, and both communities seemed to live and work together so nicely.

"Every Smetherstick village has a market of its own, but nothing like this one," Hickory said as they stood on the periphery. "This is the very heart of the Settlement. People come from all over to do their trading."

The market, though busy and bustling, came to an abrupt halt -- all commerce stopped, all conversation interrupted -- as the foursome entered.

"*Intruders*," came a booming voice from across the square. "What business do you have here?" A large and commanding man emerged from the silent crowd. He had dark skin and a thick neck, and was dressed in elaborate layers of fine, robustly died fabric.

"We're not looking for any trouble," said Hickory quickly. "But our friend's gone missing and we think that you may have been the last to see him. His name's Wallace."

"There is no one by that name here."

"An' what about Allegra?" Tess said. "Is there an Allegra we can see?"

At the mention of this name, the man's face morphed from a look of stern confidence, to the strangest mixture of submission and mistrust. The man looked cautiously around at the many patrons of Nourim Market, who were all frozen and staring curiously at Livi and her band of outsiders.

"*Come*," said the man sternly.

They trailed uncertainly behind the stranger, arriving in front of an unremarkable wooden cabin. Inside was sad and plain. Dust rose in clouds from the soft, dirt floor, and a lantern cast shadows around the small, austere room.

"I am Castil, the High Priestess's first aid. What business do you have with her?"

"Our business is our own," said Kip sharply.

The man glared at him suspiciously. "The Priestess is not here. Go now, and do not return."

"Please, just tell her we're here," Livi begged, stepping forward and staring courageously up at the enormous man. "Ask her if she knows anything about someone called Wallace. If she refuses us, we'll stop bothering you."

Castil was about to protest when the door to the cabin creaked open.

"There will be no need for that," said the elderly

woman who entered.

Castil cleared his throat. "May I present to you, Allegra, High Priestess of the Smetherstice People."

Allegra had pale eyes, white hair, and profoundly wrinkled dark brown skin. She walked with a a distinct limp, despite her crutch, but she was bold and utterly confident, making her poor posture, or otherwise weak comportment, irrelevant.

She smiled crookedly. "You are all so very young. Or perhaps I am just old."

Livi cleared her throat. "We were hoping you could help us, ma'am. We are looking for-"

"You are here about Wallace," said the Priestess.

"So he has been here?"

Allegra shook her head. "It's true I knew him once, but I haven't seen him in a great many years."

"Then where is he?"

"The man you think you know, you don't. When did you see him last?"

"One week ago. He was on his way to find *you*. If he's dead -- if you did something to him-"

"Wallace is not dead. He has only been taken," said the old woman calmly.

"*Taken?* What do you mean *taken?* Who took him?"

Allegra hesitated and then drew from her pocket a piece of parchment. On it, she drew three columns of scribbled shapes and lines.

"Those are Smetherstice characters, aren't they?" said Hickory, knowledgeably.

"You are a smart boy. And, yes, this is an old Smetherstice trick -- an equation of sorts."

"What does it say?" asked Livi.

"These character here refer to yesterday," she explained touching the left column lightly with her forefinger, "this one, to today," she pointed to the center column, "and this last line, shows tomorrow," she said, pointing to the right column. "We add the first two together, to predict the third."

"So what does it say?"

Allegra drew a deep breath. "There comes a point when one must weigh her devotion to the past, against her desire for a future. The equation does not read well for you. If you go through with your rescue, you will be risking much more than just your lives. Are you children truly prepared to sacrifice so much for Wallace?"

Tess glared at the old woman. "Well, he'd sure as cinder go lookin' for us. Jus' go on and tell us what it says a'ready."

Allegra nodded, as if this was the right answer. "Much of this has no translation in your language, but I will explain what I can." Her finger scanned the page, reading the columns from top to bottom. "You must walk where Wallace walked to find the answer -- through Pettersbee, and in-between. But be warned, the truths you find will not please you."

Tess pinched her face up in disbelief. "If that ain' cracked like a caldron after Sunday."

"The High Priestess knows all," said Castil contemptuously. "How dare you doubt her?"

"A'right, a'right so who took him, then?"

"An old friend stole Wallace. A leader, a love."

"Someone we *love* kidnapped Wallace?"

"Someone *he* loves. Or loved once."

"That's ridiculous."

"The equation does not fail."

Livi gritted her teeth. She was beginning to agree with Tess -- that all this was just a lot of nonsense. But what other choice was there? "Okay, so where is he? In Pettersbee? Can you take us?"

Allegra hesitated. "The line between true courage and spectacular foolishness is thin. Are you children very sure you wish to walk it?"

Kip glared ferociously at the small woman. "Aren't you supposed to be Wallace's friend? Shouldn't you *want* us to save him?"

Allegra sighed. "To find your friend, you must enter the Fauxs."

"Aw, now I know she's crazy," said Tess. "The Fauxs

are about as real as the Giants of the North -- just some ol' rubbish from the Ancient Times. Let's get on outta here, a'right?"

"The outcasts, the exiled, the darkest of the dark, they are what survive, what grow, deep down in the Fauxs," Allegra continued mysteriously, ignoring Tess's doubts.

"But Tess is right," said Hickory. "The Fauxs are only a legend, ma'am. I mean no disrespect, honestly, but no one really believes in them anymore."

"And what is legend, really? Legend can be truth, as fact can be fiction. The Fauxs are told as legend not for lack of truth, but for lack of virtue. Those who know, know not how to handle such great terrors, so they mar the truth until it appears as nothing more than fantasy.

"I won't try to convince you, but you must trust me now, for later will be too late. If you still wish to find Wallace, the closest passage is through Pettersbee Dam, three villages over. I can take you there now, if you like."

• • •

The night was young, the sky was clear. Castil held the reins, directing a pair of red-spotted Smetherstice stallions as they pulled Allegra's old covered wagon down the dirt road.

"The Fauxs are an in-between," the High Priestess explained as she crouched next to Livi inside the cramped, dusty wagon. "They're not part of this world, or the next."

"An in-between?" Livi echoed.

"A nook or cranny. A wrinkle in a clean sheet. Niether here, nor there -- why, they do not belong at all -- but they exist nonetheless, and to our detriment. There are many in-betweens, but none so dark as the Fauxs."

As if there was not already enough to fear, Allegra continued her tale, weaving an image of grave uncertainty: "It's a land of deception and turmoil and cruel injustice. Do not trust your eyes, for they will fail you. Do not trust your mind, for it will lie."

In the Fauxs there were no rules. Up could be down,

and right could be left. A mountain might be a river, and river, a wall. Some in-betweens acted as passages, and some as hideaways. But the worst and most dangerous in-betweens were those like the Fauxs: those that had become other worlds entirely.

It was the thick of night when they arrived in Pettersbee village. Like Nourim, it was small and simple in design. "Pettersbee is a fishing village," said Allegra as they drove swiftly through the town. "Most local commerce is generated from Pettersbee Pier, down by the Noauxware River. The dam is absolutely vital to the villagers' prosperity. Destroy the dam, destroy Pettersbee; upset the Fauxs, and destroy all of Eaux."

Kip nodded seriously. "We'll be careful."

They had arrived at the dam by now and everyone filed out. Allegra handed Livi an old lantern and a book of matches. "Use these sparingly. If you run out, you'll be good as blind."

"Aw don' worry about that -- I've got at least three pouches of Sun Sand," Tess said, patting her rucksack affectionately.

"Your magic won't work down there, I'm afraid. At least not in the way you intend."

"Does that mean I can't-" Livi stopped short. There was no easy way to explain what she was. Fortunately, Allegra seemed to already know:

"Lumae magic is different: your Luma is inside of you, it is part of you. I cannot say for certain, but I expect it won't bring you trouble."

"Still, Livi, it's better you don't risk it," said Hickory.

"He's right. Don't turn unless you have to," Allegra said. "I'll leave you now. Good luck."

"But wait!" Livi cried as Allegra turned her back on the group. "Where do go we from here?"

"Three quarters of the way across the dam is a trapdoor. Make sure to close it just right. Too much light passing through will cause terrible damage to this world and to the in-between. And just remember, nothing is ever as it seems. Go in together, come out together. Everything in-between isn't real."

The thick wall of stone looked vulnerable against the constant pressure of the flowing river. In single-file, the gang ascended the steep stone steps that were carved into the side of the dam. The air was damp, the wind blew strongly, and the ground felt slicker with every step. There was no hint of an interruption in the smooth stonework and the foursome had to cross three separate times before finding the trapdoor. Even then, it was by sheer luck, when Kip tripped over a perfectly camouflaged metal hinge hidden amid the stonework. With some difficulty, Kip lifted the tiny metal latch, and he and Hickory together raised the heavy stone door.

One-by-one they stepped down into the cold, black passage. Livi was the last to enter, and she closed the door carefully above her head, just as Allegra had specified. In the last bit of light that lingered, she saw a flight of stairs, steep and winding, leading down into the Fauxs.

20

THE
FAUXS

THE STAIRS BECAME A SLOPE, and the slope, a black hole. Down and down she fell, until finally, Livi hit the rocky, unforgiving earth with a great *thud*.

"*Hello?* Hello, is anybody there?"

A hand grazed her shoulder. Kip's voice echoed through the darkness: "Right here, Liv."

"Me too," Tess called out.

"Over here," said Hickory.

Livi lit the lantern Allegra had given her and the cave filled up with orange light. Then, she felt her eyes grow wide as she surveyed their new surroundings: calcified limestone and massive sinkholes, reflecting pools, and enormous black boulders decorated their new landscape. Rocks dangled from the top of the cave, like icicles in winter, and columns of stone -- blackened with dirt and age -- protruded from the ground and connected seamlessly with the cave's upper limits.

Every crack and crevice, every burrow and nook, was distinct and extraordinary. But the Fauxs' peculiar beauty did nothing to ease Livi's nerves. How would they ever navigate the labyrinth of caves and tunnels that lay before them? One dark, unwelcoming passage led into another, connecting and intersecting, and so on and so on, for as far as her eyes could see. The could get lost down here forever never reaching Wallace, never getting the medicine to Violet.

"So what now?" Kip asked, vocalizing Livi's owns doubts, as he peered into a gaping sinkhole, the core of which comprised tapered, crystal-like structures.

"Now's when the real adventure begins. Come on, let's try this way." Hickory directed them to the widest, most easy to maneuver tunnel. "Everyone be careful now, and look before you step."

As they walked, Hickory sketched out a rough map using some charcoal and a piece of old parchment he found at the bottom of his rucksack. At first it felt as though they were walking in circles, but after a while the landscape began to change, and with it Hickory's map grew larger and more comprehensive.

They'd been walking for an hour, at least, without anything to indicate that they were on the right track, when a chilling wind and a fierce, bloodcurdling cackle, sent the gang running as fast as they could down the jagged, eroded black rocks.

Kip pulled Livi into a sprint but a freezing, sucking, wind grabbed hold of her and started to suction her backwards. And then, she fell. Plunging through a sinkhole, tumbling and twirling, spiraling downward, until *crash* -- she landed in another cave.

"*Livi*? Livi, is that you? Are you all right?"

"Kip! Where are you?"

A moment later there was another crash, followed by a husky, pained groan. "Well, that was about as nasty as the Nothings of the North," said Tess irritably.

A few second passed, and then, with a final bang, Hickory landed face-first between Kip and Livi. "What *was* that?"

"Felt like a shiverwitch, if ya ask me," Tess said, standing up and dusting herself off. "Never met one pers'nally but Emelda's told me all sortsa things. Her sister Marla, is one herself. Terrible creatures, they are -- or so I've heard. Will freeze ya to the bone if ya let 'em."

Livi struck another match and relit the lantern. In front them, a lake blocked their path. She edged up to the water and looked into its gritty depths. The water was too deep to cross on foot, but a little way down, a makeshift bridge was strung together using half-rotted planks of wood and ancient, blackened rope.

"Do you think it's safe to cross?"

"No, but unless we wanna turn all the way around it's our only choice. We'll just have to be careful."

They crossed the dilapidated bridge one at a time, the planks swaying and creaking with every step. Hickory was the last to cross, arriving safely on the other side of the lake just seconds before the bridge collapsed into the water.

A half dozen slimy, serpentine creatures leapt from the water to greet the fallen bridge. Everyone watched as the beasts wrapped themselves around the rotting planks, sinking their enormous teeth into the wood, and forcing the bridge beneath the lake's oily black surface.

Tess stared ominously into the water. "Whew, that coulda been your legs, Hick."

"I don't know about all that, but it was closer than it should've been, that's for sure."

After enjoying a collective breathe of relief, the foursome continued their journey. The caves tunneled linearly now, narrowing and shrinking with every step. But as Hickory's map got larger, the space around them shrunk away. Soon they were they were forced into single file, and then onto their hands and knees.

Livi ended up in the front of the line, struggling to keep the torch lit as she padded along. It was getting harder to breathe, now, and she felt like she was spinning.

"Can't ya move any faster up there?" Tess called from directly behind her.

"I'm trying but I can't see anything. The fire's gotten

too low."

"That means we're losing air," called Kip from the back of the line. "Everyone just keep moving. The tunnel's gotta widen soon."

They crawled on several more feet but Livi was getting too dizzy to continue. She collapsed suddenly onto her stomach. "You guys, I feel like -- well, I think I'm seeing things."

"Livi, if you're losin' it, then so am I," Tess said, who had moved as far up as she could and was peering over Livi's shoulder. "I can see 'em too."

Just inches from her face, three tiny creatures, equal in stature and in gruesome physique, stood side-by-side, blocking her path. Naked and ugly, with large eyes and thin lips, the tops of their bald, gray heads did not even graze the ceiling of the narrow tunnel.

The first creature extended a stick that was at least twice as long as it was tall, and poked Livi in the forehead. "*Intruder!*" a mousey and utterly unfamiliar voice screamed. "Do not move."

"What *are* you?" Livi asked, wide-eyed.

The creature in the middle snorted derisively. "What are *we*? What are *you*?"

"*They* are intruders," said the first creature, poking Livi again in the forehead.

"What's going on up there? Why'd we stop?"

"Just relax a minute, will ya, Hick?" Tess called back. "There's somethin' up here."

"They're not intruders," said the third creature to first and second. "They're *imbeciles*."

"Pooooor imbeciles," cooed the first, still clutching its stick. "I think they are lost. *We* are imps. We will help you! Tulli is my name, and these are my sisters."

"I am Tark!" shouted the second imp proudly.

"Timl!" screamed the third, gesturing to herself with vigor.

"What do you want?" asked Tulli, hands on her hips.

"Where are you going?" questioned Timl.

"What are you doing here?" rounded out Tark.

"We're don't want anything. We're just trying to find our friend. His name's Wallace, have you seen him?"

"We are imps! We cannot *see*."

"*Oh*. I'm sorry, I didn't know."

"But all imps cannot see," said Timl.

"It's not their fault," Tulli whispered to her sisters. "They are imbeciles."

"Would ya stop callin' us that, a'ready?" snapped Tess, who was practically lying on top of Livi now, struggling to get a good look. Livi elbowed her hard in the shoulder. "What? They're the ones callin' us dumb."

"But only an imbecile would ask the way from those who cannot see."

"I'm sorry, but it's like I said, we didn't know you were blind."

"Blind? Did we say we were blind? We are not blind, we simply cannot see."

"Who sent you here?" Tulli snapped accusingly. "Out with it, out with it, you fool."

"No one *sent* us. We came on our own -- for Wallace."

"Wallace? What is a Wallace?"

"I already told you, he's our friend. The one who's been taken."

"*Taken*? Where's he been taken?"

"We don't know -- well, somewhere down around here, obviously."

"An intruder!" exclaimed all three imps at once.

"The intruder must be captured!"

"Captured? No, but it's not his fault, you can't hurt him. He's our friend, and he's in trouble."

All of a sudden, Tulli burst into tears, throwing herself onto the ground, in violent, shrieking sobs. Not to be outdone, Tark and Timl cried out with equal vigor, bending over each other and wailing dramatically.

"Oh the poor Wallace! The poor, poor Wallace," shrieked Timl.

"The poor imbeciles. The have lost their friend," Tulli choked out, through her tears.

"The poor imbeciles!"

"We will help you," cried Tulli. "We will show you the way."

"But aren't you bl-bli-"

"Ya can't *see*," Tess spit out, aggressively. "Ya said it yourself, ya can't see."

"And what's that got to do anything at all?" said Timl, abashed.

"You just told us," Livi began carefully, so as not to set their rages off again. "You can't give directions. You don't know the way. You did say it, don't you remember?"

"Directions? Who said a thing about directions?" said Tulli.

"No directions!" agreed Timl. "We will go with you. We may not see, but we know the way. We can smell an intruder from miles off."

The imps pressed their noses to the ground and moved aggressively down the tunnel, leaving Livi, Kip, Tess, and Hickory scrambling to keep up. They cut right at a fork and the tunnel broadened a bit, then a bit more. Finally, it got large enough for Livi and others to stand up again. And soon after that, it got so enormous that it no longer felt like a tunnel at all, but a massive, endless cave.

The expanded space and ample oxygen made following the imps a much easier task. And as unusual as they were, the imps knew the land well and they proved to be excellent guides. They never hesitated or disagreed. They moved swiftly, but carefully, talking occasionally, but always staying focused.

As they travelled even deeper into the Fauxs, things that once felt extraordinary became common and uninteresting. Livi passed by walls of tapered purple crystal; she didn't flinch when the caves started closing in
or feel relief when they expanded; and she barely noticed the elaborate paintings that frequented the dusty cavern walls. Only a few hours ago, she would have dedicated half-a-day's study to any one of the aforementioned spectacles, but now she had little patience for them.

In time, Livi even grew accepting of the frequent

howls, the indistinct hissings, and the slithering of snakes' tales, that echoed constantly through the caves; this was why, when she heard the flapping of their wings and their shrill, screeching voices, she thought little of it. It was only once she saw them that she began to worry.

Bats, thousands of them, filled the tunnel, flying together in a thick dark cloud. They swooped down and descended upon her. A hundred sets of claws dug into her back, her scalp, her legs and arms. She fought and struggled against them, but for every pair of claws Livi pried out of her skin, in sunk a dozen more. They worked in unison, picking her up and lifting her high, their small, leathery wings flapping ferociously as they carried her down the deep, black tunnel.

The air was sticky and the wind was hot as it blew across her face. Kip's voice called out for her somewhere nearby. She tried to turn her head, tried to see if the others had been picked up as well, but every movement sent a sharp pain coursing through her body. She stayed still, she closed her eyes, and she tried not to be so afraid.

Livi was flying hours, or minutes, or days, caught in the grasps of a thousand bats, when finally a tortured, anonymous cry stopped their' tiny, pulsing wings in mid air. Their claws retracted and Livi clambered suddenly to the ground.

With three more loud thuds, Tess, Hickory, and Kip crash-landed beside Livi. The imps were nowhere in sight, and their surroundings seemed more foreign than ever. If only Hickory had kept up with their map; if only Wallace was here to tell them what to do next.

She stood up and took a deep breath. But before she could hug her friends or look to see where the bats had disappeared to, a terrible cracking noise ripped through the air and a sharp pain slashed through her stomach.

It was as if someone had reached inside of her and was twisting and tearing her insides apart. It was an agony she'd never before experienced; she was doubled over and vulnerable. She reached for Kip, but he was not there. No longer beside her, no longer anywhere, her pain turned to panic.

"Kip! It's Kip, he's gone. Something's taken him!"

Hickory and Tess stared at Livi, bewildered.

"We can't just stand here. Come on, we've got to find him."

Hickory reached out to touch her shoulder, but his hand went right through her. Tess said something but her words came out as gibberish. Kip was gone, but everyone was calm. Kip was gone and no one seemed to care.

And so she searched alone, running in circles, probing every nearby crack and crevice, and climbing through the shadows on her hands and knees. She was numb and her vision was fuzzy, but she kept going. Whatever took Kip couldn't have gotten far.

Finally, she saw him, slumped over in the dusty grey corner, smelling of must and mildew. All the life was drained out of him and his eyes were glazed over and empty.

She cried and cried but no one could hear her. Everything was black and she was all alone.

21

WHAT LIVES
BELOW

LIVI WOKE UP SORE, like she had fallen from a great height. A long, thin bruise claimed half her torso, and her chest ached with every movement. How did she get here? And where were the others?

Thick green vines sprouted from between the cracks in the solid stone ground, and trees lined the enclave where she rested. The cold cavern ceiling was a sad reminder that she was still very far from home, but where *was* she? The lush underground forest in which she sat was nothing like the rest of the Fauxs -- nowhere that she remembered, at least.

Then, *clank-clank-clank*. Someone or something was just beyond the trees.

"*Hello?*" Livi called out. "Is anyone there?"

"*Livi*. It's Livi, she's awake!" cried a great, familiar voice bounding through the trees. It was Kip, and steps behind him were Tess and Hickory.

"Kip! But you were dead, I saw it."

"I'm right here," said Kip, leaning in to hug her.

"But I saw it."

"It wasn't real," said Hickory, pushing Kip out of the way and trapping Livi in a spine-crushing hug. "It was just the phantom messing with you."

"The what? What are you talking about? Where *are* we?"

"You were struck by a phantom," Tess clarified. "Made ya see some things that weren't the truth and then ya fainted."

"You'll be fine in a while," said Hickory. "You only need some rest."

"A *phantom* did this to me? A *phantom* made me go crazy?"

Kip shook his head. "You didn't go crazy. Well, almost -- but ya didn't. You're fine, we all are."

"An old hermit out on a hunt interrupted the attack just in time," explained Hickory. "He scared off the phantom and saved you before it could do any permanent damage. Then he took us here so you could rest."

"And the imps ran off right around the time the bats got us," said Kip.

"Some friends *they* turned out to be," said Tess.

"So how are you feeling? Do you think you can walk? We've already lost a lot of time; we should leave as soon as possible."

"Sure, I can walk. We'll leave right away."

Just then, a very old man in a gritty brown cloak, with only his long nose poking out from beneath his hood, entered the enclave. "What are you doing up and about?"

"Livi, this here is Eame. He's the one who saved you."

Livi smiled and tried to stand up but Eame pushed her down.

"*Sit*," he snapped, digging his hard calloused fingers sharply into Livi's shoulder-blade. "A phantom blew through you not one day ago. You must rest."

"I want to thank you so much for saving me, sir, it was so kind of you. But now we really have to get going."

The old man snorted. "Well, I didn't do it for you. The last thing I need is a phantom-spirit hibernating within healthy human flesh. If I hadn't stopped it, that phantom would have fed from your body until the thing was ten times more powerful."

"Well, it doesn't matter why you did it, we're all very grateful," said Hickory diplomatically.

Tess nodded. "But now it's high time we get goin'. Got some business to take care of 'cross the caves, ya see."

The old man let his hood slip to his shoulders, revealing an enormous scowl. "Do what you wish but if you leave tonight, you will surely regret it. A colony of Undar lives just through the trees, and they'll be very happy to have some fresh meat for dinner."

"I've heard stories of the Undar," said Hickory. "Tiny things, aren't they? But a highly organized species. And supreme fighters."

The hermit nodded. "They are vicious animals, and they've only grown worse since aligning with the Shepherd."

Livi shivered. It was the first time anyone had mentioned the Shepherd since they arrived in-between, and the mood got suddenly tense. "Well, I'm sorry, but we can't wait."

The old hermit shrugged. "They'll kill you, but so be it."

"Don't worry now, we can take care of ourselves," Tess said.

"And besides, we don't have a choice: Wallace needs us," added Livi.

"Course that's if Wallace is even down here," said Tess. "*What?* I'm just sayin' out loud what everybody's thinkin'. We've been runnin' round based on some prediction made by a kooky old lady. For all we know Wallace could be down south, lyin' on the beach somewhere."

"We've come this far, Tessajune. No use doubting ourselves now."

Kip nodded and then put on his most winning grin. "So, Eame, you know this area better than anybody, wouldn't ya say? Well, like we explained, our friend's in danger and we've got to head out tonight. What do you think about helping us out with the Undar?"

"Oh no. No, no, no. I'm not risking my hide for you unappreciative little vermin, not again," Eame shouted at the gang. He had no intention of helping them any more than he already had. He was a hermit; he looked out for only himself. And besides, it was by sheer luck that they'd gotten this far and were all still in one piece; Eame was *not* going to climb aboard that sinking ship.

But he couldn't hold out forever. After some flattery, a little bartering, and several threats from Tess, the old hermit agreed to draw out a map that would guide them through Undar Territory.

The map laid out all of Undar Territory, which included most of the underground forest. Eame drew out a route for them to follow through the least populated parts of the wood. As a final warning, he advised them to move as fast as they could, stay hidden, and to "pray to the Gods above because that's the only chance you fools have really got."

They ran for miles. Livi's heart was weak and skin was raw, but she went on. She moved faster, pushed harder, and struggled to keep up, weaving and dodging the trees as she ran. Finally, the forest began to thin and the group slowed its pace. Livi hopped over a fallen tree and moved even faster, pushing ahead of the others, eager to escape the dangers of Undar Territory.

The trees here on the periphery were dry and waxen, their bark peeling at the touch, their leaves the color of ash. The closer Livi crept to the edge of the forest, more fallen trees blocked her path. All around her, branches turned to twigs, and leaves to dust. It was as if the forest died a little more with every step she took.

Soon, the trees stopped all together and the cavern floor turned to rubble; the forest had disintegrated right before her eyes. A few feet ahead of her, the floor dropped off completely, creating a sharp cliff, dropping into a dark ravine of sand and rock several feet below.

"What in Astor's name!" exclaimed Kip, slowing his

pace just in time to avoid falling into the ravine. "Did we go the wrong way or something?"

"Couldn't be," Hickory said, standing carefully on the edge of the cliff. "I've been following the map precisely."

Hickory jumped skillfully down into the ravine, landing on his feet. He took out his compass and set it next to the map Eame drew. "Yes, this is exactly right -- another half-mile west and we should be right back where Livi got attacked."

Tess jumped into the ravine and landed right next to Hickory. "Lemme see that." She ripped the map from Hickory hands. "But it's not on the map, Hick. Ya sure we didn't-"

"I can follow a map, Tessajune. Come on, let's just keep going."

"You're right," agreed Kip, taking a running leap into the canyon. "There's no use in trying to figure out what happened, not in a place like this."

Livi was the last to abandon the comparatively smooth cavern floor for the uneven, rubble-filled canyon. Though Hickory stopped occasionally, taking samples and making notations, their voyage down the ravine was swift and steady, until they reached an enormous crack in the ground that divided the path in two.

Hickory frowned at the small, crinkled map. "This fork isn't on the map: the tunnel should continue straight. Hm, well, this way, I suppose -- *yes*, yes this way."

The group started down the path that bore right, but they hadn't taken two steps when a familiar, shrieking voice cried out: "The imbeciles are going the wrong way!" Three imps stomped out from behind a rock, shaking their disproportionately large heads.

"Timl, Tark, Tulli, where have you been?"

"Where have *we* been? Where have *you* been?" yelled Tark, her eyes wide and unfocused.

"They expected *us* to find *them*," said Tulli.

"But we are imps, we cannot see!"

"Yeah, yeah, we got it, we remember," said Tess shaking her head.

"Can you tell us what happened to the road?" Livi asked.

"We smelled it coming," said Timl, prancing around on her tiptoes. "We smelled it coming and so we ran."

"And we hid," added Tulli.

"Until it blew through," concluded Timl.

"What was it?"

"A phantom. And it was very angry. It got bigger and bigger," Timl explained, swelling up her chest in imitation of the phantom.

"And tore up the whole ground," said Tark, lifting up a rock twice her size and chucking it easily across the ravine.

"Then we didn't smell it anymore," said Tulli.

"So we came out," continued Timl.

"And stopped hiding," concluded Tark with a slight nod of the head.

"It's gone now. Far away, far out of here," added Tulli, twirling happily and beginning down the path that bore left. "Come now, the intruder is down this way."

And so they walked on, trudging across the broken ground, and falling deeper into the gloomy, winding in-between. Though the gang was still technically in Undar Territory, they were out of the forest, and safe, at least for now. Hickory handed the job of guide back over to the Imps, and Livi breathed a sigh of relief and she moved even farther from the underground forest.

According to the imps, Wallace smelled closer than ever. They led the gang confidently down the ravine, humming as they went. They were almost out of Undar Territory now, and a new wave of confidence bolstered the group. But then, a few miles along, a wind came from no where and blew the lantern out.

Something dropped from above, and then something else. The beasts were back for Livi, and this time there were five, or ten; this time there were hundreds.

"Quick, get a match," said Hickory as body after body dropped into the ravine, surrounding the four friends. "Come on, come on, hurry."

"I'm lookin'," Tess shouted. "I'm tryin'."

Livi could hear Tess searching frantically through her bag for the matches. It was too late, though. A cackle cut the air. "Bring me the girl," the familiar, high-pitched voice of the leader said, almost calmly this time.

"Wait, I found 'em, I got 'em," Tess said frantically. A second later she struck a match and the cave was bathed in soft golden light. Immediately, a strange nimble beast, scabby and brown, charged toward her, aiming for the lantern.

"*No*," the leader ordered, causing the creature to freeze inches from Tess. "Leave the light. She's on our territory now, there is no threat. Let the girl watch as we kill her people."

Finally Livi could see her mystery attackers, finally she could give them a name. The Undar: part-man, part-beast, these creatures were strong and small, and covered in dark, scabbing splotches. As Hickory foretold, they were brilliant fighters, but their weakness was their size. Still, in large numbers, they had no match.

The leader's back curved gently forward, pushing his shoulders in front of his large hairy feet. He stood in front of his men, just slightly, baring his teeth and wielding a long, jagged knife.

The imps had run away again, leaving nothing but dust between Livi and a hundred glowering Undar. Each was smaller than the last, each was uglier, each was crueler. They surrounded Livi and her friends, backing them into a tight, unforgiving cluster.

"Back away," ordered Hickory. He aimed his bow and arrow at the Undar-leader's forehead, steadying his hand and narrowing his brow. "Back away and we won't hurt you."

"It is not our blood that will be shed today," the creature said through a cackle. He whistled and an Undar dropped into the ravine and landed directly on Hickory's shoulders. He ripped Hickory's bow and quiver from his body and shoved him savagely to the ground, snapping every last arrow in half, leaving a pile of twigs where a weapon once lay. "You're in our territory now, boy. We have the numbers, and we have the brute."

The talk ended there. Like each time before, the fighting broke out suddenly and brutally. This time, however, the rules had changed: First, and most advantageously, Livi and the others had sight to guide them. But this seemed to matter little, when they were outnumbered ten-to-one.

The Undar army moved in careful, almost choreographed movements: when one dashed right, another moved left; when one threw, another caught; if one went down, another was there to pick him up. Every step was purposeful, designed to cause the optimum amount of damage and to best protect their people.

Not even Tess's quick maneuvers or Hickory's sheer brute would get them out of this mess. They were impossibly outnumbered, but they still fought bravely. Hickory threw knives and Tess shot arrows. Kip wrestled three Undar to the ground at once, using only his bare hands. But Livi was alarmed, afraid, and off her guard. A minute after the fighting began, one of the small, scabby creatures already had her by the throat.

Livi grabbed her knife from the sheath on her hip and slashed the Undar across the face so hard that she felt his cheekbone grind against her knife. The creature's blood stained Livi's blade, trickling all the way down her arm. A cocktail of fear and power, guilt and exhilaration, coursed through her veins.

The animal had recoiled momentarily, but now was charging back at her. This time, when Livi tried to fight back, he seized her knife and hit her hard in the gut with his small, powerful fists, forcing her to her knees.

Livi's mouth was full of the coppery -- and now all too familiar -- taste of blood. She tried to call out for help, but when she looked around all she saw was defeat. Each of her friends was fighting two or three or five or ten Undar apiece. Hickory and Kip, though they had managed to keep their weapons, were bruised and beaten and only half standing. Tess, like Livi, had been forced to the ground.

Her friends were dying. *She* was dying. She knew that she had to transition into her Luma, but she could not tune out the bones breaking or the blood splattering, the yelling or the cries of pain. Maybe it was because she was down in the Fauxs, or maybe it was the heightened chaos all around her, but changing into her Luma didn't feel natural anymore.

She forced herself to try again, and this time she imagined that she was back in the Befallen Forest and giant herd of Unthinkers had her surrounded. Slowly, every thought and fear and idea faded away. She left everything behind and let herself go.

Livi's body went limp against the Undar who held her. Everything that she was, morphed into a cool, glowing ball of white light. Every head turned her way, and for a split-second, the fighting ceased.

She had to act quickly. First she flung herself at the Undar that held her body down, enveloping him in light and sending him flying across the small, rocky battlefield. She did the same to creatures holding Tess and the ones fighting Kip and Hickory, but there were a hundred more to take their places. *There are just so many,* Livi thought. *If only they were afraid of me like the Unthinkers were.*

Then Livi had a new idea: If she could she could melt into the shape of a key to break into a room, then why couldn't she melt into something that would break into the Undar's mind? Livi found the Undar-leader, who was standing slightly away from the pack, calling out orders. She morphed into a thin, pointed spiral of white-hot light and shot herself into the back of his small skull.

Once so brazen, now the Undar-leader was overwhelmed with fear. He knew Livi was inside his head, that she was listening. His thoughts were scattered and spinning and nearly impossible to understand, but what Livi did make out, she could not believe.

Call off your army, Livi ordered, shouting her thoughts to him as loud as she could.

Never, his thoughts screamed back, accompanied by a mad, cackling laugh that echoed through his mind.

Do it, or I'll tear you apart from the inside out.

Just try little girl. I was ordered to catch you, and I shall. But waves of doubt corrupted his confident mind. Livi was making him nervous, making him hesitate. Flashes of worry, and tension and failure, entered the Undarleader's mind and Livi could feel as he tried to force these thoughts back. Livi listened as he retraced his missteps -- the moments he almost had her, but failed. He couldn't fail again, the Shepherd wouldn't give him another chance.

Then an image of a discombobulated man in front an old shipwreck flashed across the Undar-leaders mind.

Wallace? Livi thought to him excitedly. *Was that Wallace? Did you see him? What did you do to him?*

You mean the man I caught at the shipwreck? the Undar spoke through his thoughts. Livi could feel his confidence returning. *He denied he knew you but I knew he was lying. What's your interest with him?*

He's here? You have him! Where is *he?*

Get out of my head and perhaps I'll tell you. The Undar had found his bargaining chip. Livi could feel his confidence bolstered. He was no longer afraid of her; he had something she wanted, something she'd travelled all the way to the Fauxs for.

YOU'LL TELL ME NOW she wailed pressing against his mind with all her might, winding around his insides, constricting his every thought, his every impulse, until he we nothing but a fragile, sniveling mess.

I-I gave him to the Shepherd, he whimpered. *I-I was sent there to get you, but only the man was there, so I took him instead.*

Who sent you?

The Shepherd, of course, the Undar answered promptly. *I failed by bringing the old man instead of you. This is my last chance. My whole people will be killed unless I capture you now.*

A note of sadness tinged the Undar's scared, angry voice. He was fighting for his people; in his own way, he was admirable. Through the Undar-leader's mind, Livi saw the battle, still raging. Her people were losing. She had to do something.

Call off your army, Livi thought to him again. *Let my friends go, and I'll let you take me to the Shepherd; I won't fight you, I promise.*

Livi listened to the Undar thinking her proposal out: if he said no, she would kill him, and she might even be able to escape his army. Her people might be lost, but his would be too. *Fine*, the Undar thought bitterly to her, and she could sense that it was not in his nature to make deals. *But get out of my head now, and don't come back.*

Livi left the Undar-leader's mind and transitioned swiftly back into her body. Good to his word, the Undar-leader called his troops to an immediate halt.

By now Kip had two black eyes, a deep gash lined Hickory's left cheek, and Tess could barely stand. They all looked confused about why the battle came so such a sudden halt, but Livi didn't have time to explain.

"Go find the Imps. Make them show you a way out. I'm going to get Wallace and bring him home."

"But Livi-"

"Just go," she ordered, her tone leaving no more room for argument. "I'll be right behind you, I promise."

"Livi wait!" Kip called after her, catching her by the elbow. He pulled her into his arms and locked his hands around her waist. There was nothing gentle about the way he held her -- nothing friendly or safe. Their eyes met and suddenly he was kissing her, slowly at first, but then with vigor.

His kiss was full urgency and necessity, and as soon as it was over, Livi was left with the terrible, sinking feeling of finality.

Livi did not turn back as she let the Undar drag her away, down the dark, lonely tunnel.

22

WALLACE

THE TUNNEL SPIT LIVI AND HER CAPTOR OUT into a very large cave. Glowing orange torches dotted the gritty walls, casting strange shadows onto the warped, calcified slabs of stone. The dim light revealed two figures: the first was a woman, tall and narrow, veiled in black, and wielding a glowing white scepter. And the second was a man, average in height and weight, and with an expression so full of despair spread across his gently wrinkled faced, that Livi did not immediately recognize him as Wallace -- her usually jovial teacher and guide.

"You crossed me, William," the woman was saying. "What did you expect would happen?"

"That was five lifetimes ago. It's over, it's done."

"It will never be done!" Suddenly, the strange woman had Wallace by the throat. He fought to break free, but it was no use: her long, bony fingers curled determinately around his stubby neck, turning him purple, and sucking all his strength away.

"Let him go!" Livi shrieked, stepping out from the shadows. "You're killing him -- let him go!"

The woman glared at Livi and then threw Wallace carelessly to ground. "Well, aren't you a sight." She waved her scepter, bathing the cave in light, and allowing Livi to finally see her face: her eyes were cold and her stare was narrow; her lips were thin and fixed into a stiff straight line, and her icy blonde hair sat in a tight bun at the top of her head.

"I caught her, madam," the Undar lied boldly, yanking Livi hard at the elbow and forcing her to step forward. "I caught her, just as you desired. The others got away, but-"

"The others do not matter. Very good, Grier; you may go."

The Undar bowed so low that his long nose brushed the ground and then backed out of the cave, disappearing down the tunnel.

"Livi, you must run!" Wallace yelled feebly, between desperate, sputtering gasps of air. He was strewn pathetically across the ground, recovering slowly from nearly getting choked to death. "Go -- it's a trap, I beg of you, run."

"Don't mind William, he's just a bit grouchy," said the woman. "I'm so pleased you decided to join us. It seems Grier finally did something right."

A cold shiver ran down the nape of Livi's neck. "*You*? *You're* the Shepherd?"

She smiled, baring her bright white teeth. "Very good, little one. And now to business: I believe you have something of mine." The Shepherd flicked her scepter and sent Livi crashing into the cavern wall. Then, with a second blithe flick, invisible restraints bound Livi's arms and legs to the wall.

She pushed against the force of the scepter, trying to break free, but it was no use. She was outstretched and vulnerable and utterly useless, just as the Shepherd had planned it. The Shepherd strode over to Livi, reached toward her chest, and ripped the small silver clock from her neck.

"*That's* what you're after?" Livi cried. "But it's old and broken and I nearly forgot I had it."

"Broken? Ah, you *are* as stupid as you look. Just like your fool of a mother."

Livi's heart dropped into her stomach. "You knew my mother?" *It couldn't be.*

The Shepherd's smile grew broader. "One can only keep a secret so long before it comes back *biting.* Yes, I knew you're mother. And your father too; the idiot thought he could save her."

Wallace didn't matter now; getting home could wait. Curiosity had overtaken Livi, and she held her breath, praying the Shepherd would say more.

"She was a boring, silly little person," the Shepherd continued. "No ambition, no plans of her own. Why, the only remarkable thing ever to happen to your mother was when she got involved with Hubert."

Hubert Horridor? Livi thought to herself. *What did my mother have to do with Hubert Horridor?* She wanted to ask but she couldn't form the words. Some combination of fear and surprise and utter disbelief kept her frozen, her lips clamped shut.

The Shepherd sighed, looking pensive. "Not to say Hubert's much better. He and Mary almost ruined everything."

"You mean Mayback?"

"Of course I mean Mayback," the Shepherd snapped. "I warned him -- I told him not to touch the First Crown -- we weren't ready yet. And what does he do? He and that manipulative little rat go behind my back and nearly get themselves caught. Everything could have been ruined -- all my plans foiled before they'd even begun!"

Livi couldn't believe what she was hearing. Crown Horridor wasn't trying to destroy the Triangulation so that *he* could rule Eaux -- he did it for the Shepherd. But *why?* None of it made any sense.

"Oh, but none of that matters now," the Shepherd said, clutching Livi's locket to her chest. "I don't need them anymore, not now that I have this. I've spent three hundred years searching for this after *he* stole it right off my neck." She glared savagely at Wallace. "I finally tracked it to a little town in the East, but by the time Grier and his team of ham-fisted *morons* had gone to fetch it for me, it already found a new owner. Now, it took some convincing but the old shopkeeper finally gave up the name of the little girl he sold it to. And from there it was easy."

"*You* killed Mr. McCloud?" Livi cried. "He was just an old man. He was harmless."

"He gave my locket away to the first utterly unworthy creature to pass through his shop. He had to pay. And besides, he was of no use to me anymore. I had your name and that was all that mattered.

"Now, I'll admit, getting you down here was tricky. I sent Grier to catch you, but again and again, the little rodent fell short. All he could come up with was dear old William, here -- fortunately *he* proved slightly less useless than the olds days; he got you here at least."

Livi did not understand what she was hearing. The Shepherd talked about Wallace as if she knew him, as if she had known him for a long time. But that was impossible, it had to be. "Wallace what's she talking about? And why is she calling you William?"

"You've got what you wanted," said Wallace to the Shepherd, ignoring Livi's question entirely. "Now let her go."

"Oh hush now, William; we'll get to all that."

"Wallace listen to me," Livi demanded. She had a terrible feeling that she had missed something very important. "Why does she keep calling you William? What's going on?"

The Shepherd eyes lit up. "She doesn't know, does she?" Wallace raised his head imploringly, but the creature only laughed. "Yes, William and I have been enjoying a little reunion while we waited for you to come looking. And I dare say he's just as charming as ever."

"What's going on? What is she talking about, Wallace?"

"Oh, but you're such a pretty thing," the Shepherd cooed, "and I do hate breaking pretty things. Well, save your tears, I'll try to make this brief: your beloved Wallace is a traitor and liar and a *thief* on top of it all."

"Shut up!" Livi wailed, struggling more than ever

against her restraints. "Wallace is the most caring person I know, and no lies you tell will ever change that."

Wallace met the Shepherd's eye, begging her to stop. "Well, someone's got to tell her," she said, answering his gaze sweetly, "and it's you or me, my love."

Wallace's face fell. "All right, Helena. Fine, you win, I'll tell her."

Wallace began by recalling a story that he told Livi a few weeks ago -- the one about Helena Horridor and her mysterious lover: the man who stole Helena from the great Marcous Astor.

"Yes, of course I remember," Livi said once Wallace had finished. "But what does any of that have to do with you -- with *us*?"

"Because, Olivia, my name is William Wallace Astor. My brother was Marcous Astor, and that woman right there -- the one you call the Shepherd -- that woman is Helena Horridor."

23

THE ASTOR FAMILY TREE

WALLACE FELL IN LOVE with Helena the moment he saw her, standing at his brother's side on their wedding day. Wallace begged her to run away with him, but Helena was the Second Crown of Eaux, and she refused to leave her throne behind. Still, she loved him, and she promised that they would find a way to be together.

From there, a plan was formed to kill Marcous Astor and usurp his throne. "I loved my brother, but Marcous had everything: glory and admiration, and the crown to match. And he was married to the woman I loved. I was jealous and spiteful, and terribly, terribly selfish, but I'm a different man now, Livi, you must understand, I'm a different man."

Wallace planned to kill his brother and to reverse the newly established Triangulation, so that he and Helena alone, would reign as King and Queen of Eaux. At the last moment, however, the newly appointed Third Crown, Salvador Lima, got wind of their plan and reported it to Crown Astor.

"They called him William the Betrayer," the Shepherd

chimed in gleefully. "It's a pity the name didn't stick."

Wallace glared fiercely at his former lover, but shame, more than anger, colored his sad, wrinkled face. Encouraged by Livi, he continued his tale:

"Helena and I were exiled to the Midlands, which back then was a sentence thought to be equivalent to death. But we survived our first winter, and many more after that."

The pair spent more than a century together, stealing others souls to keep themselves alive, and traveling all over the world in search of the ultimate power: immortality. One day, they met an old clockmaker who claimed he had a way to make them truly immortal. He forged the clock that Livi carried around her neck from silver and pearl, and he coated it in magic. The clockmaker promised Helena that as long as she wore the locket, niether she, nor Wallace, would ever age a day. All she had to do was turn back the dial at the start of each morning, resetting their time.

"I thought now that she had the necklace, she would be satisfied. I thought we could live happily at last. Oh, I was so foolish!"

Helena didn't slow down. Instead, she set her eyes on a new prize: the throne she'd been forced to leave behind. "But by then I'd had enough. I'd seen too much, and hurt too many. I wouldn't stand by while she took down all of Eaux, too. So, I took the clock and ran. I loved you, Helena," he said, staring the Shepherd right in the eye. "I tried to keep up, but you were insatiable."

Everything Livi thought she knew, she didn't. Wallace was William Astor. The Shepherd was Helena Horridor. And her mother and father! Somehow they were involved in all this too. The neat, well-configured lines of good and bad were suddenly terribly blurred.

But somehow it all sort of makes sense, doesn't it? Livi thought, her brain working somewhat wildly, her body still splayed vulnerably across the cavern wall. *It makes sense now why Crown Horridor's been working for her. And not just Hubert, but all the Horridors ...for centuries!*

The Shepherd had been controlling Eaux through her descendants, waiting for the day that she could come back and claim her crown. It was how the Horridors always stayed in power: the Shepherd had been helping them, protecting them.

And that must be why so many Unthinkers have been hanging out Eterneaux lately Livi thought, piecing things together almost excitedly. *The Shepherd wanted to protect Crown Horridor from retaliation after the disaster in Mayback.*

Across the cave the Shepherd had Wallace by the throat again, making Livi suddenly very aware of how vulnerable she was. "You thought I would die, didn't you? When you stole my clock all those years ago, you thought I would die!" The Shepherd's grip around him tightened with each syllable. "*Answer*! Answer me you coward!" Wallace was sputtering and gasping for air, turning a darker shade of purple with each failing breath.

"You're choking him, can't you see you that?" Livi cried. "He can't breathe! Let him go and he'll answer you."

The Shepherd threw him to ground and shuttered slightly, as if she'd accidentally brushed up against something foul. "How revoltingly human."

Everyone was quiet for a minute, waiting as Wallace caught his breath. When he finally spoke, his voice was weary and pained: "I don't know what I thought would happen when I left you. All I knew is that I had to get away."

Wallace climbed slowly onto his feet now, and walked to stand in front of the Shepherd so that they were face-to-face. "You're right though, Helena, I've been a coward. I should have stayed and fought you instead of disappearing into the dark. Perhaps if I was braver the Shepherd might never have risen."

"What do you think now, little one?" the Shepherd hissed in Livi's ear. "Is he still worth fighting for?"

Was he? He'd lied to her, betrayed her. He'd hidden so much. Livi's whole body felt hot. Salt ran into her eyes and she could feel her heart pulsing inside her ribcage. She wanted to yell or scream or punch something, but she was still bound to the wall. What would Tess or Hickory think?

And what about the Elders? Or did they already know? Was she the only one foolish enough to see none of this? Her mind was racing, her thoughts unfocused and dreary.

"Please understand, Livi," Wallace begged, "I've spent hundreds of years searching for a way to make things right. I spent decades trying to find Helena after I stole the locket. I was going to repair the damage I'd done; I was going to stop her once and for all. But I never heard from her, or saw her again. Until the Shepherd rose, that is."

"So you knew all along who the Shepherd was? And you knew that I had her locket, didn't you?" Livi asked hotly, remembering all the times Wallace asked her about her necklace. "You knew, and you didn't warn me!"

"I *suspected*," Wallace admitted. "Oh, but I never meant to hurt you my dear Sleeping Girl. I never meant to put you in harms way. It's just the contrary, really: I was trying to *protect* you -- to *save* you from her. The mistakes I've made are many, and they run deep. I am a fraud, Olivia, and I am sorry." Wallace then turned to the Shepherd, pleading: "You have the necklace, Helena; you've got what you wanted, now let the girl go. You can keep me if you like, but let her go."

"I wouldn't be worrying about *her* right now." The Shepherd held her scepter up above her head, and it shot out a beam of brilliant white light. A cloud of black shadows filled the cave. Shapeless and empty, the mass of Unthinkers crept toward Livi.

"All people are built for the herd," said the Shepherd, "built to follow, to copy, to reproduce others just like them. You think they've died, William, that they are void, *empty*. But it's exactly the opposite: Unthinkers are more human than you or I could ever be. They are free in ways we can never understand. You needn't worry about the girl, William; she's going to a better place. But *you* -- there will be no peace for you."

The Shepherd's voice was fading fast as a hundred Unthinkers clouded Livi's mind. She had waited too long to transition into her Luma, and now it was too late. Maybe the Shepherd was right. Maybe she'd be happier as an Unthinker; maybe it's what she was meant for.

Livi was so exhausted and confused that she didn't know up from down. She no longer cared about saving Wallace or getting the Emickus root back to Violet. She didn't even care that she was going to die here, in this dark, gritty in-between.

She was resigned, hopeless, ready to give up. But then, through the deep gray fog, she saw Violet's face, and then Benny's, and Nedrick's. She saw Tess and Hickory and Kip. *Kip*.

"No!" Livi screamed suddenly, surprising both the Shepherd and Wallace, who had thought she was already gone. "*No*."

Livi's body fell limp against its restraints as she transformed into her Luma. She flew across the cave, to where the Shepherd stood, frozen in shock. Then, she wrapped herself around the scepter and ripped it from the Shepherd's unprepared hands, smashing it against the rock wall behind her.

The Shepherd drew a dagger from her cloak and charged toward Livi, but it was too late: the globe had shattered and a white cloud filled the cave. The cloud separated into a thousand wisps of light. The restraints around Livi's wrists and ankles lifted and her lifeless body fell to the ground.

A look of pure horror maimed the Shepherd's perfect face. Then, *crack* -- like a bullwhip slicing into dried ground -- she vanished.

• • •

Livi dug into her rucksack, feeling around for the Emickus root that was buried deep at the bottom of her bag. Her fingers grazed its rough, spongy exterior, and she remembered the true purpose of this journey. It was time to go home.

She looked from the dead air where the Shepherd had stood, to Wallace, edging toward her, timid and embarrassed. Livi could barely look at him -- so old and pathetic and brimming over with guilt -- but her rage had mellowed some, and she could see that somewhere, beneath all the deceit, was the friend she'd come so far to find.

She tried to stand up but she was so tired. *It's all finally catching up to me*, she thought, smiling inwardly as she ran a mental appraisal of the pandemonium that had occurred over last several days. *I think I could go to sleep right now.* Wallace came over to help her to her feet, but as he got closer the relief drained from his face, leaving a look of cold terror in its place. "Olivia, oh Livi, you're bleeding."

Livi dabbed at her forehead and felt hot sticky blood on her fingers. "It's nothing, Wallace; it's just a scratch."

"Not your head, child." Wallace pulled her hand off her forehead and to her waist. The front of her tunic was slashed down the center, its shredded edges died dark with blood; a deep, ugly wound marred her magnolia-white skin.

I've been stabbed, she thought vaguely. *But how? When?* She remembered the knife plainly enough -- its long metallic blade, its cerated edge, its obsidian handle -- and she could see the Shepherd's slender fingers wrapped around it. But nowhere in her memory could she find the moment that the dagger met her flesh.

The shock was wearing off now, and a fierce pain shot through her. All she wanted to do was sleep.

24

HOME

THE CEILING OF THE INFIRMARY was grainy and red. Livi's body ached, her head was spinning, and as hard as she tried, she could not remember how she had gotten here. It felt as if every last bone in her body had broken, every blood vessel had shredded, like she was being held together by sheer will.

A partition separated Livi's own narrow cot from the rest of the room, and as she turned her head, she noticed a shadow move across the thin screen. "Hello?" she called out weakly.

"Livi! Oh, Livi, is that you?" The partition flung suddenly out of place and Violet burst to Livi's side. "I was worried practically to *death* over you. Wren said I might have been too late and -- *oh Livi*, we were all so worried! How are you feeling?" Livi opened her mouth to answer but Violet had already begun again: "I swear, it's all just been the biggest rush, I can't even *begin* to explain. I mean, when you got stabbed something just took over. And then it was easy, sort of natural even. Can you believe it? Can you believe I can do that?"

"Do what? Violet, what are you talking about?"

"Oh, so much has happened while you were away, I

don't even know where to begin. Wait, wait, I know!" Violet raced over to her own small cot and began rummaging through her bedside drawer. "I'm just looking for my diary, and then we can go through absolutely *every* detail together."

"*Wait*," Livi begged, forcing Violet to turn away from her cluttered drawer. Livi was remembering the bloody tunic, the searing pain, the exhaustion, and she was suddenly very confused. "Just a stop a second, and tell me what happened. The last thing I remember I was -- well, I think I almost ... did you *heal* me, Violet?"

"Well, obviously."

"But how? You weren't even anywhere near me when it happened -- *were* you?"

Violet pursed her lips. "Of *course* not, Livi. But I don't need to be near you to help. I I've just got to concentrate very hard. It hurts terribly, of course, but it's worth it. And for you, oh, I'd take a knife to the gut any day for you!"

"What are you talking about?"

"That's how it works, silly. I drain it from you -- the pain, the physical trauma, all that stuff. And now that my fever's gone, Wren's teaching me to harness my abilities without -- well, you know -- without letting them nearly kill me."

"So the Emickus worked, then?" Violet *looked* better, certainly, but she had seemed better many times before, only to end up sicker than she had been in the first place.

"Oh yes -- and I'm really better this time, it isn't like before," she added, as if reading Livi's mind. "The fever's been completely gone for more than a week now, and even Wren agrees it's not coming back."

"Wait, Violet, a *week*? How long have I been out? Where's Kip? Is he okay? And what about Tess and Hickory? Did they make it back?"

Livi struggled to sit up, swinging her legs over the side of the bed determinately. But Violet pushed her back down. "Everybody's fine, Livi. Tess and Hickory and that new boy, Kip -- they're all here, and they're just fine. But you need to rest. I mean, Wren didn't even know if -- well, you've been out for ten days, Livi."

Ten days? She couldn't believe it. *And what about the Shepherd? And Wallace -- I mean William -- no, Wallace.* Everything was coming back to her all at once and she couldn't figure out what was a dream and what really happened. Did the others know who Wallace really was? What would they think when they found out?

"I've got to see Wallace. *Now*, Violet. Go and get him or I will."

• • •

Perhaps it was her run-in with death that put things in a new light, but Livi was not angry at Wallace anymore. She had forgiven him for the lies he told, and for the lengthy deceit he took part in, but there were still some things she didn't quite understand.

They talked all morning and the vast web slowly untangled. In his explanation, certain words repeated themselves: words like *shame* and *revenge* and *death*; but for every piece of the puzzle Wallace explained, there were a dozen more that Livi still didn't understand.

"But it just seems impossible," Livi said when they came to the part about Wallace being William Astor. "If you were really Marcous Astor's brother, then you would have died centuries ago. And if you stopped winding the clock back, then not even magic could save you."

Wallace looked like he was concentrating very hard on something, like he was trying to will Livi to understand. "Immortality is a dark business, Olivia, and it can yield unexpected results. When the clockmaker put our time in that locket he forged us together permanently: I live because she lives."

"And the Unthinkers have kept her alive," said Livi, putting the pieces together in her head, "so they've kept you alive too."

Wallace nodded, ashamed.

"So if the scepter controlled the Unthinkers, and the

Unthinkers kept the Shepherd alive, doesn't that mean she should have died when I broke the scepter?" Livi reasoned.

Wallace let out a deep sigh. "I'm afraid it will take a lot more than that to kill the Shepherd, especially now that she has her locket back."

"So it was all for nothing."

"If you think rescuing me was nothing, if you think saving Violet was nothing -- then yes, it was all for nothing."

Livi frowned. The whole reason for the trip was to get Violet the medicine she needed, but for some reason, that didn't feel like enough anymore. The world was so much bigger than she ever imagined.

"Wallace, you need to tell the Elders. You need to tell them who you really are, and who the Shepherd is. And Mayback! You have to tell them about Hubert Horridor and Representative Lucidon. She's not who everyone thinks she is, Wallace -- she's trouble, I'm sure of it. They'll know what to do; they'll know how to fix things."

"The Elders know everything, Olivia, but there are some things that even their wisdom cannot mend. There is a war coming, against all good and honorable men. And nothing the Elders do can change that."

•   •   •

Over the next several days, Livi's strength improved rapidly, and visitors filled the infirmary nearly round the clock. News of her safe return had travelled quickly and it seemed everyone in the Petrichor wanted to see her. Everyone except Kip.

Hickory and Tess had a myriad of excuses for why he never came to visit, but soon Livi stopped asking. Violet moved out of the infirmary on day four of Livi's convalescence (just two weeks since she'd been treated with the Emickus root), and on day five Tess and Hickory announced they would be leaving for the North.

"Just for just a month, maybe two," said Hickory. "My sister just had a baby, ya see, and so we thought we'd go for a visit."

"I wish I was coming with you."

"No ya don't," said Tess. "Hick's parents are a nightmare, and besides, there's no action up north at the moment. You're better off down here, keepin' up the Midlands Guard."

Livi knew they had to go; she was expecting it, even: Tess and Hickory never stayed in one place for very long. But that didn't make saying goodbye any easier.

Then, on day six, Kip finally showed his face.

Livi had just woken up and she blinked groggily, uncertain at first, if it was really him. But there he was, sitting quietly in the chair by her bed. Livi forced down all the joy and excitement she felt at seeing him, and she told him bitterly to go away.

"I'm sorry," he said, sitting down on the edge of Livi's bed, "and I'll go in a second, I promise, but I just wanted to say goodbye."

"*Goodbye?*" she echoed, the harsh lines in her face that she had worked so hard to construct, melting away.

"I've been trying to come up with the words all week but I just couldn't."

"What do you mean goodbye?"

"I'm leaving, Livi. I'm going north with Hickory and Tess. Hick says he can get me a job out by the Trilinian boarder and so-"

"But there are jobs for you here."

Kip smiled, but it was a sad sort of smile. "I'm sorry, but I can't stay. I don't belong here."

"Of *course* you belong here."

Kip was so close now that they were sharing the same air, but he still wouldn't look at her. He was sad, clearly, but she didn't understand why. Everyone was safe. Everything was going to be okay. "But we only just got back and Violet only just got better. Things are finally going to be okay now, don't you see? Things are finally going to start being normal again, don't you want that?" He opened his mouth to talk, but before he could, Livi leaned in and pressed her lips against his.

They kissed for a long time, desperate to prolong the silence, to keep the goodbyes unfinished. But when they finally broke apart, things were exactly as miserable as before, and saying goodbye felt more inevitable than ever.

"Listen, I've been waiting a long time to get out of Eaux," said Kip. "There are things I've got to do now, things I've got to figure out. I don't expect you to understand, but it's something I have to do ... I'll miss you, though. I will, honestly."

Livi didn't know what to say. How could he be leaving? Didn't he care at all about her? And what was he even going to do up north, all by himself? Well, it wasn't any of her concern, he made that perfectly clear, and she would not cry for him. Her cheeks were hot though, and her eyes burned as she fought to hold everything in. "You should go."

Kip reached for her hand.

"I said *go*."

The second the door to the infirmary closed, Livi burst into tears. She wallowed embarrassedly through lunch, and well into dinner, sending away any other visitors that dared knock on her door. Until finally, someone unexpected arrived:

Livi had been waiting to see Mrs. Battlebee all week, and she welcomed Mathilda eagerly into the infirmary.

"I'm sorry I haven't come sooner," Mathilda said, sitting down at Livi's bedside. "I was down south when you got back, but I came as soon as I could. Dear, are you okay? Have you been crying?"

"It's nothing, I'm fine," she said quickly, dabbing at her tearstained cheeks. "I guess I was in pretty bad shape when I first got back, but I don't remember any of that ... But Mathilda," Livi began again, unable to endure the smalltalk, "when I was down there, down in the Fauxs, the Shepherd said she knew my parents. Was my mother working for the Shepherd, Mathilda? Was everybody right? Was she really a traitor all along?"

"Is *that* what you think? Oh no, dear, it was nothing like that. Your mother was good -- all around good."

"Then what did the Shepherd mean?"

Mrs. Battlebee pursed her lips. "Well dear, you must understand, the final weeks of your parents' lives were a very strange time for us all. Mary had just disappeared and your mother and I had just been charged with treason and-"

"Wait, wait do you mean Mary disappeared?"

"She just vanished! And not ten days before your mother and I were charged with treason. We were all so worried about her. We had no idea where she went or if she was even alive. I can't tell you what an enormous shock it was when she showed up in the Third Court a few years later; by then everyone who had known her assumed she was dead."

Mathilda paused purposefully, as if waiting for Livi to ask another question, but Livi was frozen, the information overloading in her head.

"Now I don't know how the Shepherd knew your parents, and that's the truth, but I can guess: I expect that the Shepherd was the one who ordered Hubert Horridor to perform the execution. And -- again, this is only a guess -- I expect she was present the day your parents died."

The Shepherd was behind it all, Livi thought to herself. *She was behind my parents' death and Mathilda's banishment and Mary's*-"Mary," Livi said out-loud, the final pieces of the puzzle snapping together in her mind. "It was Mary, wasn't it? It was all Mary. She betrayed you, she told the Second Court what you and my mother were going to do."

Mathilda bit her lower lip uncertainly. "Yes, Olivia, she did."

"And you've known all these years?" Livi's voice cracked as she spoke, her mouth suddenly and inexplicably dry.

"I only put things together a few months ago. I've told no one yet -- not even Jane."

"You have to tell her."

"Perhaps eventually. But it will only upset her. And there's just no use looking backwards."

"How can you say that?" Livi said, her voice filling

with sudden rage. "She banished you, she *killed* my parents. You want me to just forget about all that? She deserves to *die*."

"Do not look backwards," Mathilda said again. "Not when there is so much waiting just ahead."

Livi had been stalked and beaten, tied up and stabbed; she'd been possessed by a phantom and lied to by her mentor. But never had she felt more vulnerable than right at this moment. There was no truth anymore. She knew nothing.

Livi suddenly felt like every bit of strength she had accumulated over the past several days had been knocked out of her. She wanted cry, but she had no tears left inside. She wanted to run, but she was too exhausted to even sit up.

The infirmary was warm and the air smelled sweet. Livi closed her eyes and listened as Mathilda hummed a vaguely familiar tune. *I'll worry about it all tomorrow*, she thought wearily. *I'll fix it all in the morning*. Then, she drifted to sleep under the grainy red wood of the Petrichor.

Made in the USA
San Bernardino, CA
12 March 2015